Died Blonde

Died Blonde

A Bad Hair Day Mystery

Nancy J. Cohen

KENSINGTON BOOKS

KENSINGTON BOOKS are published by

Kensington Publishing Corp.
850 Third Avenue
New York, NY 10022

All Kensington titles, imprints and distributed lines are available at special quantity discounts for bulk purchases for sales promotion, premiums, fund-raising, educational or institutional use.

Special book excerpts or customized printings can also be created to fit specific needs. For details, write or phone the office of the Kensington Special Sales Manager: Kensington Publishing Corp., 850 Third Avenue, New York, NY 10022, Attn. Special Sales Department. Phone: 1-800-221-2647.

Library of Congress Card Catalogue Number: 2004105350
ISBN 0-7582-0656-9

First Printing: December 2004
10   9   8   7   6   5   4   3   2   1

Printed in the United States of America

Died Blonde

gh it had hit something. The pitch-black
vestigation, so she fumbled for a light
d when she flicked it on.

ve brought a flashlight. Who knew?

d her way inside, wrinkling her nose at
y been here once before, when the elec-
All she remembered was a mess of cir-
s supplies belonging to the landlord.
ty hazards and ordered to clean up, but
ans, hoses, and scraps of metal were still
lly, she nearly tripped over an obstruc-
ing was soft and lumpy. As she traced it
sensation crawled along her skin.
see what it was, right now.
ay from the door, she widened the aper-
ed her lips. Surely that didn't look like
e well enough, dammit. The shopping
ht.
led the form. Biting back a shriek, she
re thinking to feel for a pulse. Her fin-
e hand to wrist when a clattering noise
her throat. She screamed just as a dark
king into her with enough force to send
Before she could regain her senses, the
a resounding crash. Darkness over-
like a giant black hole swallowing her
reacted with panting breaths and cold,
he surge of panic, she crawled to the
f upright, she found the knob and rat-
k. The door wouldn't budge.
self to think logically, she yanked her
t and called the salon. "Luis, I'm stuck
he door won't open. Something must
e way."
"
e stopped; he'd already hung up. Any-

Chapter One

"Oh no, the power went out again. It's the third time this month," Marla Shore griped to her salon staff. She tossed her blow-dryer onto the counter in disgust. "I'm going to murder that woman."

"You don't know that Carolyn is responsible," Nicole Johnson said while sorting foils for her next highlights job. "Just because she told the electric company to cancel your account before doesn't mean she's to blame again. It could be another outage due to a storm."

"Come on, ever since she opened her new beauty shop, we've been suffering one calamity after another," Marla retorted. "I'd already be suing her for putting honey in the developer if I could prove she'd done it. Do you know how long it took me to wash that goo out of Abby's hair? She smelled like a beehive. This shopping strip cannot support two salons, no matter what our landlord says."

"Carolyn's Hairstyle Heaven is no match for your Cut 'N Dye," Jennifer Cater said from across the room. "If you accuse her of resorting to tricks to undermine your business, she'll probably slap a lawsuit on you."

"You're right." Marla nodded at the blond stylist.

"Listen up, girlfriend," Nicole warned. "I see more trouble

brewing on your face than in those summer storm clouds outside. Carolyn Sutton isn't worth your time of day. Just call FPL and see what's going on."

Marla turned to her client, Babs Winrow, senior vice president of Tylex Industries. "I'm sorry for the delay. I know you're in a hurry to make a flight. Just give me a few minutes to see what's wrong."

The attractive executive gave her a sympathetic smile. "This isn't a great way to start your workweek, is it? Go ahead and make your call."

Pulling a cell phone from her skirt pocket, Marla dialed the number she'd memorized out of necessity. "Your power is still connected," said a spokesperson for Florida Power and Light. "Have you checked the circuit breakers?"

"No, I'll do that next. You're sure nobody ordered my electricity cut off or canceled my account?"

"Yes, ma'am. You might check with your neighbors to see if they're having a problem. If this outage continues, please call us back, and we'll send the service crew out. One other place you can look is at the main connection. That might trip even if the circuits look okay."

"Thanks," Marla said before hanging up. The electrical box was located on a wall outside their laundry room in the rear. On her way past, she flung a pile of wet towels into the washer. "It looks good here," she called to Nicole. The switches were turned to the ON positions.

"Go next door and see if they're having a problem," Nicole suggested, her voice as warm as her cinnamon skin.

"Want me to go?" asked Luis, their new receptionist. After interviewing numerous bimbo types and computer illiterates, Marla had hired the Cuban-American whose charming smile and efficient manner persuaded her to give him a chance. His husky build along with dark hair, a trim mustache and beard, and sultry eyes made him a target for husband hunters, and Marla hoped she wouldn't lose him to one of them, because she relied on his competent manner. In the two weeks he'd been there, he had up-

dated h
called e
"I'll d
go with
power b

A few
ones ou
her. Mis
whirring
irons w
brought
day.

"I'll
veyed h

"Tell
voked c
into the
everyth
is respo
make m

Rum
set of k
Babs fo
client w

Push
breathe
brough
Heat b
crete b
circuits
sun-wa

This
doesn't
It's stifl

App
noticed

creaked to a stop as thou
interior didn't invite in
switch. Nothing happen
Schlemiel, you should ha

Cautiously, she inche
the stale smell. She'd on
trician had to do repairs.
cuitry and miscellaneou
He'd been cited for safe
she suspected the paint
around. Stepping carefu
tion by the door. The th
with her foot, a prickling

More light. She had to

Nudging the thing aw
ture. A cry of horror esca
a . . . She still couldn't s
center blocked the sunli

Kneeling, Marla prod
rocked on her heels befo
gers were inching from t
made her heart leap into
shape whizzed past, kno
her tumbling to the side.
door slammed shut wit
whelmed her, closing in
into its depths. Her body
clammy skin. Fighting
door. After hauling herse
tled it until her teeth sho

Get a grip. Forcing he
cell phone from her pock
in the meter room, and
have gotten wedged in th

"I'll be right there, luv

"Wait, there's a—" Sh

way, her imagination might be playing tricks on her. She'd been seeing enough dead bodies lately to conjure them in her mind. Or maybe another proprietor had electrical problems, came in here, and got a shock from the wiring. That must be it; one of the other shopkeepers must have mishandled the circuits and been felled by a jolt.

Marla waited at her post until she heard scratching sounds from beyond. "Luis, is that you? I'm inside." She pounded on the door.

A moment later, daylight blinded her eyes. "A piece of wood was jammed under the transom," Luis said in a solemn tone.

"Someone trapped me in here. You'd better see this." Gesturing, she hesitated to turn around.

"Sweet saints." He shuffled over. "It looks like . . . Switch on the light, will you? I can't see well enough in here."

"It won't work. I already tried."

Giving a grunt of impatience, Luis strode to the mains and flipped a couple of switches. "No wonder our power was out. Somebody tampered with the main circuitry." Bright light from an overhead bulb flooded the interior.

"Oh my God." Marla stared down into the sightless face of Carolyn Sutton. She didn't have to assess her further to know the woman was dead. The odd angle of her neck told the story. Although she didn't like the woman, Marla had no wish to see her life end this way.

She met Luis's somber glare. "Hey, you don't think I had anything to do with it? I just pushed past the door and there she was. Then someone knocked into me. Whoever it was slammed the door and trapped me inside."

"The cops will want to hear the details. You'll have to call Detective Vail. I'm sure your boyfriend will be delighted to find you in the middle of another, er, unfortunate happening."

Marla groaned, imagining his reaction. Lieutenant Dalton Vail was the Palm Haven Police Department's chief homicide investigator. Barely five months ago, she'd helped him investigate the murder of a fellow found in her neighbor Goat's town house.

Before that, she'd answered a plea from her ex-spouse, Stan, to solve the murder of his third wife, Kimberly. And earlier . . . Heck, no one would be surprised that Marla had stumbled onto another body. But Carolyn Sutton? Right after Marla had blurted out that she wanted to kill the woman?

Speech having deserted her, she pulled out her cell phone and gave it silently to Luis. She wouldn't miss Carolyn, but her rival hadn't deserved an untimely death.

While he made the call to the police station, she walked outside, needing to escape the close environment in the shed. "Go back to work," she told him when he joined her. "Cancel my appointments, or see if one of the other gals is free to take my clients. I'll be here a while."

She knew the routine. A local cop responded first. After he took a quick look, he called his supervisor. Soon sirens pierced the morning air. A crime-scene van pulled alongside the solitary structure, followed by Vail's sedan.

Marla's heart thudded as she watched the detective's tall frame unfold from his car. Her anxious glance noted his peppery hair parted to the side, his steel gray eyes, and his navy suit that so well displayed his broad shoulders and narrow hips. Absent from his demeanor was any hint of their intimacy as he approached her wearing a stern expression.

"I hear you've been at it again," he said with a resigned twist to his chiseled lips. "Show me."

Marla breathed an inward sigh of relief. She detected no trace of judgment in his tone, merely curiosity. "In there."

His inspection didn't take long. When he emerged, he made a beeline in her direction. "Don't go anywhere," he commanded. Signaling to his team, he issued orders, then turned to address her. "Okay, give it to me quickly."

She started with their power outage at the salon, then repeated the story she'd told Luis. "I swear I didn't know it was her." Marla's voice shook, and she felt the trembling reaction descend to her toes. She swayed like a sapling in the wind, suddenly feeling sick to her stomach.

"Sit down by the curb, and put your head between your knees," Vail ordered, pushing on her shoulder.

Marla complied, swallowing huge gulps of air.

"I said I'd kill her. I didn't mean it. You know how awful she's been to me in the past, but I wouldn't ever do anything like that, not even to her."

"I know, sweetcakes." Vail's gentle tone brought tears to her eyes. He crouched beside her, patting her back.

A clap of thunder sounded, as though the heavens were admonishing her for past evil thoughts about the dead woman. Moisture-laden clouds advanced rapidly, blocking out the sun. Rather than seeing jagged streaks of lightning, she noticed the flash of cameras from the crime techs at work. They'd dust for fingerprints; something should show up on the switches or the doorknob.

"Go ahead," she told Vail. "You have work to do. Don't let me interfere."

"I could use your help. You know the people in these stores. I'll be interviewing them, but you can keep your ears open. We'll have to wait for the medical examiner's report, of course, but my bet is the victim's neck is broken. It doesn't look like an accident."

"If you don't mind, I'd prefer to keep my ears closed and my mouth shut. I don't want anything to do with another murder, especially not Carolyn's."

Shakily, she rose to her feet with Vail's assistance. Leaning into him, she allowed herself the momentary comfort of his embrace, not caring who observed them. Everyone at the police station knew they were an item by now, anyway. After his relentless pursuit, how could she resist the lonely widower and his thirteen-year-old daughter? They'd brought out a nurturing side of her she hadn't known existed.

"Carolyn's hair is wrong," she mentioned. "A chunk is chopped off by her face. It's not that way on the other side."

Vail broke their embrace. "What do you mean?" he asked, puzzled.

Marla pictured the hairdresser's bobbed strawberry blond hair, owlishly round eyes, and pencil-thin eyebrows. Carolyn had maintained herself well for a woman in her forties, although Marla didn't think miniskirts were quite appropriate. "She wore her hair angled, but one section looked hacked off. I can't see Carolyn doing that to herself."

"Good observation." Vail glanced at the entrance to the meter room. "You can return to your salon for now. I'll catch you later. Will you be okay?"

She nodded mutely, grateful for his intervention. Imagine if another detective had been in charge of the case. Assuming Carolyn's death turned out to be something other than an accident, Marla would be considered a suspect by anyone who didn't know her. She could well imagine the questions: How long have you hated Carolyn Sutton? Did you arrange to meet her alone behind the shopping center? Was the power outage a ploy to trick your staff? She'd already been the subject of police scrutiny after Mrs. Kravitz had died in one of her shampoo chairs. It wasn't an experience she cared to repeat.

She plodded toward Cut 'N Dye, wondering who would run Carolyn's salon now that the owner was dead. If Marla was lucky, they'd close the shop. *That's nasty, and it gives you a motive for doing away with Carolyn. You should focus on who else had a reason to get rid of your rival.*

"Marla, are you all right?" Nicole said, greeting her at the rear door. "Luis told us what happened."

"Just my luck that I was the one to find Carolyn's body in the meter room."

"Perhaps luck had nothing to do with it."

Marla gave Nicole a sharp glance, but she felt too drained to really consider what the stylist had said. Before her wobbly legs gave way, she stumbled to her station and sank into the chair. Customers bombarded her with questions, but she fielded them deftly. *Been there, done that.* She smiled weakly when Arnie Hartman from Bagel Busters rushed in.

Smelling like garlic, he still wore an apron over his T-shirt and jeans. "What's going on, *shayna maidel?*" he asked with a note of concern. "Police cars are outside."

Relating her story, she watched his face bloom with surprise and dismay. "I'd just said I could kill that woman," Marla concluded, noticing for the first time since she'd returned that the lights were back on.

"If wishes could kill, you might have done it, but not in this case. Is Dalton here?" Arnie said in a gentle tone.

"Ooh, I hope that hunk of a detective comes by," Jennifer's voice oozed from across the room. "You should see how this place heats up when he's in the salon."

Marla rolled her eyes. Her relationship with the handsome lieutenant had long been fodder for gossip in the salon.

As though he'd overheard their conversation, Vail ducked inside just as the clouds burst with a torrential downpour. Rain hammered the roof, competing with the noise of blow-dryers and the chatter of customers who'd resumed their participation in the rumor mill. Flicking droplets from his windblown hair, Vail regarded Marla with a wry expression. "Got your juice going again, I see."

Are you referring to the effect you have on me, or to my salon? Suppressing her feminine reaction, Marla gestured to the nearest shampoo bowl. "You're overdue for a cut. Want me to work on you while we talk?"

Vail passed Arnie a look of understanding, as though they both knew the familiar action would bring her comfort. "If it makes you feel more in control, I can manage a few minutes. I sent my deputies over to the deceased's salon. Do you know if she's married?"

"No, she isn't . . . wasn't. I guess you'll have to find the next of kin. Her salon staff might have that information."

Leveraging his large body onto a shampoo chair, he leaned back. The salon assistant, Joanne, hastened over to wash his hair.

Marla's glance lingered on him, then she turned to Arnie. "Thanks for coming over. I can always count on you being there for me. Jill is a lucky girl to have you."

Lowering his gaze, Arnie shuffled his feet. "Yeah, the kids adore her. She won't be happy to hear this latest mess."

Arnie, whose wife had died in a car accident, had been left with two young children. While Marla had always considered him a close friend, she couldn't conceive of feeling anything more than friendship for him and had been delighted when he fell for actress and public relations specialist Jillian Barlow.

"Tell Jill hello for me. I'll be all right, Arnie."

"Don't feel guilty. You're not the only one who won't miss that shrew. It'll give the yentas something to talk about."

He sauntered out the door just as a supplier walked in. Marla busied herself with a new order until Vail dropped into the seat at her station. Glancing toward the wall clock, she pursed her lips. Her immediate clients had agreed to be done by other staff members, but Marla could handle her later appointments. No sense in disrupting all their customers if Vail didn't need her.

"Fire away," she said, aware he was obligated to ask questions. Parting his hair with a comb, she let his silken strands run through her fingers. It brought to mind other places her fingers would like to roam, so she forced herself to focus on her task. That wasn't easy because snipping Vail's hair reminded her of Carolyn's missing clump. Bile rose in her throat. Later, she could allow herself a full emotional meltdown, not now. Her movements switched to automatic at Vail's first query.

"Tell me from the beginning how you met the victim."

She knew that tone of voice. Although it projected only casual curiosity, the glint in his eyes told otherwise. Marla had no reason for subterfuge, so she gave it to him straight on.

"After graduating from beauty school, I obtained my first job as a stylist in Carolyn's salon. That was before she moved away from Palm Haven to that other dinky location. She wasn't a pleasant person to work for. Carolyn would demean people in front of their customers and never had a good word to say about anyone. It didn't please her when I left a couple of years later to open my own salon. I took my client list and some of her staff members along with me."

"That must've made her mad."

"She bore a grudge against me ever since. It didn't help that my salon thrived while hers sank into obscurity. Carolyn moved her place to save money on rent, but poor business sense led to another failure. She just wasn't good to her staff, so it came as no surprise to me. Then she seemed to get financial backing from somewhere."

"Yes, I remember you told me she subsidized foreign students at the Sunrise Academy of Beauty."

Marla surveyed his cut in the mirror. Satisfied, she picked up a battery-operated electric razor. Bending his head forward, she proceeded to shave the back of his neck. Thank goodness he didn't sprout hair in his ears like her mother's boyfriend, Roger Gold. She shuddered whenever that *fresser* walked in the door. His bulk overflowed the chair, making it difficult for her to work around him. How unlike Vail, whom she yearned to touch in inappropriate places.

"Carolyn couldn't have afforded to move back to Palm Haven on her own," she said. "It was just to spite me that she got a space in the same shopping strip. Maybe she bribed our landlord."

Before Vail could comment, a young woman breezed into the salon on a gust of rain-laden wind. "I must speak to your manager," she said loudly to Luis in an accented voice. "*Je suis . . .* I am from Hairstyle Heaven. Something terrible has happened to our owner, and we have no one to take charge."

Luis pointed to Marla. "You'll want to speak to Marla Shore."

"*S'il vous plait, mademoiselle,*" the woman said, approaching her with an imploring gesture, "you must help us. We do not know what to do."

Chapter Two

Marla glanced at the young woman, whose petite figure looked svelte in a tube top, a skirt that was barely more than a piece of fabric, and sandals with heels so high they'd make her podiatrist happy for years to come. A mass of short dark curls framed a Mona Lisa face.

"Do I know you?" Marla asked, resting her hand on Vail's shoulder. His solid musculature felt good beneath her fingers.

"My name is Claudia. I'm a hairdresser at Hairstyle Heaven. Our employer, Carolyn Sutton, is dead. It is so horrible. We know you didn't like her, but can you please advise us?"

"I didn't like her? You've got things reversed, honey. What do you want from me?"

"Your guidance, mademoiselle. Should we close the salon? Keep our appointments? There's no one to tell us what to do," the girl wailed.

"I'm sorry about your loss, but it's not my job to instruct you. This is Lieutenant Dalton Vail. He's in charge of the investigation." Knowing he had to move on, she applied mousse, rubbing it in with a little more vigor than necessary.

"Hurry up," he muttered. "I have to go."

"Sit still. I'm almost done." She dried her hand, then picked up the blow-dryer, flicking on its hottest setting.

"Miss," Vail said loudly to Claudia, "why don't you return to your salon and wait for me. Isn't Sergeant Peterson there?"

She nodded. "I told him Carolyn has a sister. He spoke to *la soeur*, but we are not certain who will be in charge. The sergeant said he'll need to check our records, look over Carolyn's belongings, just in case her death wasn't an accident." Her lower lip quivered, and Marla felt a surge of sympathy.

"If it's going to interfere with business, you might want to close for a couple of days," Vail replied.

"Why don't you call Carolyn's sister?" Marla suggested, wielding the blow-dryer to fluff Vail's hair. "She might be able to direct you to the family lawyer, and then he could tell you who's named as Carolyn's successor. If you girls want to keep working in the meantime, just collect your own money for now. The rent isn't due for a couple of weeks, so you should be okay with the landlord."

"We can stay open, *non?* Our customers want their hair done, and we need the income."

"It should be feasible. You can order your own supplies, too. When you find out who the new owner is, ask her what you should do. She'll have to change the account at the bank for a start, and talk to you girls about hours and such."

"Thank you so much, mademoiselle."

"Tell me, did you experience a power blackout this morning?"

"Pardon?"

"Did your lights go out? Is that why Carolyn went to the meter room?"

Claudia's forehead furrowed. "*Non*, Madame said she had to—"

"Thank you," Vail interrupted, casting Marla a meaningful glance. "We'll talk when I come over in just a few minutes."

Marla, aware of the listening ears around them, didn't care. She wanted to hear the rest of Claudia's response. When she opened her mouth to speak, Vail jabbed her. "Leave it for later," he said, enunciating each word.

Watching Claudia's retreating back, Marla gritted her teeth.

"Afraid I'll contaminate a possible witness? I thought you wanted my help."

His intense gaze met hers in the mirror. "I do, sweetcakes, but it's still my job to interview everyone who knew the deceased. I'd rather talk to them first. Then you can practice what you do best: encourage Carolyn's operators to talk and share confidences. You know their lingo. You'll be able to pick up subtleties that I might miss."

"Carolyn may have recruited her stylists to carry out pranks against me. I can't trust any of them."

Vail smirked. "Good, you shouldn't. That's why your viewpoint will be useful."

Shutting off the blow-dryer, Marla plunked it on the counter. "Did you see how Claudia looked away when I mentioned a power blackout? She knew about it. Probably Carolyn went to the meter room to turn off my electricity."

"Or someone else did it in order to lure you there. Someone who knew about your feud, perhaps, and hoped you'd be blamed for Carolyn's death."

"If it wasn't an accident." Using a comb, she styled his hair.

"The medical examiner will determine cause of death, but with the victim's neck at that angle, I have few doubts. If she encountered foul play, someone close to you may be responsible."

"Anyone could have attacked Carolyn, even a stranger."

Vail's bushy eyebrows lifted. "Then why did that person hang around the meter room? How often have you gone there?"

"Only once, with the electrician."

"Carolyn may have left the salon long before your power went out, for what reason we have yet to determine. Someone waylaid her, then cut the electricity to your place. You show up next. This strikes me as a predetermined plan."

Her blood chilled. "I could have been killed, but he just knocked me over."

"He or she? Tall or short?"

"I couldn't tell. It was dark."

"Any particular odors? Other impressions?"

"It stank from garbage. The bin is just outside. And from electrical wiring."

"The person who trapped you inside . . . did it occur to you that he may have tampered with the wires and left a hot one for you to stumble across?"

"That's unlikely." She rolled her shoulders, stiff from stress. "Maybe an innocent bystander discovered Carolyn's body and got spooked." Grabbing a can of holding spray, she finished his hair with a light mist.

"You believe that like I believe in fairy tales." He didn't wait for her to unfasten his cape. Leveraging himself upward, he tore it off, tossing it onto the empty chair.

"The landlord," Marla said absently, running her blow-dryer over the seat cushion to dust off cut hairs.

"Dennis Thomson?" Vail had heard her mention him before.

"He gives all the shopkeepers keys to the meter room, just in case. And he has one."

"Meaning?"

"If he'd summoned Carolyn, she would have gone. I still don't know how she could afford the rent here after she did so poorly in her previous location. You should have seen how she let things slide."

"Where does Thomson keep his office?"

"He has a place by the bank. That's where I go to pay my rent. I like to drop it off in person."

"How often does he come around to inspect the property?"

"Rarely."

"So you have no reason to believe he'd been here earlier."

"I guess not, unless someone spotted him."

"Which you could find out if you talk to people." He stepped closer, gripping her shoulders, staring into her eyes in a way that made her knees weaken. "What do you say? Will you help me with this one?"

When his mesmerizing gaze turned on her, she couldn't resist. "I'll think about it, okay? No promises."

He kissed her. "I knew I could count on you."

She wrapped her arms around his neck. "Umm, I need some more convincing."

"Later," he whispered in a husky tone before releasing her. Snickers from her staff turned his skin a charming shade of crimson. "How much?" he asked, reaching for his wallet.

"No charge. You're considered family now." More tittering laughs. "Don't mind the girls," Marla said with a smile. "They're just jealous."

She knew from experience that Detective Vail turned female heads wherever he went. Who wouldn't admire him? He wore his broad shoulders squared back like a military officer. With his angularly handsome face and the steely glint in his fine gray eyes, he was an imposing presence. When he focused that intensity on you, it was as though no one else was present. Watching him leave, she felt a familiar warmth steal through her. The knowledge that he needed her was what ultimately drew her to him.

It won't hurt to ask a few questions, she told herself, but work precluded following up on Vail's suggestions right away.

Finally finding an hour free on Friday, after a customer canceled a coloring job, Marla sauntered over to the hardware store.

Sam Levy, wearing an orange vest with the store's logo, stood behind the cash register. The silver-haired gentleman beamed when he caught sight of her. Like most of the retirees in the area, he'd migrated from the Northeast. Whereas Miami qualified for international status with its Latin American constituents, Broward County defined the southern "bagel belt" for transplanted northerners.

"Hey, Marla, how's it going? Your detective friend find out anything new about that other salon owner?" Sam said in his New Jersey twang.

Gossip traveled fast among shopkeepers in the same strip. "The medical examiner's report hasn't been released yet, but the *Sun-Sentinel* reporter is saying Carolyn died under mysterious circumstances."

"Do the cops suspect foul play?"

Leaning against the counter, Marla gazed into his pale blue eyes. He hadn't yet acquired a perpetual tan, but then his skin of sixty-some years already contained enough age spots to warrant avoiding the sun. Or it could be he just wasn't the outdoor type.

"They're open to the possibilities. I suppose you'd have to consider me a suspect in that case."

"Get out of town! You may have had problems with Carolyn, but you didn't do it."

"How do you know? After all those nasty tricks she played on me, I had the perfect motive."

"Don't think so highly of yourself. You're not the only one to hold a grudge against her."

"Oh? I didn't realize you knew her so well."

Sam coughed into a callused hand. "Not me. Some of her staff members have come in here, looking for light bulbs and such. They've complained about the way she treated them."

"Ha! I'm not surprised. I used to work for her, after I graduated from beauty school. She never had a good word to say, only criticism. In front of customers, no less." Marla remembered her humiliation as though it were yesterday.

"Has the lieutenant spoken to her girls yet?"

"Just in preliminary interviews." She glanced at him curiously. "Did any of her operators say where they were from? I understand Carolyn employed a number of graduates from the Sunrise Academy of Beauty. She subsidized foreign students there."

"I heard them jabbering in some language. Couldn't recognize it, except that it wasn't Spanish."

Bilingualism being nearly an acquired trait among South Floridians since the Cuban influx, Sam's remark didn't raise her eyebrows. But where did the women originate from if they weren't Hispanic? French-speaking Canada? "Do you think Carolyn got knocked off by a disgruntled employee?"

Sam shrugged. "Carolyn acted a bit weird. Maybe that contributed to her downfall. She could have annoyed someone in her spiritual camp."

"What do you mean?" Shuffling through several magazines on the counter, Marla glanced at the covers of *Kitchens and Baths*, *Better Homes and Gardens*, *Seventeen*, *Builders Square*, and *Gardening Today*. A customer entered, clinking a bell on the door. The fellow wasn't anyone she recognized. He seemed out of place in his sport coat and tie, as though he belonged in a downtown Fort Lauderdale office, in one of those tall bank buildings, instead of cruising the casual suburbs. Black hair was slicked off his wide forehead with something that looked more like suet than hair gel.

You want to be more kosher, pal? Drop the grease on your head and lose the suit. This is tropical territory, unless you don't mind changing your shirt several times a day. Then again, Vail always wore a suit to work, and he looked smashing. It must be the way this guy was sweating that put her off. Or maybe it was his beady eyes that scoured them as though they were fire ants needing extermination.

Sam leaned forward, lowering his voice. "Carolyn was nuts about voodoo stuff. If she let it interfere with her work, that might have made people unhappy. Whenever I talked to her, she referred to her 'spiritual adviser.' Seemed pretty hokey to me."

"I didn't know Carolyn was into that sort of thing."

"You bet. Gotta go now. Keep me informed, will you?" He turned to the customer, who'd stopped right behind Marla, practically breathing down her neck. "May I help you, sir?"

Marla stepped out of his path but didn't leave, remembering another reason why she'd come into the store.

The man glared at her as though he could wish her away. "I'm having a problem with a sink faucet. Where can I find your plumbing supplies?"

Like you're going to soil your clothes to fix a sink? Yeah, right. "Sam, there's one more thing. Remember I told you about my mother? She's coming in for an appointment this afternoon, and I'd really like for you to meet her. Think you can stop by around three o'clock?"

Sam's eyes twinkled. "I was wondering when you were going to ask me. The boss is coming in at two, so I should be able to take a break. I'll be there."

"Great, see you later."

Stepping outside, she considered what to do with her remaining free time. Get a snack? Or swallow her distaste for visiting Hairstyle Heaven? Marla had yet to step inside Carolyn's salon, because the prospect repelled her. She'd made some additional suggestions to Claudia about running the shop, since the girl had come pleading to her several times after their first encounter. But offering specific advice based on an examination of Carolyn's business practices just wasn't her place.

Vail was still looking into the legalities regarding Carolyn's heirs, while Marla secretly hoped Hairstyle Heaven would be forced to close. From what Vail had told her, Carolyn's sister, Linda Hall, did not inherit the salon. Nor did any of her other distant relatives. That left future management up in the air, while Carolyn's staffers struggled to maintain the business in the interim.

Their landlord might know who had to pay the rent. Dennis Thomson's office was a short drive away, a block across from her favorite Publix supermarket. Marla figured Vail must've spoken to him already, but maybe she could learn something new.

I'm not doing this because I care about you, Carolyn. I'll help Vail wrap this case only so he can spend more nights at home with Brianna. She didn't like for the girl to be alone while Vail worked late. Marla felt compelled to keep his daughter company, or at least to check on her often. Anger made her clench the steering wheel on her white Camry. Even in death, Carolyn was managing to interfere with her life. *Go haunt someone else,* Marla thought, sucking in deep breaths of air to calm her nerves.

She never liked visiting Mr. Thomson, especially after he'd tried to force her out of her lease. For an instant, Marla considered her ex-spouse, Stan, as a possible suspect. He'd offered to back Carolyn financially in order to ruin Marla's business. But

Stan had no reason to block her path now, not after she'd acquired his half of their jointly owned rental property.

When no one answered the knock on the locked door to Mr. Thomson's business address, she glanced at the plaque listing office hours. Drat, she'd forgotten about his limited schedule. When she'd made arrangements to deliver her rental checks, he'd mentioned this was a branch of his larger holdings. Debating whether to seek the landlord elsewhere, she decided against it. He'd be here Monday; she could visit him on her day off and pay the rent for September at the same time.

Meanwhile, Marla considered what she'd tell Vail tonight. She had a movie date with the detective and his daughter, assuming he could get away from work. They hadn't spoken lately, so she hoped to learn his progress on the case.

During the week she fixed dinner or brought take-out for Brianna when Vail wouldn't be home early. Otherwise, she stayed at her town house, preferring privacy to relax and catch up on bookkeeping chores. Friday nights, she and Vail had a standing date, as well as all day Sunday, and she usually slept over on weekends. Vail wanted her to move in permanently, but Marla wasn't ready for that step yet. She had her own key to let herself into his house, and that had been a big enough concession on both their parts.

I hope Dalton isn't too disappointed that I won't have anything new to add, she thought on her way back to the salon. It wasn't her responsibility to investigate, nor did she care to offer encouragement to Carolyn's staff. This was one occasion where she preferred to mind her own business.

Her mother had other ideas when she breezed into the salon for her afternoon appointment. Following on Anita's heels were her rotund boyfriend, Roger, and his son, Barry. Marla groaned when Barry gave her a sexy grin. The optometrist wasn't fazed by the knowledge that she slept at Vail's house. Probably Anita kept encouraging him, because she'd be thrilled if Marla married the Jewish bachelor. Having already fulfilled family obligations in that regard, however, Marla felt no further duty to comply.

"Marla," Anita said, marching toward her station, "did you see what those people from that other salon did when I got out of my car? They could tell I was heading here, and one of them rushed over and offered me a deal if I tried their place."

Marla clenched her fists. "Those schmucks have done that before."

"It was some skinny broad with a funny accent," Roger said in his booming voice. "You know what I told her? *Zolst geshvollen veren vi a barg!*"

"It's not nice to tell someone to swell up like a mountain," Marla chastised him. "She was probably following Carolyn's orders."

"Carolyn is dead." Anita's brown eyes, matching Marla's own, flashed imperiously.

"Who's running the place?" Barry cut in.

"No one yet." Marla's glance swept from his curly head of sandy blond hair, to his warm blue eyes, and down his length, noting his cotton shirt, jeans, and boots. Recently addicted to westerns, he'd adopted their mode of dress outside the office. He looked pretty good in the role, she had to admit.

Anita leaned forward, giving Marla the opportunity to critically study her white hair, badly in need of a trim. "I thought Dalton had recruited you to talk to people."

"I can't bring myself to visit Carolyn's salon. Claudia has gotten enough of my free advice. I should start charging her."

Anita's mouth pinched, and Marla recognized she was in for a lecture. Glancing at the wall clock, she turned to Barry with a sweet smile. She had to get rid of him and his dad before Sam waltzed through the door. "I thought you'd be at work today."

Roger stiffened, bringing into prominence a grease spot on his carrot orange jacket. *That meshes well with your avocado pants and ruddy complexion. I see Barry hasn't convinced you to change your wardrobe.* Ma didn't mind; color blindness affected her where Roger was concerned.

"We're catching a flight out of town and wanted to say good-bye," Roger said. "My aunt passed away, and I'm her closest relative. I'm taking a few weeks to settle her estate. Barry has agreed to help me and called his patients to postpone their appointments. I know you'll miss him, doll."

"Gee, I'm so sorry," Marla lied.

Roger gave her an affectionate punch on the arm. "Be good to your mom, you hear?"

"Right. Bye," she said, eager for them to leave. While she considered Roger to be downright obnoxious, she liked Barry, though only as a friend. He didn't seem to understand the "only as a friend" part. He kept trying to insinuate himself into her life, much to Vail's annoyance.

"Now, dear, tell me what's going on," Anita said after she'd been shampooed.

Marla settled a cape around her mother's slim shoulders. "I spoke to Sam Levy. He's a nice gentleman who works in the hardware store. Remember, I mentioned him to you?"

"I think so." Anita scrutinized her painted red nails. "Is your manicurist free? I could use a touch-up."

"We'll check after I'm done with your haircut." Examining her mother's layers, she decided to give her a bit more lift. Marla had similar fine hair, which she wore in a short brunette bob. "Anyway, Sam told me that Carolyn was into some kind of spiritual nonsense. I don't recall her being interested in that stuff when I worked for her, so this must be a fairly new development."

"Once a fruitcake, always a fruitcake, that's what I say. She was *meshuga* when you labored on her payroll. She didn't know how to be good to people then, so why change?"

"Maybe she had a revelation and wanted to redeem herself."

"I doubt it. Doesn't Vail know who inherits ownership?" Anita asked. "Maybe you can make a deal to take over management duties."

"Are you kidding? I'd be nuts to support another salon a few doors down. Why do you think I've been avoiding going in there since they opened? I'm hoping they'll fold."

Gripping a pair of shears, she glanced at the front door as the chimes rang. *Oh no, here comes Claudia again. Won't that girl ever give up?* Through the window, she noticed Sam approaching with a purposeful stride. The silver-haired man halted, greeted Claudia at the door, then pushed past her after a brief exchange.

A flash of light reflecting off metal diverted Marla's attention.

Watching from the parking lot with a scowl on his long face was their landlord, Dennis Thomson.

Chapter Three

"Marla, is that your beautiful mom? I can see the resemblance, although she looks more like your sister," Sam said with a shy smile.

Marla caught her mother's pleased glance in the mirror. "Ma, this is Sam Levy. He used to be in the building business up north. Now he works part-time in the hardware store."

"Just call me Mr. Fix-it," Sam teased, holding out a callused hand.

Anita gave him a shake; then he stood back so Marla could finish trimming her mother's short white layers.

"About that extension cord you ordered," Sam said, winking, "what length did you want?"

Marla realized he was offering an excuse for his visit. "Oh, yes, I'll come get one later." In the mirror, she caught a glimpse of Claudia directly behind, arms folded across her chest. "What is it this time?" she demanded.

The dark-haired woman pouted. "I have come to give you important information, but you are rude to me. Or maybe your detective friend already told you."

Marla raised her arms in defeat. "Ma, I'll be right back. Talk to Sam in the meantime, will you?" Placing the scissors on the counter, she whirled on her heels and gestured at Claudia.

Outdoors, the August heat penetrated her pores. In just a few minutes, her sleeveless top stuck to her back like plastic wrap. The rich smell of humus hung in air so heavy with humidity, she could almost squeeze the moisture from it. Shielding her eyes, she avoided the sun's glare that bounced off the pavement like desert sand cooked under a broiling sky. She glanced for relief to the west, where storm clouds accumulated to gather strength for their pending onslaught. Marla enjoyed the daily race against time when thunderstorms threatened to unleash their fury before she got home.

She'd forgotten about Mr. Thomson, but he had disappeared. He must have gone into one of the shops. If she was lucky, she would catch him later.

"Where are you from?" she addressed the young woman abruptly. Although Marla was taller than Claudia, her low-heeled shoes were no match for the stylist's towering sandals. The girl beat her by a good two inches in height.

"*Je suis Française* . . . I am French. From a small city beyond Paris." Claudia wore one of those tiny flowered tops that looked like a scrap of material but came from one of the higher-priced boutiques. Marla had seen the European fashions in her friend Tally's store, Dressed to Kill.

"Were you a hairdresser at home, or did Carolyn pay for your training in the states?"

"I don't see why that matters."

"Someone subsidized her, or else she took out a loan. I'm unable to fathom how Carolyn could've afforded to move otherwise. The director at my beauty school said she helped certain students pay their tuition. Where did she get the funds?"

Claudia spread her hands. "I came to offer information, not to be questioned. The policeman has already spoken to me."

"Well, he hasn't shared his findings."

Claudia's eyebrows lifted. They were thin almost to the point of absenteeism. A dark pencil gave her an artificial arch. "Madame said you were lovers."

"What else did she say about me?" Marla couldn't help herself. She still resented Carolyn, even in death.

"Madame generously gave you your first job, and you were ungrateful," Claudia replied, sniffing. "You left without giving notice, stealing her stylists to open your own place in direct competition with Carolyn's salon. You did your best to ruin her and forced her out of town."

"That's a bunch of lies!" Marla's blood seethed. "She was a terrible employer, always criticizing. She'd raise her voice in front of customers, threatened to fire us. When I got enough money from my divorce settlement, I decided to leave. Some of the other girls asked if they could join me; it wasn't my initiative."

"Madame believed otherwise."

"So why have you been coming to me for advice?"

Claudia kicked at a pebble. "We need guidance. Our new owner knows nothing about the salon business."

Marla's ears perked up. "Is Carolyn's sister in charge?"

"Linda is not the heir, at least regarding Hairstyle Heaven. Madame left ownership to Wilda Cleaver, the ghost lady. She was Carolyn's psychic friend."

"Interesting." Sam had mentioned a spiritual adviser. She wondered if Vail had followed this lead.

The stylist turned an imploring gaze on her. "Please, mademoiselle, I know Carolyn had not been kind to you, but she felt betrayed. Surely you would not take your anger out on us poor working girls? This wild woman does not know how to manage a salon. You can advise her. We do not wish to lose our jobs."

Why should I care? Despite her reluctance to get involved, Marla disliked seeing colleagues in distress. She could always suggest to this Cleaver person that they relocate the salon.

"Send her in to see me, and I'll talk to her. That's all I can promise. Is she there now?" Marla glanced inside the salon. She still had to finish her mother in time for the next customer, although Ma seemed to be happily chatting with Sam. At least that had worked out well.

"*Non*, the lady will be in next week. I'll give her your message." Claudia pumped her hand in gratitude. "Until then, may we borrow some developer? We're nearly out."

Marla winced. "When's the last time someone took inventory?"

"That was Carolyn's job."

"So now it is Wilda's responsibility, and she'll have no clue what to look for. Bless my bones, I really don't have time for this."

"Make time," was what Vail said to her that evening when they were on their way to see the latest James Bond movie with his daughter, Brianna. She sat in the front seat of his roomy sedan while Brie lounged in the rear, rocking to music playing from her headset.

"I have enough to do without worrying about your case," Marla protested, crossing her ankles. She'd changed into a sundress, carrying a sweater for the air-conditioning. Thunder rumbled in the distance, but the cloud bank edged the sky too far away to pose any immediate threat. Nonetheless, she'd brought an umbrella, a necessity during the hurricane season.

"You're not alone in disliking Carolyn Sutton, so I could use your help. People tell you things they won't reveal to me."

"I meant to speak to our landlord," she conceded. "I'll catch him next week. Did you learn anything about Carolyn's finances?"

"She's had some bank deposits that we're looking into and a series of regular withdrawals, but nothing outstanding. The sister gets whatever's left after her estate settles, minus the salon." He gave her a quick glance, warming her skin and making her nerves tingle. She liked the way he'd parted his hair to the side and yearned to fluff it through her fingers. "Why don't you give her a call? I'll give you Linda Hall's number."

"What for?"

"Express your condolences, see if she'll tell you anything new. You know, draw her out. The funeral is Sunday."

"So? I'm not going." She gave him a playful look. "If I recall, you used to warn me against interfering in your cases. Maybe I should ask for a deputy badge. There's a cute officer on your team who might be happy to oblige me."

"Yeah, Marla," Brianna chipped in. "Go for it."

"No way, lady. You're my territory." Vail patted her thigh, glancing at the amethyst ring she wore on her right hand. It had been his gift for Valentine's Day, her birthday.

Marla thrust his hand away before he distracted her train of thought. They'd been careful to confine their lovemaking to her town house, using his home only when Brie slept over at a friend's place. She still felt awkward about their showing affection to each other in front of the teenager.

"Have you interviewed Carolyn's guru yet?" Marla asked Vail. "What does she do, anyway, predict the future? I'll bet Carolyn paid her a tidy sum to look into the crystal ball. Maybe Wilda told her that moving back to Palm Haven was good karma."

"Cleaver has her own theories about Carolyn's death. She gave me a bunch of mumbo jumbo, but I'm wondering about her motives. It's likely she took advantage of the victim."

"Carolyn could've discovered she was a charlatan," Marla mused. "What kind of reputation does Wilda have?"

Vail snorted. "She has a following. I spoke to a couple of women. They were both fiftyish, looking for something to relieve their boredom, in my opinion. If anyone is missing a spark plug in her mental engine, it's the medium."

"Now you've aroused my curiosity."

His eyes smoldered. "Is that all? I'd hoped for more."

"Marla, why don't you talk to these people?" Brianna suggested. "You always find out more than Daddy."

Like I don't have enough to do: maintaining a household, running my salon, and keeping Ma from driving me crazy? "I don't mean to change the subject, but did I tell you Ma met Sam Levy, the guy from the hardware store? He's such as sweet man. I'd like to fix them up, especially now that Roger is out of town."

Vail shook his head. "You're happy to play matchmaker, but you won't settle down on your own."

She narrowed her eyes. "Life with Stan left me with a bad taste for settling down. You should be happy I'm trying to keep my nose out of your affairs for a change."

"You're closer to the people who knew the deceased. She met someone in the meter room . . . someone who turned off the power to your salon. Maybe Carolyn wasn't the intended victim."

"What does that mean?"

"Sutton may have been in the wrong place at the wrong time. The intruder might have been after you."

Marla stared at him. "That's providing she'd been murdered. Anything you want to share with me?" *Like cause of death?* When he shook his head, she continued. "I doubt Carolyn had many friends. She took too much pleasure in demeaning other people. If you counted those of us who aren't sad over her death, I'll bet you could form a line."

"Prove it to me."

"Huh?"

Brianna snickered. "He's got you, Marla. Give him a list of everyone who hated Carolyn."

Challenged, she took the bait. "All right. I'll show you who had reason to want her dead." She rattled off some names of people Carolyn had offended. "Justine Welsh must be one of them. I remember the day Carolyn reduced her to tears in front of a customer. Then there was Andy, the shampoo assistant, who Carolyn docked every time her hair washes took too long. Carolyn said time was money, and so the poor girl hardly made anything. Carolyn made plenty of enemies. I was just lured there as a patsy. If anyone else were in charge of the investigation, I'd be a suspect as well. Assuming someone plotted to kill Carolyn, we'll find out who did it and why."

Marla finally got the chance to question Dennis Thomson on Monday. Entering her landlord's office always made her uncomfortable. It reminded her of a prison cell, like the one in which she'd visited dear old Stan in the city clinker when he'd been wrongly accused of murdering his second wife. Maybe the harsh lighting reflecting off gray walls contributed, or else it was the lack of accoutrements besides the standard-issue desk, couple of chairs, and single metal trash can. Even the carpet, a mixed-color Berber, muted into dismal ash. Her mood sank along her body as she took a seat opposite the landlord.

Thomson had grown pudgier over the years. His black hair, thinning over his crown, along with small deepset eyes and an almost nonexistent chin, gave him a weaselly look. It didn't help that his thick lips were curled into a perpetual snarl.

"I wanted to talk to you about Carolyn Sutton," Marla said after handing him her rental payment. "Although we didn't get along, I felt bad about her . . . passing. I'd like to do what I can to help the police. What do you know about Carolyn's successor?" Crossing her ankles, she smoothed her knee-length skirt.

Thomson's amber eyes glowed. "It doesn't strike me as being your concern."

"Detective Vail thinks maybe I was the intended victim instead of Carolyn. I don't agree with him. Carolyn wasn't a nice person, and she may have made enemies. When I worked for her, she treated her staff like dirt." Her ears still rang with the criticisms Carolyn would say in front of customers, like *Marla will never get that cut right, but she tries hard.* What made Carolyn's girls so loyal that they wanted to stay even after she was gone? "I don't understand why her stylists choose to remain when things are in such turmoil."

Thomson shrugged. "It's a job. They need the money, and customers depend on them."

"Claudia, one of the hairdressers, has repeatedly asked for my advice. Shouldn't the new owner tell the girls what to do?" She couldn't help her resentful tone. Thomson knew she disliked his decision to bring another beauty shop to the same location.

"Indeed. I'm sure her staff appreciates your insights, but it wouldn't be wise for you to spend time at Hairstyle Heaven."

Clearly she wasn't going to get any information out of him

about Wilda Cleaver. An idea surfaced, one that didn't set well. If Carolyn had some kind of hold over those girls, perhaps she had one over their landlord as well.

"Carolyn sponsored foreign students at the Sunrise Academy of Beauty and employed them in her salon after they graduated. Where do you suppose she got the funds? Her previous location wasn't exactly a success."

"How would you know?" Sweat beaded Thomson's upper lip.

"I visited her there when she tried to take over my lease. Was Carolyn on time with her monthly rent payments?"

"She met her obligations." Rubbing his hands together, he avoided her penetrating stare. "If I were you, I'd keep my nose out of other people's affairs. Otherwise, when your term comes up for renewal, you might find a few surprises."

Marla shot to her feet, but she bit back any retort that might aggravate him further. *You're the one who will be surprised when I determine why you act so nervous.* Thomson hadn't directly answered any of her questions, but she'd bet her *bobka* he knew more about Carolyn's life than he let on. Better to acquire additional information before probing deeper.

"Thanks, I'll keep that in mind," she replied before taking her leave.

Realizing it was unavoidable, she stopped off next at Carolyn's salon in spite of Thomson's warning to stay clear. In another attempt to steal customers, her rival had opened on Mondays. That meant Carolyn's staff had only one day off a week unless they staggered schedules. Spotting Claudia working on a blonde with highlights, she waved.

The Frenchwoman's expression brightened, and she signaled Marla to come over. No one manned the reception desk, Marla noticed.

"I thought your new owner was coming in this week," she said, sniffing the familiar scents of hair spray, permanent-solution fumes, and polish remover.

"Wilda said the signs weren't right for today," Claudia said with a sneer. "I fear she will add to our problems. Have you come to assist us? Girls, this is Marla Shore from Cut 'N Dye."

Busy with customers who required cutting, coloring, and conditioning, the stylists waved while Marla's quick glance took in counters strewn with equipment and hairs littering the tile floor. Where was their shampoo assistant? In her salon, Joanne took care of sweeping chores along with other mundane tasks. Each hairdresser cleaned her own station. Apparently, no such standards existed here. She didn't see how a fortune-teller would be able to run the place without experienced counsel. Clients had to receive a significant discount to remain loyal; Marla made a mental note to check their price list.

"How are you getting on?" Marla asked, genuinely perplexed. If these stylists rented their booths, they paid a fixed monthly sum to the owner and maintained their own stores. Alternately, when a proprietor wanted more control, she employed a commission system wherein operators kept sixty percent and gave forty percent to the owner. These shared profits often led to better teamwork and a broader sense of cooperation. It was how Marla ran her salon. In return for the percentage fee, she paid for overhead expenses, stocked the shelves, and scheduled advanced training seminars.

"Detective Vail took things from the front desk," Claudia said. "Wilda promised to set things straight when she gets here, but I am afraid she may consult her crystals instead of the appointment book. We are scared, mademoiselle. If we lose this job, we shall have to go home."

A tall, model-thin brunette sidled up to her. "*Je suis* Lisette. I am sorry if Carolyn made us do mean things to you. It was not our wish to cause harm. We had to obey, or she would have dismissed us. You will forgive, *non?*"

Marla lifted her chin. "I fired that manicurist she suckered me into hiring after catching the woman pilfering our supplies. Not only did Joy talk against me to customers, but one day she put depilatory into our shampoo bottles. Carolyn must have paid her well to sabotage me. How about the rest of you? Did you get a bonus to order that truckload of toilet paper in my name? Or to cancel that delivery from Sebastian that I really needed?"

The girls exchanged glances. "We'll do anything you ask if you'll help us," Lisette pleaded. "Right, Claudia?"

The Mona Lisa look-alike nodded curtly, giving Marla the impression that the younger hairdresser looked to her for guidance. Had Claudia hoped to gain management of the salon for herself? Possibly, if Carolyn had relied on her. Surely she wouldn't expect to inherit ownership, though. Why the devil was she so desperate to keep her current job? Marla surveyed the other stylists. Were they here on work visas, meaning they'd be shipped back to France when their documents or employment expired?

She'd have to ask Vail these questions. He might be more familiar with immigration regulations, plus he'd be looking into the background of Carolyn's staff along with anyone else who had been close to her.

The detective had wanted Marla to talk to Carolyn's sister, but she'd been negligent in fulfilling his request. Avoidance behavior was something she was becoming adept at, especially in regard to any actions involving Carolyn. Now would be a good time to contact Linda Hall. Then she'd have an excuse to call Dalton with news.

"I'll come in tomorrow when Wilda Cleaver is here," Marla promised the French stylists. "Maybe we can work out some sort of agreement." *As in a noncompetition clause in exchange for my expert advice.* Too many salons existed already in nearby shopping centers, as ubiquitous as Chinese restaurants, pizza kitchens, and bagel dens. What she'd really aim for would be to persuade the new owner of Hairstyle Heaven to change locations.

Marla wished she could convince Dalton Vail to do the same. While she spent weekends at his house, she still felt uncomfortable surrounded by his dead wife's belongings. He hadn't removed a single knickknack since Pam died three years ago. It drove a wedge between them, one that she'd chipped at but barely budged. If she ever made her move permanent, a new house might be their only solution.

In the meantime, she divided her time between his ranch-style home and her one-story town house. As she drove into her driveway, she noticed her neighbor, Goat, walking his dog. The black poodle yipped and tugged on its leash, yanking its scraggly-haired owner in Marla's direction. Hearing her own dog, Spooks, bark in response when she emerged from her Camry, Marla unlocked the kitchen door and grabbed his leash from its hook. Her male white poodle bolted out the door to meet his lady love, Rita. The two poodles sniffed each other while Marla addressed Goat.

"Aren't you at work today?" she said, glancing at his parked van. Goat, whose real name was Kyle Stanislaw, ran a mobile animal-grooming business. His thin straw-colored hair, sparse beard, and menagerie of pets had given him his nickname. Today he defied the August heat in a Hawaiian shirt, shorts, and a new addition: an Indiana Jones style hat. *Probably the summer substitute of his usual fur cap.*

"Ugamaka, ugamaka, chugga, chugga, ush," he chanted, tapping his bare feet against the sidewalk. "Took some time off, to build my loft, and then I met Jenny, who tossed a penny at Walt Disney World, where we cut and curled."

"Oh, you met your sister in Orlando?" Marla deciphered his lyrics. Jenny lived in Mount Dora, a quaint town with an annual antique fair.

"You got it." He stumbled when Rita, chasing Spooks, twisted her leash around his ankles.

Marla jerked her pooch to a halt. "Spooks, behave." Their dogs joined forces to touch noses. "He may be fixed, but he still has his mojo," she remarked.

"So does Rita." Goat grinned. "How are things with your boyfriend?" Tightening his grip on the leash, he danced a jig. "Your lights go out, the house is bare, weekends go by with nary a scare."

"I'm spending time with him and Brianna. Dalton still has some issues to settle before we, uh, take the next step."

"Has he?"

"What?"

"You know, popped the question."

"No, thank goodness. I'm not ready for that yet. He wants me to help him investigate another case."

"Awesome, dudette. You're good at the crime thing."

"Not this time. Carolyn Sutton and I didn't get along. She probably made other enemies. It doesn't surprise me that someone bumped her off." Marla watched while Spooks did his business on an elderly neighbor's lawn. "I'd better go inside and make a phone call. I promised Dalton I'd call Carolyn's sister to see what I can learn."

Goat gave her the thumbs-up sign. "I'm with you, man. If you need help, you know where to find me."

Marla appreciated his sincerity and support. "I know. Have a good day. I'll talk to you later. Come on, Spooks, move."

Having delegated the role of matchmaker to herself for Anita and Sam, Marla now considered whom she could find for Goat. Poor guy, all he dreamed about was acquiring a piece of land up North to raise his animals, but he'd taken too many wrong turns. Maybe if he found the right person to focus his attention on, he'd stay on the proper path. His sister had explained his weird mannerisms as being due to shyness. What he needed was a woman who loved pets and could tolerate his shenanigans.

That wasn't her concern yet, though: interviewing Carolyn's sister came first. A promise made was a promise kept. Marla entered her house, released Spooks, washed her hands, then picked up the telephone.

Chapter
Four

"My name is Marla Shore," she said when a woman answered on the other end of the line. "Is this Linda Hall?"

"Speaking."

"I am . . . was . . . er, a friend of your sister's." Marla wondered how much Carolyn had confided about their rivalry.

"Aren't you the lady from the other salon?" Hall's sharp response answered her question.

"Yes, I'm with Cut 'N Dye. I was terribly sorry about your sister's untimely death."

"I told that detective about you."

Sinking onto a kitchen chair, Marla gripped the receiver. "Look, I don't know what Carolyn said about me, but I meant her no harm." *She was the one who played nasty tricks on me*, Marla wanted to add but held her tongue.

"What do you want?"

She squirmed at the awkwardness of their conversation. "I feel bad about what happened, and I'd like to help. Is there some way we can get together for a chat? I gather you live north of Palm Haven. I could go to your home, or we can meet somewhere, and I'll buy you a drink." Biting her lower lip to stop babbling, Marla waited.

A long silence met her request. "All right. The kids are at their friend's house, so I can spare an hour. I'm in Delray Beach. Take I-95 to Atlantic Avenue. Get off at Exit Fifty-Two, and go east six traffic lights to Pineapple Grove Way. Make a left, and look for Murder on the Beach Mystery Bookstore. A few doors down is the Seagrape Café. I'll meet you there at five."

"Okay. I have brown hair and eyes, and I'll be wearing a peach slacks set. See you soon."

Her preparations took less than ten minutes. She stuffed a large notebook into her white leather purse, changed into the peach outfit with matching sandals, refreshed her makeup, and refilled Spooks's water dish.

"Bye, precious." Scratching the poodle behind his ears, she smiled. "Guard the house while I'm gone." She set the alarm, locked the door between the kitchen and garage, and swung into her car. Putting her cell phone into its charger, she switched on the ignition.

Traffic wasn't too bad, considering it was close to rush hour. She veered north on I-95, dodging the usual assault of trucks and sport utility vehicles. Once she'd cleared the Fort Lauderdale corridor, she allowed her mind to drift into automatic gear. Time to plan the interview. *Don't let Linda know how you really felt about Carolyn, or you'll turn her off.* She would assess Linda's relationship with her sister first. Consider what Linda had to gain, if anything, from Carolyn's death. *Regard everyone as a suspect.* That was Vail's oft-repeated advice. She hoped to question Linda concerning her whereabouts the day Carolyn died. Presumably, Dalton had already interrogated the woman, but Marla would use a softer approach, especially when the funeral was just yesterday.

She found the restaurant without any trouble and parked her car around the corner. A few minutes early for the rendezvous, she stopped in the Murder on the Beach bookstore where the proprietor, Joanne Sinchuk, recommended a couple of medical thrillers for Nicole. The stylist enjoyed mysteries and was always imploring Marla to read them, but who had time? She preferred the real-life thing to armchair detecting anyway.

At the café, Marla was surprised to find a full-service restaurant instead of the coffee shop she'd expected. Already bustling with shoppers and businesspeople who had gotten off work earlier, the crowded bar had few empty seats. Nor would it lend itself to a quiet chat, she realized with dismay. Someone waved, and she spotted a woman on a barstool saving an empty seat beside her. When Marla met her gaze, she signaled more vigorously.

"I'm Linda Hall," said a heavyset blond whose lined face put her in the late forties. "You must be Marla."

They shook hands while Marla did a quick inspection. Linda's heavily mascaraed eyes made her complexion pale in comparison. Pink glossy lipstick and plum blush might have worked on a younger person, but on her they gave the impression of someone clinging to youth who was past her prime. Nor did the thick hair straight to her shoulders have any appeal. *You'd look better with a shorter cut angled to your face and more subtle makeup.* If Linda worked with her attributes, not against them, she'd be much more attractive, Marla concluded.

Smiling sweetly, she took the proffered chair and ordered herself a bushwhacker along with another white zinfandel for her companion. "I'm grateful you took the time to see me," she began, nibbling on a honey-roasted peanut from a dish set in front of them. "I guess Carolyn told you about my salon."

"She said you wanted to run her out of business." Linda's hazel eyes narrowed. "Carolyn gave you your first job, then you stabbed her in the back by walking out with half her staff. You set yourself up in direct competition, forcing her out of town."

"I left only because Carolyn didn't give me any respect. She had problems getting along with the other stylists, and that's why they came with me. As for her relocating, I suspect that was due to her business decisions rather than any influence I might have had."

"She said you visited her new place and accused her of conspiring with your landlord."

"Someone was trying to take over my lease, and I knew

Carolyn wanted to return to Palm Haven. My ex-husband, an attorney, confessed he'd set her up with the money to offer my landlord. Fortunately for me, their plan fell through."

"Didn't you bear a grudge against her? Maybe enough to permanently get rid of a rival?"

Marla stiffened. "I didn't kill her. I was grateful she'd hired me when I graduated beauty school, and then I just wanted to succeed on my own. She's the one who started playing nasty pranks on me to steal customers."

"That sounds like my sister."

"How well did you get along with her?"

Linda gripped her glass, a large diamond ring flashing on her left hand above a slim gold wedding band. No bracelets, and an inexpensive watch. Here was a lady who didn't burden herself with jewels, unless she was storing them for more important events. Diamond tennis bracelets were so common among South Florida mavens that you could pave the streets with them.

"Carolyn was incredibly jealous of me," Linda said. "In her mind, it wasn't fair that I'd met Richard and married him before I hit thirty. We have two beautiful children, a nice house, and a comfortable life. I quit my job two weeks before Kevin was born and haven't worked since."

"Go on." Marla's nostrils picked up the scent of ale mingled with barbecued beef. It made her mouth water. She took a sip of her coffee-flavored beverage, enjoying the kick from the liquor.

"Carolyn avoided serious relationships. I always attributed it to a flaw in her character, that she couldn't trust anyone. Like she projected the pettiness within herself onto others, you know? Or else she was just too kooky."

"Wasn't she seeing a medium?"

Linda gulped her wine. "I shouldn't have said that," she went on, confusing Marla about what she meant. "Carolyn did get engaged at one time to some man she thought she loved. The guy took advantage of her; anyone could see it, but my sister wore blinders where he was concerned. He wanted to start his own business and figured she could support him."

"When was this?"

"About five years ago. After he died in a car crash, Carolyn turned weird. She started visiting mediums to communicate with him."

"You mean Wilda Cleaver?" Leaning toward her companion, Marla lowered her voice to a conspiratorial tone. "Detective Vail mentioned that Carolyn had left her the salon."

Linda's face scrunched like a prune. "That woman has no right. I'm Carolyn's sister. She should've left the business to me." Taking a long gulp from her glass, she set it down, then glared at Marla. "Carolyn figured I had it all: a husband who supported me, kids, a nice roof over my head. She always whined about how she had to earn a living while I could stay home."

"You think that's why Carolyn didn't leave you the business? Because she thought you didn't need the money?"

"Partially. That witch lady brainwashed her. All Carolyn could talk about were messages from her dead fiance that she felt were guiding her. She got into crystals, candles, and seeing some shaman when she didn't feel well. Nuts, that's what she was! It's all that Cleaver woman's fault."

"So you feel Wilda unduly influenced your sister?"

"No doubt about it. She made Carolyn resent me even more. I'm surprised my sister left me her collection."

"Oh?" A large man jostled past on his way to a barstool. When he bumped Marla's shoulder, he gave her a leering grin. She shifted her position, turning more toward Linda. Her stomach growled, reminding her it was dinner hour, but she didn't want to linger any longer than necessary.

"Maybe I shouldn't be mentioning this, but Carolyn bragged that the items were valuable. Whenever I saw her recently, she said how they would be mine one day. She seemed to think that would make me happy, but she never showed them to me."

"What did she acquire?"

Linda's gaze clouded. "I have no idea. Detective Vail and I went through her place together, but we couldn't find anything worthwhile."

"Did he look in her salon? Maybe she hid the stuff there."

"No luck." Linda jabbed a finger in the air. "You know what I think? Either Carolyn was putting me on, or she had something so valuable someone killed her for it."

"You didn't tell me anything about Carolyn's valuables," Marla told Vail on the telephone later that evening. She'd driven home, fixed herself a quick dinner courtesy of a frozen meal, let Spooks into the backyard for a brief foray, then settled down to make her phone calls.

The detective's gruff voice held amusement. "I gather you spoke to Carolyn's sister. What did you learn?"

"Not so fast. You've told me hardly anything about this case. You go first."

"Want me to come over? It's easier for me to confess everything when I'm staring into your beautiful eyes."

"Forget it. I have to get up early for work tomorrow, and you shouldn't leave Brianna. Is she ready for school?"

He gave a hearty sigh. "One more week. I can't wait. It's been a long summer without Carmen."

"You have been managing fine without your housekeeper."

"Thanks to you. When will you stay here during the work week? You know I don't expect you to cook meals or wait on us."

That isn't my concern. Your house stifles me. Pam's ghost haunts the place and fills your mind with memories. "I'll think about it," she hedged. "You were telling me about Carolyn?"

"Hmph. Carolyn promised Linda she would inherit her collectibles, but we couldn't find any items of value."

"Jewelry? If a collection exists, it makes sense that they were gifts from her private benefactor. I don't see how Carolyn could afford anything else. Did she have a safety deposit box?"

"It held deeds and other papers. No jewels or mementos."

"Did you find out who funded her relocation? Subsidized those girls at the academy?"

"I'm working on it. Any other advice?" he teased.

"You might want to ask around to see who had keys to her

apartment. If someone gave her valuable gifts, he might have re-trieved them after her death." That would support what Linda theorized about Carolyn being murdered for her collection. Then again, it was always possible Carolyn had been lying. She might have made empty promises to her sister to mollify her.

"Linda all but accused Wilda Cleaver of brainwashing Carolyn. She blames Wilda for driving a wedge between them."

"Yes, I know. I'd like you to talk to Wilda, give me your im-pression."

"Why?"

"You'll see."

"I hate it when you hide things from me."

"I'm not doing that. I just don't want to color your percep-tions."

"What do you know about her?"

"She's a popular psychic who lives in Miami. Her customers think the world of her. I told you that already."

Marla pulled a nail file from her desk drawer. "Did Carolyn have any other friends, people she confided in?"

"Oh, yeah. She played bingo pretty regularly, based on some receipts I found at her apartment. According to her calendar, she met a woman named Rosemary Taylor at the Indian casino in Hollywood on a weekly basis."

Marla mulled over this news. She wouldn't have guessed Carolyn was a gambler. "You think Carolyn won big, and that's where she got the money to invest in collectibles?"

"We can't prove this cache of treasure really exists," he replied, his tone cynical. "Anyway, I can think of another secret treasure I'd rather explore."

"Such as?"

"You know." The huskiness of his voice revealed the direction of his thoughts. "I don't think I can wait until Friday night."

"Tempting. I wish we had time before then."

"So do I, but I can dream about it for now."

"Good. While you're indulging yourself in fantasies, I'm going to call my mother. Talk to you later." She dialed her mother's number. "Hi, Ma." Rolling her shoulders, she yearned for a shower. It had been a long day.

"So, *bubula*, you decided to call your mother? To what do I owe the honor?"

"Just reporting in. I visited Carolyn's sister today." Filing her nails while cradling the receiver to her ear, Marla shared her latest findings.

"You're a schnook for getting involved, unless you can influence the new salon owner in your favor. Better you should take more time to care about your family."

Here we go again. "I just spoke to Michael yesterday. He and Charlene were taking the kids to a water park."

"I'm not talking about your brother. Do you ever call Aunt Polly to see how she's getting along? She has no children, you know. It would be nice if you thought of her now and then."

"She's your sister."

"Polly won't do anything I say. She lives like a pauper and embarrasses me by the way she dresses. She'll listen to you."

Marla snorted in derision. "Like I could get her to change after how many years?"

"Seventy-two."

"No! I didn't realize she was that much older than you."

"Someday maybe you'll be interested in my family when you lift your nose out of police business."

"Since when is looking after Aunt Polly your responsibility? She manages well enough on her own."

"She's becoming forgetful, and I'm worried about her. You're the closest niece. Do me a favor and go visit. See if you can help her with things."

Just what I need when I have so much else to do. If you dump anything else on me, I'll scream. "Okay, but you have to do something for me in return."

"What's that?" her mother's wary voice responded.

"Go out with Sam Levy from the hardware store. I could tell he was taken with you. He's a nice man, and it'll give you something to do while Roger is away."

"Oh, I couldn't do that. Roger wouldn't like it."

"You have no commitment to him."

"You've made no commitment to Vail, either. Do I see you going out with Roger's son, Barry? He's a good catch."

"Things are going well with Brianna now. She needs someone she can trust. I don't want to spoil our relationship."

"*Kinehoreh.*" Ward off the evil eye. "If everything is so smooth with Vail, why aren't you engaged?"

"He hasn't asked." Finished with her nails, she put away the file. Since when had this conversation diverted to her personal life? "You want me to help with Aunt Polly, then agree to meet Sam if he calls you. Deal?"

Anita clicked her tongue. "All right, but you should have learned by now that manipulating people doesn't always lead to the outcome you expect."

After a refreshing shower, Marla phoned her friend Tally. She spent the first few minutes of their conversation complaining about her mother and then about Vail's lack of progress on the case. "Want to play bingo this week? I'd like to check out Carolyn's gaming partner."

"That works for me. I had my aura class tonight, but I'm still not getting anywhere. The instructor says my energy is blocked."

"Is that so?" Marla hadn't followed her friend's foray into the New Age.

"Maybe it's why I can't get pregnant, although Ken doesn't believe in psychic influences. All our tests have come back negative. What else can it be?" Tally said.

"Too much stress. Did you listen to my advice about hiring a manager? You put in too many hours at the store."

"Like you should talk. You won't trust anyone else to run the salon. When is the last time you took an entire week off?"

"Nicole handles things for me when I'm gone."

"I've seen those travel brochures stuffed in your purse. When do you expect to go anywhere? When you retire?"

Marla pursed her lips. "Look, you're the one who's having problems. Maybe you and Ken should take a vacation."

"Holy smokes, this is hurricane season. Ken is up to his ears in insurance claims. He just got back from South Carolina where that last storm hit."

"So how do you expect to make a baby if he's never home?"

"That's not the issue."

"No? Then what is?" Marla might not be psychic, but she sensed an underlying tension in her friend that wasn't being expressed.

"I'm hoping my yoga and meditation will relax me. That's what my guru says I should do because I'm absorbing too much negativity, and that can imbalance my chakras. Did you know that if you tighten your stomach muscles, it locks your aura?"

It does more than that. If your abs are flab, exercise makes sense-ercise. "That's good to know," Marla said wryly. "How about if we talk more about this when I see you? I need to check my e-mail."

"Okay, do you want to look into what hours the bingo place is open and give me a call? Then we'll set a time."

"You got it. I'll talk to you soon."

Marla hung up, shaking her head. Tally seemed to be turning into someone she didn't know. It saddened her that they were diverging onto such different paths; how it would affect their friendship remained to be seen. She used to have such fun with Tally, too: going shopping, night-clubbing, exploring the environs. Tally, a statuesque blonde who could pass for a model, had had a career-track mind and dreamed of expanding her boutique empire. But then she'd become dissatisfied. Marla couldn't put her finger on when or why, but Tally had started searching for fulfillment in alternate realities.

I should take her to Disney World, on the Tower of Terror ride. She'd like that ghost story. Right now, visiting the theme parks was a far more attractive option than helping Vail solve Carolyn's murder.

No matter how hard she tried to disengage herself from the Carolyn Sutton case, fate kept intervening. Marla was working on a foil highlights Tuesday morning when a woman cruised into the salon, drawing all eyes to her strange appearance. Her generous body dressed in a flowing caftan, she commanded attention with her striking features, vibrant green eyes, and flaming red hair. As an advertisement for a color chart, Marla thought, she'd serve well. Even her eyebrows, drawn in a perfect bark brown, reflected calculated expertise. What she couldn't correct without surgery were the sagging folds about her eyes, but they conveyed wisdom rather than decline.

The apparition strode straight up to Marla and introduced herself. "I'm Wilda Cleaver. You're going to help me."

Thunderstruck, Marla stared at her. "Excuse me?"

"She said to go to you, that you would know what to do."

"Oh, Claudia must have sent you." Belatedly, Marla recalled her promise to greet Wilda that morning at Hairstyle Heaven.

Wilda tilted her head, making her earrings clink. The tiny pink stones matched the odd-shaped quartz pendant she wore around her neck. "Carolyn sent me, darling, not Claudia. She has a lot of faith in you."

Bless my bones, we're dipping into fruitcake territory again. I should get you together with Tally. "Really?" Marla said, picking up her brush and resuming work. She painted on the color, wrapped the foil, then separated the next strand. "As you can see, I don't have any free time right now. I'd be happy to stop by later and have a chat."

Dalton, you owe me one, she gritted inwardly. *I'm only doing this for you.* Her glance strayed to the rabbit's foot on her counter. It had been part of a birthday gift her staff had presented her in February. She might have need of such talismans if Wilda relayed any other messages from Carolyn. *Kinehoreh,* she said, repeating one of her mother's favorite words. Not that she believed in such superstitious nonsense.

Wilda closed her eyes, rocking on her sandaled heels. "You don't believe I see things. That's because your energy pattern is disrupted. But it's not yourself you should be worried about. It's the other."

Chapter
Five

"What are you talking about?" Marla asked Wilda. She hated talking to people who spoke in riddles.

Wilda's eyes seemed to glaze with mysterious depths. "You help me, then I'll tell you about my disturbing vision. I'll be waiting." Whipping around, she stalked off at a brisk pace befitting a younger woman.

"What was that all about?" Nicole said from the next station. Her expression reflected the same avid curiosity as was showing on the faces of the rest of Marla's staff.

"Carolyn's successor is probably going to use her mumbo jumbo to entice me into giving free managerial advice. It's not as though I've given her staff enough of my time already."

Nicole clucked her tongue. "Unless she's been in the business, she wouldn't have a clue what to do." Cutting a client's hair, she snipped automatically while regarding her friend in the mirror.

"Wilda is a psychic. Why doesn't she communicate with Carolyn? She can receive instructions from the spirit world."

"You're closer to home," Nicole said, grinning.

"Carolyn left her sister some kind of valuable collection that no one is able to find, along with the rest of her personal effects.

Maybe Wilda knows more about it, although Vail likely asked her already."

"You may get a different response."

"That's true." Marla returned her attention to her client, Kathleen Marsh. The elderly patron had been listening intently. Marla already won the prize for entertaining customers with her adventures, and this would start a whole new round of gossip. So be it; people often flocked to the Cut 'N Dye to get the latest scoop. Marla hoped it would increase her coffers.

During a break in the afternoon, Marla moseyed over to her competitor's salon. Seated at the front desk, Wilda had a perplexed frown on her face as she pored over the schedule. Her countenance brightened upon spotting Marla.

"By the light, I'm glad you're here. I don't understand anything. The girls say we're running out of supplies, and I need to order them. The phone keeps ringing. Someone has to deposit these checks in the bank, plus we have bills overdue. I can't possibly handle all these details." She fluttered her hands. "How do you manage to run your place and stay behind the chair?"

Marla smiled. "Hire a receptionist. Then you won't be glued to the front desk. You'll have to ask each of the girls what hours they work in order to schedule appointments. If you're not into bookkeeping, you can use a software program designed for salons that's very helpful. Or consider working with an accountant. I'd also suggest you go to the bank as soon as possible to open an account under your name. As for supplies, set yourself a time each week to do inventory and place orders with suppliers. Why don't we start with that job?" It would give her an excuse to open drawers and search through cabinets.

Marla didn't find anything of significance other than disorganization and uncleanliness that she never would have tolerated in her place. Carolyn's station had been cleaned out by the police, and if she'd hoped to find a stash of valuables or clues to Carolyn's murderer there, she was disappointed. At least she helped Wilda get her feet on the ground as far as management was concerned, although she seriously doubted the flaky female would last long in that role.

"Didn't you have something to tell me?" she said before departing. Aware that she was five minutes late for her next customer, Marla stamped her foot impatiently by the front desk when the other woman delayed her response.

Wilda, turning to face her, donned an inscrutable expression. "I can't give you a clear reading in this place—too many negative vibrations. You'll have to visit me at home."

Marla nodded. "Where do you live?" When the psychic told her, Marla winced at the notion of an hour's drive to South Miami. "That's a long commute for you to make each day," she commented.

Wilda smiled, exposing a row of crooked teeth that would benefit from braces. "Oh, I don't intend to keep on here. It's not my calling. I'll hire someone else to take charge now that you've given me an idea of what to look for in a manager. Maybe you'd like a job as my agent."

"No thanks."

Her refusal didn't faze the woman. "Shall I expect you this evening at seven o'clock? She said it's urgent that I give you the message."

"She?"

"Carolyn. The dear woman needs your help to put her soul to rest."

Marla found the psychic's address without any problems. She'd been to the Kendall area enough times to recognize the landmarks. The small Spanish-style house was set in a community behind Kings Creek apartments, near Dadeland Mall. Marla wished she had time to run into the Container Store, but she didn't know how late it stayed open. Anyway, she reminded herself, she had a clearly stated purpose in coming here, and it didn't include shopping.

"This promises to be as much fun as getting a tooth pulled," she murmured, turning into Wilda's driveway. Drawing information from the woman might not be so easy. The lady seemed willing to talk, but how much of her material would be useful? Although Marla didn't believe in the paranormal senses, she told herself to keep an open mind. Forces might exist beyond her understanding. *Yeah, right. Like Carolyn really wants me here.*

Emerging from her air-conditioned car, Marla breathed in air thick with moisture. Not a single cloud blocked the brilliant sky, meaning rain wouldn't be cooling the evening hours. At seven o'clock the sun had begun its welcome descent, but heat still radiated from the street and sidewalks.

Wilda's lawn brought shady respite. Purple crape myrtle shrubs shared a front corner with white pinwheel jasmine, while a butterfly garden displayed scarlet milkweed, golden dewdrops, red pentas, firebush, and lantana. Marla noticed pots of parsley, mint, and dill placed among planted vegetables: lettuce, tomato vines, and eggplants. The scent of sun-warmed tomatoes mingled with fresh herbs, making her glad she'd grabbed a bite to eat before hitting the highway.

Tugging her tangerine shorts set into place, she rang the front doorbell. Her eyebrows shot up when Wilda answered wearing a pair of jeans and a blousy top, sans jewelry, her hair fastened back with a large clip.

"Hi," Marla said, swallowing her startled reaction.

Wilda smiled, standing aside to let her pass. "Surprised I'm not wearing a robe and turban? I dress like that for show, because people expect it. I don't have to put on airs for you."

Marla wasn't sure how to take that, but her attention was drawn elsewhere by the clutter that met her eyes. *I'm entering the Twilight Zone,* she thought, her gaze alighting on the stones and statues covering every surface. She'd never seen so many tchotchkes in one place. Crystals vied for space with candles, replicas of Buddha, pipe pyramids, and books.

"Interesting stuff," she murmured.

"Come, we'll sit on the patio. There's a decent breeze, and I don't have much free space in here, anyway. I'm in the process of rearranging my books. Can I get you a drink?"

She shook her head. "I'm fine, thanks." Maybe her first impression had been based on preconceived notions. She'd reserve judgment till their upcoming interview. "So how long had you known Carolyn?" she asked once they were seated on a couple of lounge chairs.

The screened patio faced a backyard shaded by black olive and mahogany trees. No citrus trees were present, or perhaps they'd been cut down under the citrus-canker eradication program. Marla had learned more than she'd wanted to know about that political hot potato when investigating her neighbor Goat's disappearance.

"Carolyn started coming to me about five years ago, after the man she loved was killed in an accident," Wilda related, folding her hands in her lap. "She was referred to me because I feel the presence of spirits. It's a gift mentioned in the Bible, you know. When I started in spiritualism, I questioned myself after I gave people information and it came true. That blew my mind. Through the years my gift has strengthened."

"So Carolyn wanted you to communicate with her dead boyfriend?" Marla withheld the skepticism from her voice, careful to keep her expression neutral.

"That's right, but we don't acquire messages upon request. Spirits communicate with us telepathically. I receive images that are more symbols than words."

"So were you able to help Carolyn?"

"It was more a matter of her helping Julius. He died in a car crash. People who depart life suddenly remain unfulfilled. These unfortunates refuse to understand they have transitioned, and they may wander for months. We can steer them toward the light and their true path. Religious rituals aid in this regard."

"In the Jewish religion, we have a mourner's prayer called the kaddish, but it doesn't mention death. It praises God. Are you saying that our prayers encourage departed souls to move on?"

Wilda nodded. "Organized religion serves its purpose, but the power of the light is ultimately more important."

"So you don't follow any particular faith?"

"I believe in Spirit. Life is continuous; death is merely the door into the next dimension. You have to be careful because the door to this unseen fourth dimension remains open."

Marla struggled to understand. "You call yourself a psychic. How do you distinguish what you do from other practitioners?"

"Psychics may be sensitives, intuitives, prophetics, psychometrists, or healers. I feel the presence of spirits, but I also do healing, and sometimes I can tell what's going to happen. So my powers are mixed."

Wilda picked up a smooth hematitic stone and stroked its shiny surface. "Let me tell you a story," she said, glancing at Marla through half-lowered lids. "I was in New York for a gift show in the early days when I had a store. We stayed at one of those high-rise hotels near Times Square. One night we got all dressed up for a party. My roommate and I were barely on time, and we caught the elevator on its way down. Although it was packed, we could've squeezed in. But when I looked inside at the people dressed in their fancy evening wear, I saw no auras. I got a terrible feeling, and I held my roommate back. We signaled they should go down without us. The door closed, and we heard a strange sound. Moments later the elevator crashed, killing everyone aboard."

I've heard that one before, pal. "Amazing," Marla murmured, pretending to be impressed.

"Listen to this. One day, I was sitting at home, and a stranger pulls up to my front door. He says he's from out of town and he's here on a business trip. But that's not the real reason for the visit. He's come to exchange energy. Now, understand, I have a connection on the astral level where there's no time or space. My body emits magnetic energy without my being aware of it. The stranger locked arms with me, and my marrow started boiling. My body ignited as though I were on fire. This man had been suffering from too much energy, and he'd been drawn to me for his salvation. After the transference, he felt much better. That's how I heal; through bioenergy. Some healings take a lot of work; others are spontaneous like that one."

Marla's throat felt parched, as though Wilda were sucking away her energy on the astral level. "I see."

"No, I don't think you do." Wilda's gaze speared hers. "I can see people's auras. You know what an aura is?"

"My friend Tally takes a class on it. Supposedly, it's an energy field that surrounds us."

"That's partly correct." Pursing her lips, Wilda gazed into the distance. "Energy permeates everything around you, even inanimate objects. The human aura is a luminous body that surrounds your physical body. It has several layers composed of vibrations. The higher the layer, the more I must expand my consciousness to perceive it. As you progress through life, you can utilize these expanded realities if you're open to them."

"Huh?"

"The more energy you let through, the healthier you'll be. Illness is caused by an imbalance of energy, or when the flow is blocked. You need to keep your channels open. Let me tell you about the time a woman brought her daughter to me. The girl had a terrible case of shingles and was in a lot of pain. I neutralized the shingles by putting my energy on her. While she was sitting there, I noticed the mother's aura was diminished. She said she'd been plagued by arthritis and nothing helped. My healing energy shattered her calcifications."

"Are you saying you can cure anything?" Marla scoffed.

"Not at all. I'll recommend that people consult medical professionals and stay away from home remedies. My type of healing complements traditional methods of treatment. Sometimes my healing works where they fail because they're not addressing the true cause of the problem. The more I heal, the better I feel."

"What did you mean when you said I should be worried about someone?"

Wilda glided to her feet and began pacing. "We'll get to that in a minute. It's part of Carolyn's message to you. You have psychic ability, too, you know."

Marla wished she would get to the point. "I don't sense anything." *If I did, I'd know you were taking me for a ride.*

"In your instance, I get a reading of turmoil. You're losing your humanity by focusing on work too much. You may be a lucid, no-nonsense type, but what you need is more diversity. You have to relax, to go with the flow."

"Don't we all?"

"You're too uptight. You should take time to smell the roses. Otherwise, you'll obstruct your channels. People who are psychic and block it get different maladies."

"You mean if people get stressed, they're more susceptible to illness. That's common sense."

"You're not hearing me." The older woman wagged her finger. "You're setting yourself up for problems."

Did I come here to get analyzed? "You're right. I get so caught up in my job that I don't have time for anything else." *Especially when you add in murder investigations.*

"You also have to learn to protect yourself against negative energy. Quartz crystals guard you with their reflective nature." Wilda pointed to her pendant. "You can wear them as jewelry, put the stones around your house, or go to the beach. Wade through the shallow water, and let your bare feet sift the wet sand through your toes."

A walk on the beach would dispel anyone's anxieties; this was nothing new. How could she return the topic of conversation to Carolyn?

"Do you have plants in your house?" Wilda said before Marla could marshal her thoughts.

"No, I kill plants."

"Ah." The psychic gave her a look connoting superior wisdom. "You may have too much electricity. Try running the faucet at home and putting your hand on the metal spigot. It will ground you. You should keep citrus and mint around, too. Mint opens the channels; citrus harmonizes them. It's been proven that mint provokes business. You know about aromatherapy? If you dispense mint fragrance in your shop, people spend more."

Again, that made sense. Marla always noticed when she walked into a store and it smelled pleasant. This was a given sales principle. *Tell me something I don't know.*

Wilda closed her eyes. "I'm seeing chairs, heavy wooden chairs. You're picking up negative energy from them. You've heard of wood nymphs? These are unseen things from the other dimension that live in wood. It could be coming from them, or maybe not."

Marla gave the medium a startled glance. "My boyfriend's late wife filled their house with antique furniture."

"You don't care for that style, do you?"

"The stuffy pieces remind me of a mausoleum. I'm trying to encourage Dalton to clean out his place, but he won't get rid of anything belonging to his dearly departed wife."

Wilda's lids snapped open. "You're absorbing the negative vibrations. You must protect yourself. Put out a bowl of water in the room. Water attracts negative energy. Dump it outside and replace it each day. Antiques can be dangerous; you don't know who owned them before you bought them. Let me tell you about this woman who came to me once. She'd bought a settee. Every time she sat on it, she got irritated. Well, after I visited her, I could tell why. The couch came with two ghosts."

Marla smirked, shifting in her seat. "Maybe that's why I'm uncomfortable when I stay at his house. Pam's ghost still haunts the place."

"Don't make jokes about it. Keys, rings, furniture, clothing, everything carries a story. You have to avoid bad vibrations. That's why I don't shake hands with people. I don't want to pick up their negative energy. It's all around us, and we must guard against it."

Who did Carolyn have to guard against? Marla stood and stretched, inpatient to move on. "Linda Hall mentioned a collection that Carolyn had left to her. Something valuable, but the sister didn't know what it was. Do you?"

"I wouldn't trust what that woman says. She felt a lot of resentment toward Carolyn. She even went to a root lady once to put an evil spell on her sister. I was able to block the influence, but it wasn't easy."

Root lady? Somehow Marla didn't think that referred to hair roots. Her mind conjured an image of an old hag brewing herbs over a steaming cauldron. Wait until Vail heard these stories. She could imagine his incredulous expression.

"Linda told me that Carolyn was jealous of her," she said.

"Just the opposite, dear." Wilda's expression clouded. "Carolyn needs your help. She can't rest until her murderer is exposed. She wants you to find her killer."

"Why me? Carolyn hated me. She tried to sabotage my business when she moved back to Palm Haven."

"That's not what she told me. She said you forced her out of town initially, and she was only returning to her origins. But your relationship is not the issue here. You're good at solving crimes. If anyone can help Carolyn's spirit find its way to the light, it's you."

"What else did she say?" Marla asked.

"Someone close to you needs to see a doctor."

"How could she tell you that? I thought you received messages in symbols, not words."

"It's nothing written out in sentences," Wilda snapped. "I get a feeling that comes through. Someone associated with you is ill. Carolyn will reveal who it is when you find her murderer."

"What is this, some sort of spiritual blackmail?" Marla snatched her purse, uncomfortable with the turn of dialogue.

"I am merely delivering a message from the higher spiritual plane."

And I'm a schlemiel to have wasted my time here. "I'll consider it. Tell me, do you have any suspicion who might have killed Carolyn?" *Other than you, since you inherited a fairly lucrative business.*

Wilda raised a hand to ruffle her thick red hair. "That's for you to determine, dear."

"What about this collection Linda said she inherited?"

"I've no idea. Carolyn never said a word to me about it."

"Did Carolyn mention receiving negative vibrations from anyone?" Marla tried, speaking in Wilda's terms.

"You mean, anyone besides you? That's not for me to say. Our sessions were confidential."

"Well, if you think of anything else, you'll let me know? It will make my job easier."

Wilda's face creased into a grin. "I knew you would help. I could foresee it." Her expression sobered. "I'd suggest you work fast. Your loved one's aura isn't strong. I sense . . . it ceases in the near future."

"What does that mean?"

"Transformation occurs. To a higher plane of existence."

"You mean someone dies?"

"Within months, but delay may be possible with the proper treatment." She gripped Marla by the elbow. "Heed my words. I'm not a nut case. This is the message I'm receiving."

"It's just your interpretation." Perhaps Carolyn had left a ghostly residue. That might account for the fading aura Wilda visualized. But in the event her words held any truth, Marla considered what other questions to pose on her way to the exit.

"Why did Carolyn go to the meter room that day?" she asked. "Were you able to gain any information from her staff?"

"No, but that's a good angle for you to work on."

Marla sidestepped an obelisk on the floor. "How could Carolyn afford to move in the first place? I thought her other salon wasn't doing too well."

"She had her resources. Sometimes people can turn around their fortunes with the right attitude. Let me tell you a story about this man who came to see me."

Recognizing another lengthy tale about to begin, Marla raised a hand. "I really have to go. Thanks for your hospitality." Her temples throbbed, and she longed for the comfort of her own home. An hour's drive wouldn't help her mood.

"Wait, you have a headache. Let me relieve it." Stepping forward, Wilda pressed her fingers to Marla's brow.

"It's getting late," Marla protested, strangely hesitant to move. Maybe she was just hungry. She felt oddly weak.

"Do you feel anything? A sensation of warmth?"

Marla stared at Wilda's age-crinkled face. "Nothing."

"You're not receptive." Wilda regarded her knowingly. "It's okay. Just remember to protect yourself. Absorbing too much negative energy will bring you down."

Chapter Six

"I can't decide if Wilda is for real or not," Marla said after describing the interview to Tally. Speeding down I-595 in her Camry, she gripped the steering wheel. They were on their way to the bingo hall in Hollywood. By seven o'clock on Wednesday evening, most rush-hour congestion had cleared, although it mainly affected the opposite lanes. She couldn't conceive of why anyone would move farther west, despite the prestige of a Weston address, when you'd commit to fighting bumper-to-bumper lines crawling east every morning and the reverse every evening. Maybe she just wasn't a commuter.

Tally turned her blond head to gaze at Marla with wide blue eyes. "You don't think Wilda is a true medium? Or is it that you don't believe the soul lives on after death?"

"It's not a matter of what I believe. Why would Wilda say Carolyn wants me to find her murderer?"

"Perhaps she did get a message from beyond."

Glancing at the rearview mirror, Marla grimaced. An edge of storm clouds marched from the west. She pressed the accelerator, hoping to beat the torrential tropical downpour. "Wilda claimed messages come through in symbols, not words. Telepathy is the means of transmission. So how do you think Wilda received this message, as an image of Carolyn's dead body? And where did I come into the picture? Give me a break."

Tally's eyebrows arched. She'd darkened them with pencil, her natural color being so light as to be almost invisible. "Carolyn knew you solved crimes. It's possible she truly does want your help. Her soul will be doomed to wander until justice is served."

"Ha. Then what about those crimes that never get solved? Police files are full of cold cases."

Sadness altered her friend's expression. "Let's hope the victims find peace."

"Wilda said people who die suddenly can't understand what happened to them. They may linger in the same spot for months, and a medium can pick up their negative energies. She advised me to protect myself. Maybe this was her oblique way of warning me against someone who is very much alive."

"Could be."

Marla took the turnoff for State Road Seven heading south. Overhead, the sky darkened as the encroaching clouds blotted out the sun. "As if her message from Carolyn wasn't enough incentive, Wilda hinted that someone close to me should see a doctor. Doesn't that sound like a threat?"

"Do you consider Wilda capable of harming someone?" Tally's raised tone indicated it had never crossed her mind to include the psychic as a suspect.

"Why else would she imply one of my relatives is ill? Couldn't she just as well be talking about a consequence if I don't comply?" Focusing her attention forward, Marla ignored the passing stream of used-car dealerships, gas stations, and adult video stores. This wasn't the most scenic part of town. Like any avenue that had once been a central hub, it had gone downhill after communities expanded westward.

"Why do you question everything she says?" Tally countered. "It's just as likely Wilda truly communicates with Spirit."

"I'm grounded in reality. And I think Wilda's words serve an ulterior purpose." Uncomfortable with their conversation, Marla brushed a strand of hair off her face. While she conceded that psychic powers were possible, logic dictated that Wilda must have a vested interest in her cooperation. Although the reason for that eluded her, she was determined to track down the truth. She didn't like it when people pressured her into acting on their behalf.

Shifting in her seat, Tally gave her a sly glance. "There's one way for you to tell if Wilda is a fake. Go to Cassadaga."

"What's that?"

"It's a spiritualist camp in Central Florida. Residents are certified healers and mediums. They offer all kinds of classes, readings, and healing sessions. The people in my drumming circle have talked about hiring a bus for a weekend. I'm sure they'd let you join us."

Oh, joy. Just what I'd like to do on my day off, ride on a bus with a bunch of New Age enthusiasts beating drums in the background. Nonetheless, it was a good idea to check Wilda's prediction against another medium's reading, sort of like getting a second opinion from a doctor.

"It sounds like a worthwhile trip, but I'd rather go alone. Maybe you'd like to come with me. With fewer people, we'd have a better chance at getting appointments with the mediums we wanted. Less competition," Marla added as an incentive. She could imagine Dalton's reaction if she invited him. Just the thought of his cynical expression made her smile.

Her attention was diverted by the sign announcing the Indian reservation, and she scanned the area for the bingo hall. She had never been inside the place; not being a gambler, she'd always passed by without a second glance.

The sand-colored building with burgundy awnings wasn't as garish as the Miccosukee gaming resorts in the area. Those were gambling palaces, complete with restaurants, entertainment, and a variety of ways to lose your money. Marla never had enough disposable income to risk on games of chance—plus, she'd rather spend her excess on clothes.

Across the street, signs offering live turtles, genuine western wear, a produce market, and a native village tempted tourists.

"Look at all the pawnshops," she said. "That must be for people who lose at the gaming tables. I wonder how many different tribes run these places."

"Haven't you read your Florida history?" Tally teased.

With a broad grin, she pulled a guidebook from her handbag. "Always be prepared, that's my motto." She flipped open the pages. "Ponce de León arrived on our shores in 1513. The Spanish explorer named the land Florida, which means 'full of flowers' in Spanish. At that time, about ten thousand Indians lived here. They belonged to four tribes: the Calusa and Tequesta in the south, and the Timucua and Apalachee in the northern territories."

"So the Seminoles weren't here initially," Marla said as she searched for a parking space.

"That's right. Warfare and diseases brought by the whites killed many of the Native Americans. That left the territory open for other settlers. In the early 1700s, a band of Oconee Indians migrated south from Georgia. *Sim-in-oli* means 'wild,' so that's where their name originated. Other groups joined them. They all spoke a language called Hitchiti until another band arrived who spoke Muskogee."

"Were those the Miccosukee?" They seemed more prevalent; Marla had noticed their land on Alligator Alley heading west toward Naples and on the Tamiami Trail in Miami.

Tally shook her head, tendrils of blond hair escaping from her twist. "The early Seminoles clashed with whites over escaped black slaves, hunting grounds, farmland, and other issues. Sometime after the War of 1812, General Andrew Jackson attacked the Seminoles, destroying their villages. Those remaining were herded into reservations, but not all complied. The government tried to get rid of them, and thus started the Second Seminole War. Some Native Americans retreated to the Everglades. They differentiated into the Hitchiti speaking group known as the Miccosukee, and the Creek Seminoles who speak Muskogee."

"Their problems brought them together in one respect,"

Marla commented, pointing to the casino. "Now they all speak the language of money." A loud crack of thunder ripped the air. Pulling into an empty space just vacated by a Caprice, she switched gears and cut the ignition.

Outside, Marla surveyed a confusing array of building entrances. Jackpot . . . Do-It-Yourself . . . Bingo. A few droplets of rain hit her head. They'd never make it to the third entry before the deluge.

Tally took the lead, pushing open the first door they encountered. "I'm sure we can get through to the bingo section from here. Holy smokes, this is like Las Vegas."

Dazzled by row after row of slot machines, Marla hesitated. While thunder rumbled outside, clinks and bells filled the cavernous interior. Somber patrons sat on green vinyl seats, punching buttons on devices that swallowed their money. Mustering her nerve, she strode forward, noting that the minimum bet was one dollar.

"Not Las Vegas," she commented wryly. "There you can play for a nickel."

Gold Rush, Super Touch Lotto, Golden 7s, Joker Poker. These were games she'd never heard of. What happened to the old-fashioned slots with an arm that you pulled, hoping to get cherries or a row of bars?

"I wonder if all the tribes have casinos," she murmured, glancing at the carpet underfoot. It sported a vibrant design of tangerine sunbursts. She noted similar colors in the paintings on the walls that depicted various Indian scenes: riders on horseback, women in colorful skirts in a chickee hut, warriors on a hunt. Thatching rimmed the ceiling, creating the effect of being in an encampment. Modern amenities intruded by means of mounted televisions playing sports games and radio music blaring from loudspeakers.

"Cocktails, cappuccinos, expresso," called a server circulating through a section of poker tables inhabited mostly by men with solemn expressions.

Pushing past a glass door, they entered the bingo room, where

cigarette smoke tinged the air. Apparently the state law prohibit-
ing smoking in public places did not apply to the reservation.
Marla's nostrils clogged while she noted the guards hovering
about the exits and the white-shirted attendants roaming the
crowd.

"I guess we have to go over there," she said, pointing to a line
snaking from another door.

When it was their turn to pay, Marla drew out her wallet.
"We're supposed to meet Rosemary Taylor here," she said to the
cashier, a woman whose world-weary face barely glanced at hers.
"I understand she comes regularly."

"Oh, yeah. That's her over there." Waggling her finger, the
woman indicated a dirty blonde in a lavendar dress. Rosemary sat
at a long table, one of many that reminded Marla of the tables in
a school cafeteria. Unlike their school counterparts which would
have resounded with noisy chatter and laughter, these tables
were surrounded by deathly silence except for the shuffle of
bingo paraphernalia. It appeared bingo players took their occupa-
tion seriously.

"Which pack do you want?" the attendant asked.

"What are my choices?"

"The twenty-two-dollar pack plays a four-hundred-dollar
game; for thirty-three dollars, you can play the eight-hundred-
dollar game; and for forty-four dollars you can play the eleven-
hundred-and-ninety-nine-dollar game. Then you can buy extra
books and specials." Selecting a handful of brochures, she thrust
them at Marla.

"Uh, I'll just take the first one."

"Paper or handset?"

"Excuse me?"

"Do you want a paper pack or computer?"

Marla glanced at some of the players already seated. They had
cards laid out before them, and some had miniature tabletop
computers. Her eye caught on colorful tubes that looked like
paint. "What's the difference?"

"With the paper, you have to mark off each number. You can buy your own dauber in the machine over there."

"I see." She noticed a lady testing her dauber by blotting colored circles on a blank piece of paper. This was a far cry from grade-school bingo where you put tokens on a gaming card. "Does the computer automatically mark the numbers called?"

"You still have to key in the number, but you don't have to locate it on the grid. The computer will do that for you. It's a lot faster if this is your first time. The game gets intense. Some people use both methods because they get bored."

Marla studied the brochure for the evening session. Eighteen games were interspersed with brief intermissions. "What's this *Ko Na Wi* where the prize starts at twenty-five thousand?"

"That costs one dollar to enter, and you pick six numbers ahead of time. It's like the Lotto. If your numbers are called, you win. We only call sixteen numbers total."

Marla bit her lower lip. "I'll just stick to the regular bingo game." Aware she was holding up the line, she paid quickly and grabbed her power box. Now to figure out how to work the thing. Fortunately, a couple of seats were vacant on either side of Carolyn's bingo partner.

If she ever entered a contest for bag ladies, Rosemary Taylor would win the prize, Marla thought. She couldn't decide which sagged more: the lines of dissipation on the older woman's face, or the shift she wore that looked like a recycled drapery from the flowery sixties. Dry blond hair with brassy highlights stuck out in clumps from under a battered felt hat. Her limpid blue eyes, lashes heavy with mascara, gave Marla a quick glance.

"Hi, are these seats taken?" Marla began. She introduced herself and Tally after Rosemary indicated the spaces were available. "This is our first time here. I hope I can understand how this thing works." After settling in, she pushed the power button on her unit, watching as the screen lit up. Rosemary had sheets of paper laid out in front of her plus a computer and a row of daubers in different colors.

"The warmups will get you oriented," Rosemary said in a raspy voice that ended in a cough.

Observing the stubs littering the woman's ashtray, Marla wasn't surprised when Rosemary lit a cigarette as long and slim as a pencil. Her throat constricted, and the lack of windows contributed to her oppressed feeling. It must be raining, but she couldn't even hear the thunder. Very few people conversed with each other, and those few got disapproving glances. It felt as though she'd entered a prison where you weren't allowed to speak, and breathing the smoky air was part of your sentence.

"My friend used to come here often," Marla said, focusing on her purpose. "She kept urging me to play, but I couldn't find the time. I'm so sorry she isn't here tonight. Maybe you knew her? Carolyn Sutton."

"Oh my. Carolyn was a friend of mine, too. Poor dear."

Marla lowered her voice. "They say she was murdered."

Rosemary's face pinched. "*Oy gevalt*, it's horrible."

"Are you Jewish?" The woman did possess Mediterranean features. It was possible she came from the Sephardic strain.

"I'm Irish-Italian, honey. You live around here long enough and you pick up certain phrases. It's necessary in my line of business."

"And that is?" Tally asked, inclining her head to listen.

They spoke in low tones but still attracted attention. Not that anyone cared what they said. The glares they elicited indicated people were more concerned about the interruption to their focus—even though the games hadn't even started—than they were about eavesdropping. Marla shuddered. What kind of lives did these women lead that this was their sole means of recreation?

"Don't tell anyone, but I'm a scout," Rosemary whispered.

"You work for the Girl Scouts?" Marla must have heard incorrectly. Rosemary didn't look like a troop leader.

"Trail scout, talent scout, you know. I scout out the opposition."

"Oh, like you work for someone else?"

Rosemary nodded. "This is the enemy camp," she said, glancing furtively over her shoulder. "I'm here to keep my eye on the mark. Mustn't let them get on to me."

Marla watched her rearrange the paper cards on the table in a repetitive shuffling motion. *Am I missing something here, or does Rosemary lack a few stairs on the way to her attic?*

"I've heard people aren't happy about the new hotel and casino down the road," Tally commented. "Didn't it cost two hundred million dollars to build, while the surrounding neighborhood is one of Broward County's poorest areas?"

"You're right, honey," Rosemary said, puffing on her cigarette. "You can see the mobile-home community from the highway."

"Doesn't the income provide for better living conditions on the reservation?" Marla cut in. "I would think the new construction provided a lot of jobs."

"Not for us. Our area has more traffic, more crime, and more car accidents. We have no say in what the tribe votes on, while their decisions affect everyone in the neighborhood."

"If you dislike it so much, why do you support them by coming here?" Marla challenged.

Rosemary shot her a waspish gaze. "It's my job."

"You mean someone pays you to gamble?"

"I told you, I'm a scout. Shh. Don't let anyone hear us."

Tally signaled to draw Marla aside. Using the excuse that they were getting a snack, they headed for the concessions. "I remember a case in a newspaper a while ago," Tally told her. "The Internal Revenue Service investigated the tribe's finances after some men were accused of stealing from them. The men were acquitted, but tribal leaders admitted they didn't pay taxes on gifts they gave people. In a three-year period, council members spent more than eighty million dollars on gifts."

Marla gawked. "They make that much money?" After South Florida voters turned down proposals for casinos that would draw tourists, she'd never considered the reservations as gambling magnets.

"They've made millions since this place opened. Each tribal

member receives almost forty thousand dollars per year. Not bad for an allowance, huh?"

"How do you know all this?"

"I read the newspapers."

"Do you really think Rosemary is telling the truth about being paid to play bingo?"

Tally frowned. "She can't gather too much information if she sits in the same spot all day."

"Rosemary isn't spending her funds on grooming, I can tell you that. Did you see the dirt under her fingernails? And she smells like she hasn't seen a shower for days. I wonder why Carolyn liked her."

"Let's go back and find out."

When they returned to their seats, Rosemary gave them each a furtive glance. "Did you see him? He's out there," she said, grasping her blue dauber. Thankfully, she'd finished her cigarette, but smoke lingered in the air, tightening Marla's throat.

"Who is?" Marla croaked, sipping her coffee. She hadn't been impressed by the snack bar. Dirty linoleum floor, bare block tables, worn chairs, glaring overhead lights. Fearing the kitchen nurtured a variety of wildlife, she hoped the heat from the liquid had vaporized any germs.

"The one who watches me. I have to be careful. Their assassins have tried before, but I foiled them." Uncapping her red dauber, Rosemary stabbed the tip on a margin of paper as though demonstrating their attempt in a mock circle of blood.

"Maybe they got to Carolyn first," Marla suggested.

Rosemary sucked in a sharp breath of air. "You could be right. She told me about the evidence. I warned her that it was dangerous to keep those things, but she didn't listen."

"What things?"

"You know, her collection."

"What exactly did Carolyn have that was so valuable?"

"I guess you weren't that close of a friend if she didn't tell you."

"Do you think the killer was after this evidence?"

"Probably, but she kept her stuff well hidden."

"I spoke to Carolyn's sister. Linda is supposed to inherit her collectibles, but she hasn't received anything."

Rosemary sneered. "That sister, now she was a jealous one. She wanted everything that Carolyn had."

That confirmed what Wilda said. "Linda told me Carolyn was envious because she didn't have to work and had a family."

"Are you kidding?" Rosemary's eyebrows soared like a wingspan on liftoff. "It ate Linda's heart out that Carolyn had her own business and didn't need a man. She would have traded places in a minute."

"Maybe you're right, although Carolyn left the salon to her spiritualist rather than her sister. So what's this prized collection she granted to Linda?" Marla tried again.

Rosemary cackled. "You'd like to know, wouldn't you? Why, honey? Are you working for them?"

Marla curbed her impatience. "I have no idea who you mean by *them*." She tried a different tack. "Who do you think killed Carolyn? Can you give me some names?"

"Sorry, my lips are sealed."

"I'll put in a good word with the police for you. The cops might be able to provide protection."

"I can take care of myself, thanks. That's how I've survived this long. *They* know I'm a tough cookie." Rosemary narrowed her eyes. "There's someone else, though. Carolyn went to a chiropractor I'd recommended. John Hennings treated her for a neck problem, and she felt better afterward.

"On her last night here, Carolyn spent a lot of money playing the big jackpots. Said she'd found out something about Dr. Hennings that gave her a profitable edge on him."

Chapter
Seven

Thursday morning, Marla shared her evening activities with Nicole at the next station. "I won four hundred dollars," she concluded, grinning. "Maybe I should try for a bigger jackpot the next time."

"Would you really go again?"

"Probably not. My clothes smelled like cigarette smoke when I got home. I threw them right in the washer." She wrinkled her nose. "It clung to my hair, too. You stink like a chimney when you come out of that place. I don't know how people can stand it, but, then, all they care about are their winnings."

"At least you came out on top," Nicole said, winking. "Have you told Dalton what you learned?"

A different image of coming out on top popped into her head, a more erotic one then playing bingo. "He's picking me up later. I didn't schedule anyone past four o'clock today. I figured we'd exchange news then."

"Uh huh."

"Get your mind out of the gutter, girl. He's taking me to an appointment related to Carolyn's case."

Nicole's customer asked a question, diverting her attention. The young woman exemplified the typical client who had dyed her own hair with unfortunate results. A natural auburn, she'd come in with orange splotches all over her head and white re-growth. Now she required professional intervention by means of a costly color correction. If she'd learned a lesson, hopefully it was to consult an experienced colorist and pay up front rather than pay more, later, to correct her mistakes.

This brought to mind a new marketing ploy, a Bad Hair Day when customers with hair disasters could come in for free advice. When Carolyn began siphoning off her clients, Marla had figured a special event each month might help draw in newcomers. Last week they'd done a hair drive to benefit Locks of Love, a non-profit organization that provided hairpieces for disadvantaged children who suffered from medical hair loss. Those who do-nated their hair received a free cut-and-style at the salon. Hair donations had to be at least ten inches long, as it took ten to fif-teen ponytails to make one wig. Marla felt good when she con-tributed to the community. And a Bad Hair Day clinic would be a good way to introduce potential customers to her salon.

Satisfied that her new marketing ideas would work, she took a break at lunchtime to run over to the hardware store to see how Sam Levy felt about her mother.

The older man beamed at her from behind the counter. "Hey Marla, what's up? How's that beautiful mom of yours?"

"Why don't you call her and find out?"

"That sounds like a swell idea. How can I contact her?"

Marla hesitated to give out her mother's phone number. Even though she'd like to see them get together, that struck her as being too pushy. "Are you on e-mail? You could send her an ad-vertising blurb about the store, you know, nothing personal. See if she responds, and you can take it from there."

"Okay." His pale blue eyes glowed. "Is she on AOL?"

"Yes. She uses her first initial and last name."

"Thanks, I appreciate it. It isn't easy for a widower like me to meet decent ladies. Your mom has a lot of class. I can see her in you."

"Gee, I guess that's a compliment." Her ears picked up the

sound of pounding rain. "Can you believe it's raining? The sun is shining."

Sam pointed to a cloud bank. "Not over there, it isn't. Did you hear the weather report? That tropical depression is strengthening."

"It's too far away to worry about." The hurricane season was full of storms that swirled off to sea and dissipated. Rarely did one hit the coastline, although all you needed was a maelstrom like Andrew to cause widespread destruction. "School starts next week. I just hope the weather holds up when Brianna goes to class."

"You have a child?" His furrowed face reflected surprise.

"She's Dalton's daughter. He lost his wife to cancer over two years ago. Brianna and I have grown close. I probably spend more time at his house now than my own."

"How old is she?" Sam pulled over a catalog on moldings and fingered the pages.

"Brie just turned thirteen."

"A difficult age."

"No kidding. She wants to wear makeup and those scraps of clothing that teenagers call outfits, while her father is still in the dark ages where his daughter is concerned. I'm caught in the middle, because I understand her need to blend in with the crowd. On the other hand, Brie doesn't have the judgment an older woman develops."

He leaned forward, lowering his voice. "Teen girls wield a lot of power. They give out signals that can cause trouble."

"That's because they don't know any better. It's just immaturity." Sam didn't have any children, so perhaps he wasn't attuned to their mindset. Marla had enough teenage customers that she heard their angst, plus her own conflicts with Anita helped her to empathize.

"Are you telling me that when they lead a guy on, they don't know what they're doing?" Sam said, lifting an eyebrow.

"That's right. They need guidance from an adult, even though they won't admit it. Anyway, you know how to reach my mother if you're interested. I've got to go back to work."

"Thanks, sweetheart. Need any batteries, light bulbs? We're having a sale today."

"I don't think so. See you later, Sam."

She ducked outside where the rainfall had let up and glanced at her watch. Four more long hours until Vail came by. He'd been mysterious when she had asked him where they were going, and ever since, curiosity had drilled a hole in her stomach. Or maybe it was hunger; she hadn't eaten anything except yogurt for breakfast.

Dashing into Bagel Busters, she encountered Arnie in his customary apron. The proprietor smiled beneath his droopy mustache. "Marla, my *shayna maidel*, what brings you here?"

"I'm starving. Can you get me a quick corned beef on rye?"

"Sure." Unable to leave his checkout post, he signaled to Ruth, a waitress, and placed Marla's order. "So what's new?"

She gave him a quick rundown. "You hear any gossip about Carolyn?"

He shrugged, his broad shoulders encased in a T-shirt that had seen many washings. "Those French girls of hers have come in here looking for croissants. They're worried about their status, and if they'll be allowed to stay."

"I thought Wilda had reassured them she wasn't making any staff changes."

"It's not that. I think they're here on work visas. Assuming Carolyn sponsored them, they must be concerned about remaining in the country."

Later that afternoon, Marla brought up the subject of Carolyn's staff again while she and Vail drove in his car. "Are these girls the same ones from the Sunrise Academy of Beauty?"

"Yep." Vail's peppery hair, parted on the side, didn't move a strand when he nodded his head. She'd have to speak him about lightening up on the holding spray. "They obtained immigrant visas through a local attorney, Peter McGraw. We're on our way to interview him. He's the same fellow who drew up Sutton's will."

Her eyebrows lifted. "Why bring me along?"

His sidelong glance heated her blood. "It may throw him off guard if I show up with a woman. You know . . . we're on our way out to an early dinner and we're stopping by for a brief chat. Nothing formal like an interrogation, so he'll think I'm only interested in talking to him as a matter of form."

"So I'm your cover. While you drill him, I flutter my eyelashes and distract his attention."

He chuckled. "You do that and I'll want to take you somewhere private. Just listen and observe, and contribute to the conversation if you catch something I don't. Remember how we worked together to interview Jeremiah Dooley?"

"Right." Although it wasn't his customary practice to have her accompany him during investigations, they had teamed up previously to interview the tilapia farmer after Kimberly Kaufman's murder.

Playing her part, she smiled at the receptionist in the lawyer's office and clung to Vail's arm like a symbiotic vine. Her practiced gaze took in the fine furnishings, and she quickly tallied the attorney's rates. He must charge at least two hundred fifty dollars per hour to afford the tooled-leather chairs and polished mahogany tables. Confirming her impression were the magazines available to clients: *Fortune, Money, Stock Futures & Options*, plus the daily *Wall Street Journal*. None of them were on her leisure reading list.

The selections reminded Marla of the first time she'd entered Stan's office as a trembling nineteen-year-old forced to defend herself against a potential lawsuit from Tammy's parents. She hadn't wanted to drag her own family into the ordeal and instead stooped to a humiliating job to pay for a lawyer on her own. Purposeful negligence on her part as baby-sitter couldn't be proven; it was determined the toddler drowned by accident, like so many other unfortunate occurrences in South Florida with its predominance of backyard pools.

"Are you okay?" Vail asked in a low voice after he finished speaking to the woman behind a glass partition.

Marla clutched her stomach. "I'm remembering how I first met Stan. He was a lifeline to my sinking ship. I don't think I would've gotten through that year without him."

Vail's mouth tightened. "He took advantage of you, a beautiful young girl in distress. Professionals shouldn't date their clients."

She smiled wryly at him. "He was the perfect catch: an attractive Jewish lawyer who'd never been married. How could I resist?"

"He never knew what you did to pay for his legal services, did he?"

"Thankfully, no." She hung her head. "He might not have been so interested then. It was a whirlwind courtship that salvaged my self-esteem. I'll always be grateful to him for that much."

"You've paid your debt."

"Yes, I have." Together, she and Vail had discovered who'd murdered his third wife. She owed Stan nothing more.

"You should be proud of all you've accomplished," he told her, cupping her chin and lifting her face. His smoky eyes imparted admiration along with something deeper.

A surge of affection swept her. Raising to her toes, she kissed him. "I feel that I can do so much more because of you."

His hands found her shoulders, but before he could draw her closer, an inner door opened. They sprang apart, Marla flushing guiltily and Vail grinning.

"Detective? Please come in," said a balding fellow in an impeccable suit. His few remaining hairs were brushed over his crown in an attempt to hide his shiny pate.

You could have used some of that secret hair-growth formula I chased down in March, Marla thought. Too bad the prototype got slurped by her neighbor Goat's pet snake.

The lawyer's private enclave was every bit as plush as his waiting area. Marla stood for introductions before taking a seat at one of two upholstered armchairs facing his massive desk. A huge picture window showed a distant view of traffic on Broward Boulevard in downtown Fort Lauderdale. Usually heights didn't bother her, but after September 11th she'd become more wary. Regarding the tiny cars below, she felt a twinge of discomfort at being on the top floor of a high-rise building. The sooner they concluded their business, the better.

"I'm Pete McGraw," the man said in a rich baritone voice. "It's nice to meet you in person, Lieutenant."

"I'd hoped to get here sooner, but other things were more pressing. You told me most of what I needed to know on the telephone." Vail's broad smile widened as he draped his arm around Marla's shoulder. "This is Marla Shore, my fiancée. We're on our way to Las Olas to grab a bite to eat, so I thought we'd stop by. I just have a few more questions to ask."

"Of course. Please take a seat."

Marla, gaping at Vail, sank into the nearest chair. What did he mean by introducing her as his fiancée? Although she wore his amethyst ring on her finger, it by no means signified a commitment. He'd never asked her to marry him, and she hoped he wouldn't anytime soon. Just because they'd used this ruse before to disarm a suspect didn't give him leave to resurrect the pretense. Then again, maybe Dalton had a particular purpose in mind. She'd reserve judgment until later.

"You've been in touch with the people named in Carolyn's will, I presume," McGraw said, assuming a nonchalant expression.

"That's right," Vail replied. "Her sister hasn't found any collection. Nothing turned up in the victim's apartment, nor in her safety deposit box, except legal papers and stock certificates."

"Can't help you there." McGraw straightened his tie. "My client never described the particulars about this collection of hers. She just wanted to make sure her sister received the things. I assumed Mrs. Hall knew about them."

"Did anyone else have a key to her apartment?" Marla suggested. "A cleaning lady, or a maintenance man?"

The attorney leveled his gaze on her. "Do you think someone

stole the items? That implies Carolyn told someone else about it other than her sister."

"Indeed." Vail glanced at her thoughtfully.

"You know, Rosemary mentioned Carolyn's collection. She said Carolyn kept it well hidden."

"And Rosemary is?" McGraw said, leaning forward.

"Rosemary Taylor, Carolyn's bingo partner. I don't think they were actually friends. They met at the bingo parlor every week."

"What did you say you do, Miss Shore?"

Oy, she'd forgotten to play her part of the dumb broad. "I'm a hair stylist. My salon is in the same shopping strip as Carolyn's," she said, offering him a business card from her purse.

His sharp glance penetrated her. "Oh, yes, I believe I recall the poor woman mentioning you."

"We weren't on the best terms, but that's irrelevant now. Wilda Cleaver has asked for my help in managing their shop."

"Ah, the psychic. She shouldn't need any help if she communicates with the dead. Carolyn can tell her what to do. Har har." He laughed at his own joke.

"When she made out her will, did Carolyn tell you why she was leaving the salon to her spiritual advisor instead of her sister?" Vail persisted.

"She said Wilda had brought her a lot of comfort."

"Wilda doesn't know anything about running a salon," Marla inserted.

"Neither would her sister," McGraw pointed out. "I gathered there was some animosity between them."

"Oh?" Vail raised his eyebrows.

"I really shouldn't reveal my client's confidences," McGraw stated, rocking back in his executive chair. "Confidentiality and all that, you know."

"Your client was murdered." Vail squared his shoulders. "Everything you tell us will be helpful in finding her killer."

"Carolyn sponsored students at the Sunrise Academy of Beauty," Marla cut in. "She employed the same girls when they graduated. I'd visited her previous salon, and I wasn't impressed by its prosperity. How do you suppose she coughed up the funds to support these foreigners as well as make the move back to Palm Haven?"

McGraw's expression clouded. "Perhaps she had a generous benefactor."

"You mean, someone who paid her rent, or someone who paid for the girls?"

"Client privacy prevents me from giving any further information. I'd suggest you focus your investigation on those people who knew Carolyn intimately, Lieutenant. Or check out a competitor, one who might have been offended by Carolyn's intrusion into the same shopping center."

Resisting the urge to smash the smug grin off his face, Marla dug a fingernail into her palm. "I resent your implication. While I'm not exactly grieving over Carolyn's demise, I am sorry to see her life end so prematurely."

"Then why don't you concentrate on running your salon instead of hers?" His eyes gleamed. "Or maybe it's entered your mind to make an offer to Wilda Cleaver."

Unable to keep still any longer, Marla shot to her feet. "Why would I want two salons in the same shopping center?"

"You tell me."

Vail lazily drew himself up to his full height. "I understand your practice includes immigration law."

The attorney leveraged out of his chair, tugging on his suit jacket. "That is correct."

"What kind of visas would those French stylists need to enter this country as students and then be employed in a salon?"

"That depends." He shuffled a few envelopes on his desk.

"They're worried about being sent home," Marla added, swallowing her anger. While provoking McGraw might have been part of Vail's plan, she'd overreacted while he maintained his cool. The attorney knew which buttons to push to rile her.

"Perhaps the hairdressers are concerned about being dismissed by their new employer," McGraw offered in an oily tone.

"Wilda said she'd keep them on, and business would continue

as usual. I wonder why Carolyn brought them in at all. Maybe
she hoped to increase her prestige by having French stylists."

"Maybe." The attorney's shuttered expression hid his opinion.

Marla's glance caught one of the envelopes that had flipped in
her direction. It had a single name, Iapetus, scrawled across the
front in sloppy handwriting. No return address, or anything else.
Peculiar, especially since the name rang a bell in her mind. She
opened her mouth to pose a question when she saw the look on
McGraw's face. Scooping the envelope into a drawer, he gave her
a pasty smile.

"I can see why you'd have a special interest in this case, Miss
Shore, but I certainly hope your relationship with Detective Vail
won't cloud his judgment. He's apt to be less objective with you
involved."

She laughed. "Oh, don't worry about him. He doesn't ever let
me interfere in his investigations."

Strolling toward the door, she heard Vail's snort of derision.
Like he'd had a choice. After she'd helped solve some of his earlier cases, he'd given up trying to discourage her involvement.
Little did the lawyer know that she'd become his unofficial assistant, using her conversational talents and contacts to snoop
where the homicide detective dare not go. He valued her contri-
butions, while she prided herself on her astute observations.

Nonetheless, their teamwork did not allow him to batter her
reputation around town. She'd already acted once as Arnie's pre-
tend fiancée, and that news had spread like schmaltz among her
friends and relatives. Vail had no right to use the same ploy.

She waited until they were seated in his car driving south on
Andrews Avenue to let out her emotions. "Why did you introduce me as your fiancée? If he blabs about our interview, everyone will find out. You could have at least forewarned me."
Folding her hands primly in her lap, she glared at him.

Vail gave her a sexy, disarming grin, and took his hand off the
steering wheel to pat her thigh. "Is that such a bad thing? Maybe
it's time we made it official."

"What?" Her pulse leaped. Did he mean what she thought?

"Well, you know," he said, jostling his attention between the road and her. "We've been going together for several months now. I like having you in the house when I come home from work. You and Brianna are getting along fine. Why not get hitched?"

"Why not? Because . . . because . . . is this a proposal?" She couldn't think of a single thing to say. Flabbergasted, Marla thought of all the reasons she didn't want to get married. Obligations of keeping house and cooking dinner. Having to modify her schedule to suit someone else. Attending school functions. And the most important deterrent: she couldn't stand living in his house. It reeked of memories of his dead wife.

"We'll have dinner on Las Olas. I know it's early, but we can stroll around a bit. I thought we'd look in some jewelry shops, you know, so you can pick a ring."

At least he wasn't planning on presenting her with Pam's engagement trophy. He probably intended to give it to Brianna when she was older.

Marla held up her right hand. "You already gave me an amethyst ring."

"I want you to have a diamond. You deserve it, because you brighten my life. Making you happy is important to me."

Marla swallowed. "This is rather sudden. I need some time to think about it."

"Not too long." He spoke with the confidence of a man who knew she'd give a positive response.

Chapter
Eight

"What did you think about the lawyer?" Marla asked Vail on the drive home.

They'd scoured the jewelry shops on Las Olas Boulevard, but Marla felt Vail could get a better price elsewhere. At least that was the reason she gave for not selecting anything. Vail had noted her ring size and what style solitaire she liked, so he could make the choice. It would allow her time to adjust to the idea. Uncertain of her feelings, she'd made him promise not to tell anyone yet. While she felt secure in his presence and lonely without him, too many obstacles loomed before their union could be blessed.

In the past she'd listened to her family in regard to selecting Mr. Right, and each time her ideal had turned into Mr. Wrong. Dalton appeared to be wrong for many reasons: a widower still attached to his dead wife, with a teenager in tow and a risky job. But maybe for once she should listen to her heart. She and Dalton could confront those barriers together.

Reassuring herself that when the time was right, she'd know her answer, she drifted back to their conversation.

". . . he's involved somehow," Dalton concluded.

"Sorry, I missed that last part."

"I said, McGraw is more involved with Carolyn's staff members then he's willing to admit."

"The shyster was concealing information," Marla agreed. Remembering his furtive movement of slipping the envelope into a drawer, she considered whether to tell Vail. Better wait until she could look up the name scrawled on top, Iapetus, to see if it meant anything. "I'll bet he knows who was funding Carolyn."

"Perhaps." Vail's stern profile revealed little about the direction of his thoughts.

"Do you have any other leads?"

"I'm still checking into the backgrounds of everyone connected with the deceased."

She'd filled him in on her recent findings. "I think I'll make an appointment with the chiropractor Rosemary mentioned." Rubbing her neck, she gave him a coy glance. "I've been working too hard, and my muscles are cramped. I could use a neck adjustment."

The corners of his mouth lifted. "How about a massage? I'll be working late tomorrow night, but there's always Saturday."

Disappointment swept through her. "I thought we were going out to dinner on Friday."

"Can't. Would you mind giving Brie a ride to her friend Corey's house? I'll make it up to you, I promise."

His infectious grin won her heart. "All right. I guess I'll just stay at your place on Saturday night then."

With her plans changed for Friday night, Marla called her mother after she got home. Forcing herself not to jump the gun by blurting out Vail's proposal, she offered to accompany Anita to synagogue.

"I thought you might want some company since Roger is gone," she explained. "By the way, has Sam Levy contacted you?"

"Not at all." Ma's reproving tone told Marla what she thought about her matchmaking efforts.

An idea hatched in her mind with the brilliance of a level-ten hair color. "Uh, are you doing anything on Sunday?"

"I have a luncheon at noon, that's all. Why?"

"Keep the evening open. I'll tell you about it tomorrow night when we go to services."

Anita gave an exasperated sigh. "Polly is starting in on me again about driving on the Sabbath. I brought her some tomatoes yesterday, and, do you know, she wouldn't take them? She claims to be so religious, and then she roots around in the trash for things to recycle. You need to go over there, Marla. I don't know how my sister lives as she does. It would be a real mitzvah for you to help her."

Marla didn't understand the source of the sisters' antagonism unless it was just that they had such different personalities. "She's survived this long on her own."

"Well, she's not able to get around like she used to. I'm afraid she isn't eating properly. When can you get there?"

Marla rolled her eyes. "I'll go on Sunday. I'm free during the day. We were just going to take Brianna shopping for school supplies." Maybe she'd ask Vail to accompany her, unless he had to go into work. On the other hand, it might be a good idea to wait before introducing him to the more eccentric members of her family. She didn't want to scare him off.

Marla called Vail from her salon the next day to propose her idea. "Ma has agreed to leave Sunday evening open. I'll ask Sam if he has plans. If not, we'll have them both over for a barbecue."

His sputtering reply made her smile. "B-but your mom has never been over to my house."

She noticed he didn't say *our* house. *Therein lies the crux of the problem*, she noted to herself. Anita's observations might prompt his awareness of their difficulties in that regard. "It's as good a time as any to win my mother to your cause. Roger and Barry are out of town. She can't use them as buffers."

"We'd have to clean up. I haven't cut the grass, and—"

"Tch, tch. Let me handle everything. It's about time we started entertaining together, especially if we're considering, you know, being together." She still couldn't say the words "getting engaged." The idea seemed unreal. "Brie can invite some friends to come. I know you've taken her pals out in return for them having her over, but it would be nice to feed them at your house for a change."

"It's been a long time. Brianna won't admit it, but she's missed having a mother at home."

"Yeah, well, I'm not exactly her mother, but I hope she considers me her friend. I'll talk to her more about it later, when I pick her up." She hesitated. "Thanks, Dalton. I know this must be difficult for you." *Never mind how I feel in your house, where Pam's ghost follows me everywhere. Maybe I need to take Wilda's advice and guard against negative influences. Or maybe I have to accept that Pam will always be part of our lives, and that she would want you to find happiness with me.*

As long as she was near the telephone, Marla decided, she might as well look up the business number for John Hennings, the chiropractor Rosemary had mentioned. Having secured an appointment for later that day, she realized one more item needed her attention, and a glance at her watch told her she had barely ten minutes to spare before her next customer walked in the door. "I'm running over to the hardware store," she called to Nicole. "If Lisa comes in, have Joanne shampoo her. I'll be right back."

Fortunately, Sam was on duty. The silver-haired gentleman cracked a smile at her entrance. "Hey, Marla. Whaddya need? Don't tell me you ran out of batteries for your razor again."

She didn't mince words in making her offer. "Nope. I've come to invite you to a barbecue on Sunday. My mother will be there, and it's the first time she's visiting Dalton's house. She may feel awkward, so I thought if you came, you'd help her out. You'd be doing me a favor, and we'd love to have you."

Appealing to his sense of chivalry might work, she figured. At least, it didn't appear to be such a blatant attempt to get them together. Although playing matchmaker had worked in the case of Arnie and Jill, her mother's admonition about manipulating people came to mind with a rush of guilt.

"I'd be delighted," Sam said to her relief. His eyes crinkled. "What time, and where's the address?"

As she scribbled the details, she considered the preparations. *Lord save me, I have a lot to do.*

The rest of the day passed by in a blur as she rushed to finish early and get to the chiropractor on time. When she picked up Brianna later, she'd see if the girl wanted to invite any friends for Sunday. Hot dogs and hamburgers were out: too ordinary. Chicken would be good, along with side dishes that appealed to the younger gang as well as seniors.

Food fled from her mind as she approached Dr. Hennings's office on foot at five-thirty. Squeezed between an insurance office and a print shop, the unimposing door held a modest sign advertising the doctor's services. Glad to see a couple of other patients in the waiting room, Marla advanced toward the receptionist and gave her name.

A few minutes later, she took a seat clutching a standard medical questionnaire. As she plowed through the reams of paper with queries ranging from her birth date to her bowel habits, she surreptitiously glanced around the lobby. A sign above the reception desk read MAKE LIFE A LOT HEALTHIER FOR FAMILY AND FRIENDS. RECOMMEND CHIROPRACTIC CARE. One pastel blue wall held a large poster of a human spinal column and nervous system. Scanning the area, her glance rested on an aquarium with a rock formation and tropical fish in varied colors, but its soothing qualities were counteracted by a blaring television on a Lucite pedestal.

It annoyed her how every doctor's office or hospital visitor's lounge had a television. Once when Marla had been waiting for her mother to undergo a medical procedure, she'd turned off the TV so she could read a magazine. An irate nurse had come bustling in to turn it back on, saying it was mandatory to keep the television going so relatives couldn't hear what went on beyond the doors. Marla had wondered if the nurse didn't want families to hear the conversation among the medical staff or the screams of their patients.

Shifting her feet on the blue carpet, she filled in her medical history, then paused to survey a child's table in one corner complete with chairs, preschool toys, and an ugly troll doll. For adults, magazine racks held pamphlets on headaches, carpal tunnel syndrome, and other common ailments. Old issues of *Reader's Digest* littered another table.

She finished her questionnaire as one of the other patients was called. A howl of pain came from the inner sanctum, making her wince. She'd never been to a chiropractor, preferring the established medical system, but she knew this type of treatment helped scores of people.

Nonetheless, when her turn came, her heart beat alarmingly fast. Dr. Hennings was a handsome fellow, with curly black hair and engaging brown eyes. Younger than she'd expected, he ushered her into a treatment room with crisp efficiency. Unlike medical doctors, he didn't wear a white lab coat. A standard dress shirt and trousers were his uniform. A quick glance showed her the only objects in the room were a padded treatment table like you'd see in a massage studio, a small stool on wheels, a single chair, and another poster of the spinal column.

"What brings you here, Marla?" he asked after glancing through her medical questionnaire. She'd put down her reason for coming as "neck pain."

She rubbed her nape to demonstrate. "I've been working long hours lately, and my neck hurts. I thought you might do something for it."

"Have you ever seen a chiropractor before?" His eyes twinkled as he regarded her face-to-face.

"No, this is my first time."

He pointed to the chart. "You see the spinal column, and the nerves radiating from it? Nearly all your problems can be accounted for by a disruption in blood flow. If your column is misaligned, it impinges on nerves, and this in turn diminishes blood supply. My job is to find where the blockages are and make adjustments to allow for the normal transmission of nervous impulses. This may take several sessions."

Not to mention several payments. At least his services were cheaper than going to her regular doctor. She'd asked about his rates at the front desk.

"I can feel a knot right about here," she indicated on the side of her neck.

Moving behind her, he placed his large hands on her shoulders. His fingers explored her stiffness. "Boy, these are bunched tight. You must have years of strain piling up on you."

"Tell me about it." His manipulating fingers massaged her knots of tension. "Ah, that feels good."

He ran his hand up her spinal column, carefully palpating her vertebrae. "You're pretty straight through here. That's good." Bending her head forward slightly, he prodded her neck. Then he placed his hands on either side of her head, and before she knew what was happening, he gave a sharp twist that made her shriek.

"The first time is always a shock," he said with a hint of a smile in his voice. "Now hold still, here's another one." *Thwack*, he snapped her neck again, and she cried out, her senses reeling from the jolt.

"That was in the opposite direction from the last one you did," she gasped. "Didn't you just reverse the benefit?"

"They're not the same vertebrae. You should feel a difference."

"I don't know about my neck, but I feel dizzy."

"Stay with me, now." Wrapping his arms around her from behind, he jerked her so suddenly that she stumbled when he let go. Each sharp adjustment made her feel like her bones were cracking. Or more likely, slipping into place. One wrong move, and he could do serious damage. She wondered if anyone had ever been paralyzed by a chiropractic treatment. Or worse. Remembering the weird angle of Carolyn's neck, she shuddered.

"Lie down on the table, and let me have a look at the rest of you. Put your face through that hole."

Lying on her stomach, she muttered, "My friend, Carolyn Sutton, referred me to you."

"Oh?" Starting at the base of her spine, his fingers climbed northward. After finishing his inspection, he pressed on her spinal column as though testing its flexibility.

"It's a shame what happened to her. I can't believe she was murdered."

He pushed on her lungs, forcing her to expel trapped air. "I thought she died in an accident."

"Homicide is investigating. When she came to see you, did Carolyn mention any problems she might be having with some-one?"

"Why are you asking me?" His wary tone put her on alert.

"She had a habit of learning things about people that could annoy them," Marla said, hoping to prompt him into revealing any secrets he might harbor.

"How close were you as friends?"

He's trying to find out how much Carolyn told me, she thought. So Rosemary was right; Carolyn did have a hold over him. What could she have found out? That he had malpractice claims against him? Something else? She'd have to tell Vail to check into the man's background.

"I knew a lot about her," Marla hedged. "I believe the detective said her neck had been broken." *You wouldn't know anything about that, would you, doctor?*

A moment passed before he spoke, while he lifted his hands from her body. "I'm not supposed to reveal patient confidences, you understand, but since you were a friend of hers, and Carolyn isn't here anymore, I guess it won't matter." Avoiding eye contact, Dr. Hennings helped her into a sitting position. "When Carolyn started coming to me, she needed treatment for a neck problem, like you. She'd been stressed out by a court case involving her former partner."

Marla, dangling her legs over the edge of the table, gave him a sharp glance. "What partner?" Could this be Carolyn's benefactor, a silent partner?

"Peg Krueger used to own an interest in her salon. They ended up in court when Peg accused Carolyn of swindling her. The case dragged on for years but finally came up for trial."

Sliding to her feet, Marla faced him. "What happened?"

"All I know is, Carolyn wasn't happy about the outcome. Unfortunately, other people had to pay for her mistakes." He spoke bitterly, as though he'd been personally affected.

"I see. Is there anything you'd like to add? Detective Vail is in charge of Carolyn's case. He stops in at my salon from time to time. I'd be happy to pass along any information you think would be useful."

His gaze chilled. "Enough said for now. You can make an appointment for your follow-up treatment."

"Well, thanks for your time, Doctor." She twisted her neck from side to side. "Hmph, it does feel better."

Outside, she strolled through humidity so thick you could almost drink it. She must've just missed an afternoon shower. Puddles flooded the asphalt as she headed for her Camry. Lost in thought, she wondered how she could trace the Krueger woman. Maybe Vail already knew about her, in which case, he hadn't mentioned it to her.

Vowing to ask him when they got together again, she concentrated on driving home. Solving Carolyn's murder was the detective's chore. Better for her to concentrate on their relationship.

Maybe I should ask Wilda what to do in that regard. Counseling people is what she does, aside from her healing sessions.

Yeah, right, her other inner voice answered. *Don't fool yourself. You prefer crime investigation because it distracts you from personal issues.*

"Has Peg Krueger's name come up in your investigation?" Marla asked Dalton on Saturday. Proud that she hadn't let slip to her mother anything about their status the previous evening at services, she regarded the homicide officer across their table at J. Alexander's restaurant. Brie had wanted to stay home and watch a movie on television, so it was just the two of them.

"I spoke to her." His gray eyes glinted. "Krueger said she'd put that episode behind her. I didn't get the impression she was hiding anything, but you can talk to her."

"Did she put up the money Carolyn needed to move to Palm Haven?"

"No, this is something that happened ages ago, but it took a long time to get to court. When Carolyn opened her first salon, she and Krueger invested together. According to her former partner, Carolyn booted her out and took over the business. Krueger has been trying to get repaid with interest for the amount she contributed."

"Would the grudge she held against Carolyn have led to murder? Whatever happened to the medical examiner's report?"

Vail stiffened. "No question it's a homicide. Somebody knew what they were doing."

"Dr. Hennings studied anatomy. Have you found out anything about him?"

"I'm looking into his practice."

When Vail's face folded into a frown, Marla realized that was all he'd say concerning the chiropractor. Maybe Anita knew someone with an ailment he'd treated. No doubt a repeat visit was in her future. Her muscles knotted just thinking about Carolyn.

"I wish I knew if Wilda Cleaver was on the level. Nobody I know is sick, but she implied one of my relatives or close friends is ill. Oh, no." A thought struck her with unpleasant connotations.

"What?"

Marla spotted the waiter heading their way with salads and held her silence until he left. "Tally and Ken have been trying to get pregnant. Well, you know what I mean. Something doesn't seem to be quite right between them, or at least that's the impression I've been getting. I hope she doesn't have some disease that's affecting fertility."

"Emotional reasons can be just as much of a deterrent."

"Nonetheless, I'll speak to her about it. She's probably gone through a battery of tests already."

"There may be nothing wrong that a long vacation together wouldn't fix."

Stabbing her fork into a piece of lettuce, she gave him a scrutinizing glance. "Are you speaking from experience?"

His wry grin stole her heart until she heard his subsequent words. "Pam had some trouble. We saw a specialist, and he helped us. When we were least expecting it, she conceived."

"Oh." Marla chomped her salad, swallowing it past a lump in her throat.

Leaning forward, he grazed her mouth with his glance. "Now that you've grown to care for Brianna, have you thought about having one of your own?"

Choking, she coughed. "No way."

"You used to be afraid of losing a child you loved. You're taking that risk now. Don't you know the quote: 'It's better to have loved and lost than never to have loved at all.' "

Putting down her fork, she shook her head. Strands of hair brushed her face. "I'd be terrified."

"You'd be a better mother because of what you experienced. Do you believe you're not responsible enough to be a parent? Tammy's drowning was an accident. It wasn't your fault."

"Tell her parents that and see what they say."

His lips compressed. "Give yourself more credit. Look at the tremendous progress you've made with Brianna. She asks for your advice, likes you to take her shopping, respects your job."

"Yeah, and if anything happened to her, I'd be a basket case." She truly had become very fond of the girl.

"Can you imagine the age difference if we had a child? Brie is thirteen. We'd have a built-in sitter for our baby."

Oy vey. That wasn't the life she'd envisioned for herself. His proclamation made her want to run home.

"Aren't you rushing things?" Marla asked.

His lazy gaze surveyed her body. "Sweetcakes, just the thought of making a baby with you sends me into hyperdrive. When do you think you'll be ready to set a date?"

Chapter
Nine

Sunday morning found Marla looking forward to confiding in her mother when Anita came for dinner. She hadn't given Vail a direct answer on when to set a date for their nuptials other than to promise it would be after he solved Carolyn's case. Although she needed to get that load off her shoulders, it also served as a convenient excuse. Or maybe she was just waiting for him to present her with an official engagement ring, relieving her of any decision. After their night of lovemaking, no doubt remained that they belonged together; it was merely a matter of working out the details. But definitely a discussion about having children was in order. Marla figured caring for Brianna would be enough of a responsibility; she still wanted space to further her dreams, which didn't include childbearing.

Before they'd even begun barbecue preparations at Vail's house, Anita called Marla on her cell phone.

"You'll have to forgive me, *bubula*, but I have to cancel dinner for tonight. I'm not feeling too well."

Alarm frissoned up her spine. "What's the matter?"

"My head feels like it's going to explode. It must be my blood pressure. I'll go down to the drugstore and get a free reading. I've been feeling out of sorts lately, so I might need a change of medication."

"You didn't say anything to me on Friday." Working in Vail's kitchen to make breakfast, she put aside the kiwi she was slicing and dried her hands on a towel. She cradled the phone on her shoulder.

Vail glanced up from the table where he labored on a crossword puzzle from the Sunday newspaper. He'd started the coffeemaker and squeezed fresh oranges from a farmer's market for juice. She knew he still felt bad about losing his citrus trees to the state agriculture crews, but it didn't stop him from taking advantage of Florida's sunshine crop.

"I didn't want to worry you," Anita replied in her singsong tone. "I'll be all right, but I'm not up to a dinner party. I'd like to enjoy myself when I see your beau's house for the first time."

Great, now she'd have to get hold of Sam Levy and postpone their plans. "Okay. Should I come over?"

"Don't bother. You have so few days off; I'm sure you have a lot to do. I'll put in a call to my doctor if my pressure is too high."

"I'm seeing Aunt Polly today. I could swing by your place." Polly and Anita lived about ten minutes apart.

"I might be napping. I'll phone you later."

Her mother's weary tone made Marla cut the call short. Now what? She surveyed the kitchen, strewn with breakfast ingredients and implements. Guilt urged her to rush to Anita's house, but she'd promised Brianna an omelet. They had to go shopping for school supplies, then Marla planned to visit Aunt Polly. Resolving to cruise by her mother's, she tacked on a stop at her town house to get Anita's spare key.

Spooks licked her ankle. While he liked staying at Vail's home to play with the detective's golden retriever, the poodle resented any attention she paid to the other dog. Sparing a few minutes to scratch him behind the ears, she murmured endearments.

The phone rang again, this time for Vail. Shortly thereafter he left for the station. The body of a missing fourteen-year-old girl had been found. Disturbed by this news, Marla cleaned the kitchen while breakfast for the teenager turned into brunch. In the meantime, she located Sam and postponed their dinner plans.

"Th-that's okay." Sam almost sounded relieved. "I've just gotten a load of mulch for my yard, so I'll keep busy here."

"We'll make it another time," she promised.

Her restlessness grew until Brianna woke, well past noon. Reheating the omelet, she discussed which mall they should hit.

"It sucks that tomorrow is the first day of school," Brianna said after they finally got started on their shopping tour.

Regarding the girl's profile as she sat in the car, Marla felt a twinge of anxiety. With her clear complexion, toffee ponytail, and minimal makeup, Brie radiated the picture of innocence. Feeling a surge of protectiveness, she smiled gently. "I would think you'd want to go to school to be with your friends."

"Yeah, but I have Mrs. Strickland for history this year. I heard she's a tough teacher, and that's my worst subject. Mr. Rodriguez for Spanish is the same as last year. If you do bad on tests, he lets you make it up with special projects."

"What else are you taking?" Marla asked. If she were the girl's mother, she'd probably have her schedule memorized.

"English with Miss Jackson. I heard she assigns a lot of reading. Mr. Moore is pre-algebra; he hangs out at the teacher's lounge and hits on the pretty women. Then there's science with Mrs. Fox. She's okay if you don't mind her buggy eyes and that she sneaks cigarettes outside during lunch break."

"I'm glad my school days are over."

Brianna looked at her. "It'll seem strange coming home tomorrow when no one is there. You wouldn't be getting off work early, would you?"

Marla gripped the steering wheel. "I'm off on Mondays, remember? I have some errands to run, but I'll show up in time to throw something together for dinner. You can fill me on your day then."

"Why don't you stay over tonight?" Brianna said, her offhand tone not fooling Marla.

"I have my own things to do."

"Are you and Daddy getting married?"

Marla gaped. "Where did that come from?"

"I don't know. He seems happier lately, and he's always mentioning you. I thought maybe you two had talked about it."

Marla heard the wistful note in her tone. "It would be a big change for me. Don't get me wrong, I want to be with you and your father. But I'm uncomfortable in your house. I'd have to leave my place, and I'd probably rent it out, but where would I put my things?"

She couldn't quite bring herself to confess that it was Brianna's mother who inhibited her. Call it negative energy, using Wilda's terms, but Pam's ghost, or at least her family's memories of her, filled that house. "I'd want us to start over," she blurted. "That would mean you'd have to move, too. It's probably too much to ask."

A hurt look entered Brianna's young eyes. "What if we pack away a lot of stuff, and Daddy lets you redo the kitchen? I know you hate it."

"It's not only that; it's the bedroom. You know, he and your mother slept there, and that bothers me. Even though I want to honor your mother's memory, I can't help the way I feel. I'm not sure how we can get around this obstacle."

"Where there's a will, there's a way," Brianna quoted, jutting her jaw in determination.

Admiring the girl's resolve, Marla wished she saw a solution. Until one arose, she couldn't give Vail a definitive answer to his proposal.

Their awkward silence dissipated when they entered the Fashion Mall. Following Brianna through the Juniors department at Macy's, Marla gritted her teeth with impatience. A couple of hours breezed by while the teen searched through scores of blue jeans, tops fitted for stick figures, and lingerie that Marla wouldn't have been allowed to wear at her age.

At the makeup counters, Brie hesitated. "I need some advice," she said, her ponytail flicking as she turned her head toward the Chanel display. "I don't know how to line my lips. Mostly, I use a gloss, but I'd like to learn how to use lipstick. I can't get it right."

Examining the contours of her mouth, Marla smiled. "I usually advise people to cover their lips with foundation when they're putting on their base makeup. Then use a lip liner to carefully draw your new lip line. Be careful not to make your mouth too small or you'll look like a geisha, or too large so you look like a clown. The lip gloss is fine for someone your age. *Glamour* did a survey regarding what guys like on women, and lip gloss was in the top ten."

"Can I buy some polish?" Brianna pointed to a metallic blue.

"At these prices? I don't think so. We'll go to the beauty-supply place where I get a discount. Come on, it's late, and I have to go see my aunt."

After dropping Brianna off, Marla transferred Spooks to her town house, where she freshened up, grabbed a snack, and collected Anita's key.

"I should get a key to Polly's place," Marla growled after pounding on Polly's door at a condominium complex where all of the units looked the same. Depression settled over her like a curtain as she watched the elderly residents shuffle through their daily routine. It saddened her how many senior citizens were reduced to living in a small apartment, their proud accomplishments forgotten beneath the sands of time. Those whose grown children lived up North suffered loneliness just at a stage in life when their faculties were failing but a stubborn sense of dignity prevented them from seeking help.

Fortunately, Marla had been able to assist Miriam Pearl, an old gal who had plenty of spunk despite her troubles. She'd spruced up Miriam's hair along with her social life, getting her out of the house to meet her cronies at the mall. Miriam's new nurse had started taking her to a senior activity center, too. She had Marla to thank for these changes. And solving the murder of the woman's granddaughter had strengthened their relationship. She felt a wave of guilt about neglecting her own relatives. Why didn't

Polly answer the door? She banged louder, calling her name. At last she heard an answering reply. Moments later, the door swung open. Polly glanced at her through spectacles held together with adhesive tape.

"Eh? Is that you, Marla?"

Marla spoke in a loud tone. "I was passing by the area and thought I'd stop in to say hello."

"Well, this is a pleasant surprise. Don't just stand there. Come inside." Anita's older sister plodded into her living room, scruffy slippers barely covering her feet. She wore a housecoat that snapped up the front, its hem hanging loose on one side.

Marla's glance rose inescapably to Polly's scraggly gray hair hanging straight to her shoulders. Her aunt had split ends like you wouldn't believe. Remembering that her purse contained a pair of shears, Marla wondered if she could convince the elderly lady to submit to a free trim.

"Free" was the operative word as far as Polly was concerned. Hot, humid air worse than outside accosted Marla after she closed the door and pursued her aunt. "I can't breathe in here. Don't you have the air-conditioning on?" she croaked, gasping for air. Thrusting her purse on the dining room table, she veered toward the thermostat. Sure enough, it was turned to the OFF position. Lowering the temperature, she switched it on automatic. A comforting whoosh of cool air blasted the room.

"*Tanteh*, how have you been?" Marla said, sitting on the lone sofa covered with a ragged sheet. A polished wood buffet table held family photographs while the rest of the furniture looked like garage-sale additions.

"Eh, whassat you say? I'm too thin? Nonsense, girl, I've still got an appetite." Suspicion narrowed her filmy eyes. "Did Anita send you to check up on me?"

"Not at all. I haven't seen you in a while and was wondering if you needed help with anything. Are you able to go food shopping?"

"Huh?"

"Shopping! Can you get food?" Realizing Polly had grown more hard of hearing, Marla shouted into her ear.

Her aunt's wrinkled face crinkled into a smile. "Didn't you eat lunch already? Would you like a cup of tea?"

"No, thanks." She sighed in exasperation. "Can I fix you something?"

"I'm all right, dear. So tell me about your family."

"Ma isn't feeling well. I'm going to stop over there from here."

"Your daughter isn't well? What's the matter with Rebecca?"

"Aunt Polly, I'm not Charlene." She didn't look anything like her brother's wife. "I think you need a new pair of glasses and a hearing aid." Things were worse than she'd expected. How did Polly manage on her own? No wonder Ma wanted Marla to help her aunt.

"I don't have any Kool-Aid, dear. Would you like some orange juice?"

Lord save me. Rising, Marla smoothed out her khakis. "May I use the bathroom?" This couldn't get any worse.

Wrong. Inside the lavatory she surveyed a cracked vinyl toilet seat, age-old stains in the bathtub, and blouses soaking in a sinkful of water. Aunt Polly probably didn't spend a dime to do her laundry. Her gaze fell on the distorted lump that passed as soap. Impossible. Anita had set her an impossible task. Quickly using the facilities, she emerged and headed for the kitchen, afraid of what she might find there.

Peeling wallpaper, a nearly empty refrigerator, and a lack of any modern conveniences confirmed her fears. Polly didn't even possess a toaster. Next visit, she'd bring some groceries to stock her shelves. "You have to get help," she told her aunt, striding into the living room. "I don't see how you can live like this."

Struggling to her feet, Polly waggled a finger at her. "I know your mother sent you. Anita is always telling me what to do. She'd better mind her own business, and so should you."

"She's worried about you, *tanteh.*"

"I'm fine the way I am. Anita always puts me down. She criti-

cizes what I wear and how I do things. Just because I try to be re-
sourceful rather than wasteful, she's on my back. Anita is too
high-strung, I tell you. That's why her blood pressure bothers
her." Polly's voice climbed a notch in pitch. "Tell her to mind her
own affairs and to stop sending you to do her dirty work. I know
she's behind it. She's never liked me."

Realizing this tirade could continue, Marla retreated toward
the door. "Time for me to go now. I'll look in on you again, Aunt
Polly. I really am concerned about you, and I'd like to help."
Yeah, right. Like I need this headache. No wonder Ma gets agitated.

"She's getting in trouble, your mother is." Polly advanced toward her, a fanatical gleam in her eyes. "Running around with
that man, Roger. Flaunting herself like a trollop. It's disgusting.
It'll lead her to a bad end, you mark my words. People talk about
her, and it isn't nice."

"Who talks about her?" Marla snapped, feeling the need to
defend her mother's reputation even though she didn't care for
Roger, either.

"They do—our mutual friends. It embarrasses me."

Marla couldn't leave without at least fixing her aunt a snack
and swiping her counters with a clean cloth. Diverting Polly's attention, she busied herself in the kitchen while her aunt ate.

An hour later found her at Anita's house.

"Polly is full of it," Anita said, dipping her hands into a bowl of
chopped-meat mixture to form a meatball. "She's jealous of me. I
have a lot more friends than she does, and she can't stand it that
I'm dating anyone."

"Regardless of your personal problems, Aunt Polly really does
need someone to look after her. She doesn't hear or see well, and
she barely has any food in her refrigerator."

"Well, you'll just have to convince her to hire a girl." Dropping
the meatball onto a plate rimmed with others, Anita speared her
daughter with a dark look. "You have your work cut out for you,
angel." ·

"I'm no angel, and I don't have time. It's not my problem."

"You're her closest niece. She won't listen to me." Anita

placed the emptied bowl in the sink before washing her hands. Crossing to the stove, she centered a heavy stockpot on the larger burner. One by one, she tossed in the contents of a jar of grape jelly, a bottle of chili sauce, and a fifteen-ounce can of tomato sauce. "Hand me those chopped onions, will you?"

Marla complied silently, watching Anita stir the onions into the bubbling sauce over a medium-high temperature. Once the ingredients were blended, Anita added a sprinkle of garlic powder and tossed in the meatballs, stirring the entire mixture until the meat was well coated. Turning the heat dial to low, she covered the pot.

"I gather your blood pressure was all right," Marla commented, wondering if her mother's headache was a ruse to get out of their barbecue.

"I took a couple of Tylenol, and they helped."

"Uh huh." Tired of interfering in other people's lives, Marla decided to let Sam approach Anita on his own.

"How is the case regarding Carolyn Sutton proceeding?" Ma queried, untying her apron.

"Dalton was called for another murder this morning. Some young girl was found dead. I don't know how he can deal with things like that without thinking about Brianna."

"It must be tough on him. Just don't let it bring you down."

"He says I help erase the ugliness from his life," she said wistfully. "The man needs me, Ma."

"Being a policeman's wife won't be easy . . . if you decide to go that route." Anita gave her a questioning glance.

"We'll see." Averting her gaze, Marla helped herself to a cinnamon twist pastry in a box on the counter. "Regarding Carolyn, I want to follow up on another lead. Her chiropractor told me she'd been involved in a court case with a former partner. Peg Krueger works at a Haircuttery across town. They're open on Mondays; I thought I'd catch her tomorrow."

"Don't neglect your customers while you're chasing down suspects."

"I won't. You can do something to help. Can you ask your

friends if anyone knows Dr. Hennings? Rosemary Taylor, Carolyn's bingo partner, said Carolyn learned something about the chiropractor that gave her an edge against him. Maybe one of your acquaintances has seen the doctor for treatments."

"You should ask around at Polly's complex. Those people have probably visited every doctor in town."

You're right. Sitting in the doctor's office is the main form of entertainment when you get to that age. "I'll think about it. In the meantime, please see what you can find out."

Marla's spirits lifted as she left Anita's house to complete a list of errands before returning home. Relieved to enter the sanctuary of her town house by four o'clock, she unloaded a trunkful of groceries before letting Spooks outside to the fenced backyard.

After putting away the perishables, she retrieved her Saturday mail and was shuffling through the envelopes when the phone rang.

"Thanks for taking Brianna shopping," said Vail's gruff tone. "She's really come to rely on you."

"Are you still at work?" Holding the receiver, Marla sank down onto the desk chair in her study.

"Yeah."

"I left Brie some spaghetti pie. She'll be able to heat a slice for dinner if you're late. I said I'd stop by tomorrow after work to see how her first day of school went."

"That's thoughtful of you."

His unusual silence made her wonder at the purpose of his call. "Was there something you wanted to tell me?"

"That girl they brought in, you know, my new case? A shank of her hair is missing. It isn't much, and I might not have noticed it ordinarily, except you've got me looking at things like that now. Her layers don't match."

Marla's blood chilled. "You mean it's similar to Carolyn's uneven haircut?"

"Right."

She swallowed, unable to ask how the girl died. "Maybe if you solve one case, it will relate to the other." That wasn't a comforting thought. They could have a serial killer running around town, although the age difference between Carolyn and a teenager discounted that possibility.

She heard the click of her call-waiting system. "I'm getting another signal," she told him. Sensing he needed comfort, she added, "Want to wait, or talk to me later?"

"I'll catch you another time. See ya." He rang off.

"Hello?" she said, after hitting the FLASH button.

"Marla? This is Linda Hall, Carolyn Sutton's sister. I have something urgent to tell you."

Chapter
Ten

The sun blazed its descent at seven o'clock on Sunday evening when Marla met Linda Hall at an outdoor Starbucks on Atlantic Avenue in Delray Beach. Comfortably attired in a linen slacks set, Marla sipped her coffee while regarding the harried housewife across the table. Usually vibrant with shoppers, the busy district quieted by the end of the day except for restaurant-goers. Other tables were jammed with shorts-clad residents exchanging gossip.

Thunder rumbled in the distance, making Marla aware she hadn't listened to the weather report recently. The latest tropical depression had spun into a named storm, but she hadn't been following its course. Too many stormy waters closer to home drew her attention.

Scratching her forearm, itchy from the hot, sticky air, she focused on the papers Linda withdrew from her purse.

"While I was sifting through Carolyn's personal stuff, I came across these," Linda said, pushing the pages across the table. They looked as crinkled as their new owner. Her heavyset figure didn't tolerate the heat well. Sweating beneath her foundation, Linda appeared pale, her blond hair limp. She'd extended her lip liner too wide, the result reminding Marla of the Joker.

"This looks like jewelry," Marla said, indicating some scanned photos on the sheets she held. Brooches, rings, bracelets. Where were these from?

"That's not what I found in Carolyn's safety deposit box. If they're part of her collectibles, they could be worth a lot of money. Those are pieces of Victorian mourning jewelry."

"What's that?"

"I looked it up in the library. In the days of Queen Victoria, people wore accessories created from the hair of deceased loved ones. It served as a keepsake of the dead and as a reminder that death could strike at any time. If you look at the listings, Carolyn had some antique jewelry worth a small fortune."

Marla shuffled through the papers. "Wow, this is something else," she said, noting a couple of cameos worth over two thousand dollars. "Where did you find these documents?"

"In a folder labeled income tax." Linda slurped a Coke, keeping her eyes on Marla. "Read the history part; it's fascinating."

Marla summarized aloud. "Queen Victoria, who was widowed at forty-two, wore mourning dress for the next forty years of her life. After the aristocracy followed suit, this practice extended to other classes as an expression of dignity and social status. Magazines outlined the length of different mourning periods. Initially, women didn't wear jewelry, but in later stages, it became quite fashionable."

"They cut off part of the dead person's hair to make jewelry from it," Linda said with a grimace. "I think it's pretty morbid, although I suppose it's no different than pasting a lock of your loved one's hair in an album."

"Victorians created their own hair jewelry using instructional pamphlets featuring patterns, or they hired professional hair workers," Marla read on. "This presented a problem because often these workers didn't use the deceased person's hair. Sometimes they sold items made from purchased bulk hair." She glanced up. "In other words, they practiced fraud. How would you know who the hair belonged to if someone else created the jewelry?"

Linda suppressed a belch. "Some people still like to wear

lockets containing hair or photographs. Did you see where it says the mourning jewelry could include precious stones like diamonds? The Victorians also liked to engrave their gold fittings."

"Often a wearer added more hair to the piece when additional relatives passed away," Marla continued, then stopped and said, "Yuk, I don't think I'd want to wear something that reminded me about death. It's supposed to warn the wearer to lead a good life because death was just around the corner. That's gruesome, don't you think?"

"Look at how much some of that stuff is worth." Linda's hazel eyes narrowed. "I wonder what happened to my sister's collection. Obviously, someone stole it, but who?"

"I can't believe these prices," Marla proclaimed. "Here's a hair ring with seed pearls that represent tears for six hundred and ninety-five dollars. This hair brooch with three different colors of hair weaved into a crisscross design goes for five hundred and fifty. Carolyn wouldn't have had to possess that many of these things for them to add up to a fortune."

"Look at the items on the next page. Those are regular antiques. Carolyn didn't collect only mourning jewelry. If I recall, there's a gold and tortoiseshell barrette worth twelve hundred dollars, and a garnet necklace for more. I can't understand how she could afford to buy these things, unless they were gifts. Carolyn didn't talk much about her love life, but she did date."

"If you're right, then her boyfriend might have retrieved his property after her death. Who had a key to her place?"

Linda snorted. "Her homeowners association, that friend she met at bingo, her spiritual guru, and God knows who else."

"Rosemary Taylor, the bingo player, said you envied your sister's lifestyle and wished you had her independence." Marla exaggerated a bit, hoping to provoke Linda into fuller disclosure.

"What housewife wouldn't trade a day of drudgery for more freedom?" Linda straightened her shoulders. "That doesn't mean I'd discard my family. Sure, I get tired of the same old routine, and I admired Carolyn for running her own business, not that she did so well. But I wouldn't want her life."

Marla eyed the encroaching cloud bank. They'd have to move inside if it rained. Swatting at a mosquito, she continued. "Who's watching the children tonight?"

"Richard is home."

"What did you say he does?"

"Actually, he's out of work right now. He got laid off last month. I'm thinking of looking for a job until he can find something worthwhile."

"You must've been really annoyed that Carolyn didn't leave her salon to you."

"I wasn't surprised. She always felt my life was perfect. I'm lucky she left me anything at all."

Pushing away her empty coffee cup, Marla folded her hands on the table. "I gather the jewelry wasn't insured."

"Too bad, isn't it? We could have used the money." Giving a yawn, Linda stretched, then rose to her feet. "I'm hoping you can find out who took these things, Miss Shore. You seem to be good at getting people to talk. Cops make me nervous, so I'd rather chat with you." She hesitated. "Don't think I'm only interested in getting my due. I want to see my sister's killer brought to justice."

"I appreciate your calling me. I'll let you know if anything significant turns up in the investigation."

"Thanks, kiddo. Hey, maybe the two of us can do a night on the town sometime. Richard doesn't mind when I slip out with the gals. He said it prevents me from turning into a New Age junkie like my sister."

"Er, sure, when I have some free time," Marla lied.

"If you don't mind, I'll keep those." Snatching the papers, Linda stuffed the lists into her generous handbag as she got up to leave. "It's my only proof of what I have coming to me."

As Linda hastened along the sidewalk, Marla shuffled her chair back when she realized they hadn't paid the bill.

"Why, you schnorrer," she grumbled at Linda's retreating backside while reaching for her purse. "I suppose you consider this your payment for information." But then, she reasoned, if operatives on television paid informants, why shouldn't she? At least they hadn't met in that fancy seafood restaurant on the corner. They could easily have run up a high tab for dinner in there, and if Linda's husband truly had lost his job, they must be hurting for cash.

An inheritance would come in mighty handy right about now. Linda may not have acquired Carolyn's business, but according to those papers, she could get a substantial amount by selling her sister's Victorian jewelry. Maybe Vail had connections with antique dealers in the region. He could ask Linda for a copy of the lists and scour the shops for recent sales, a tedious job Marla would readily turn over to him.

"What's up?" Vail asked in a weary tone when she called him at the station later. It was nine-thirty, early by her standards, but late for him to still be at work. A twinge of guilt hit her for selfishly wanting to stay home instead of keeping Brianna company. Although she didn't like the idea of the teen staying alone, making other arrangements wasn't her responsibility. Yet. *You have to deal with those guilt trips, Marla. Too many people impinge on your good nature. Put the energy into yourself first, or you won't have any left to give.*

"I drove to Delray Beach to talk to Linda Hall," she told Vail. "She'd been looking through Carolyn's papers and discovered a list of collectible items. It appears Carolyn acquired Victorian mourning jewelry and other accessories from that period. Appraisals show they could be worth a small fortune."

"You say Hall has a list?" His voice sharpened.

"That's right. An article explained how people in the Victorian era wore jewelry containing clippings from a deceased person's hair. It reminded them of their loved one. Rings, brooches, hairpins, and lockets were fashioned out of gold, often with diamonds, pearls, or garnets included. Sometimes the hair would be woven into designs."

"Mourning jewelry . . . hair clippings . . . dead people. Hmm."

"Oh no. You're thinking about . . ."

"Often a killer takes a souvenir from his victim. Maybe that's why Carolyn was missing a clump of hair."

Sitting in her study, Marla didn't answer, grabbing a pen while chills rippled down her spine.

"I'm not saying anything conclusive," Vail added. "Now that there's concrete proof this collection exists, though, I'd like to locate it."

"So would I. Linda believes the jewelry was stolen. She mentioned that Rosemary Taylor and Wilda Cleaver may have had keys to Carolyn's place. Have you spoken to her landlord or her neighbors?"

"Of course."

"Linda's other theory is that Carolyn had a boyfriend who gave her the jewelry as gifts, since there was no way Carolyn could afford an investment like that herself. Possibly this boyfriend returned to regain his property after her death."

"That would work in with your idea that Sutton had a benefactor." He gave a heavy sigh, and she heard a tapping noise, like a pencil on his desk.

"Have you eaten dinner?" she asked with a touch of concern.

"I had a snack from the vending machines. Look, I've got to get back to work."

"If this new case with the teen has your attention, who'll solve Carolyn's murder?"

"Sergeant Peterson is working on it. But if you find out anything new, let me know. I'm worried about the way the wind is blowing, and I don't mean that tropical storm festering offshore."

"That reminds me, I meant to listen to the weather report. I'll talk to you later. Good luck," she said, hanging up before he could mention anything else about the slain teenager. Just thinking about it made her stomach churn.

After her second call of the evening to Brianna to reassure herself the girl was all right, she turned on the television to the weather station. Exactly ten minutes before the hour, the storm report came on. Watching the perfectly coiffed female meteorologist, Marla listened halfheartedly to her report on how the storm in the Caribbean was strengthening into a distinct rotary circulation with wind speed of up to fifty-five miles per hour. That wasn't the matter uppermost in her mind.

Carolyn Sutton's image conjured itself in her imagination. Once again she saw the woman's body lying on the ground in the meter room, with that uneven patch of layered hair. What could it mean, and how could two cases with victims so diverse in age be related, if indeed they were? She shook her head. That was for Vail to determine. In the meantime, she could help him by interviewing Peg Krueger.

By eleven o'clock on Monday morning, Peg Krueger already had clients backed up, and the receptionist told Marla bluntly no openings were available. Catching an opportunity when she spied Peg heading for the rear, Marla charged after her. The woman at the front desk had pointed her out. She'd look right at home on a battlefield, Marla thought. The woman had a head like an aircraft carrier, with a flat-top haircut and a chin that drove forward like a jet on patrol. Her bland brown hair, dry as straw, would have suited the military, just the same as her rigid posture and trim, tailored clothes. In contrast, Carolyn's soft strawberry blond hair and miniskirted figure must have provided the antithesis in their partnership.

"Why the hell should I talk to you?" Peg snapped after Marla introduced herself. "I'm doing a touch-up; I have no time for this. Besides, the cops already questioned me." Yanking a color tube from a shelf, she squeezed the contents into a bowl, then added developer. She didn't impress Marla as a woman to engage in an argument.

"Just tell me briefly what happened between the two of you," Marla pleaded, glancing at the well-stocked supplies. "You and Carolyn were partners once, right?"

"Until that bitch cheated me." Peg mixed the solution vigorously with a stiff brush.

"I'm not sure I understand." Sniffing the familiar chemical scents of a salon, Marla smiled encouragingly.

"We were friends, like, you know, before we went into business together. Carolyn and I opened the salon as partners because we shared the same dream. It was going to be our nest egg that we built up for our retirement someday."

"So things went well for a while?" Leaning against the counter, Marla folded her arms across her chest.

Peg bobbed her head in time to her stirring motions. "Then Carolyn, like, gets grandiose ideas. She claimed I managed the salon poorly and lost money. After filing for bankruptcy, she took over the business, and it flourished after I left."

Doesn't that tell you something, pal? Keeping her expression bland, Marla pushed onward. "Some people have good business sense; others have talent and should stay behind the chair. You seem happy here. Maybe you weren't suited to running a business. Being an owner/manager adds to your responsibilities and takes a lot of energy."

Peg glared at her. "That's not the point. Carolyn owed me money for my investment. When we signed the lease, the building wasn't open yet. We each put down five thousand dollars toward security and rent. I had no credit card and no checking account, so I took money from my savings. What I didn't know was that Carolyn just sent in her payments."

"You mean the landlord thought Carolyn was the only one paying on the lease?"

"Exactly, and this happened every month. She said I wasn't paying my share of the rent. Carolyn, like, just wanted to push me out, so she discredited me to Mr. Thomson."

"Dennis Thomson was your landlord?"

Peg's lip curled into a snarl. "That man had the nerve to evict me, and I hadn't done anything wrong. It was all Carolyn's fault. She'd paid her part. Since her name was on the lease, he gave the shop solely to her."

"What happened to your money?"

"Carolyn said she used it to equip the salon. Like, to buy

shampoo bowls and such, you know? Plus it was her job to pay the utility bills, so she spent some of my cash on the telephone and electric."

"Let me see if I understand correctly. You believed you were paying your share of the rent, yet Carolyn ended up using it to stock the salon and pay for utilities. Weren't you supposed to split the cost of these items, too?"

"Well, sure, but I had no choice in anything she ordered. Look what it cost us before we even opened: six hundred and seventy dollars each for the stations, three hundred and fifteen for shampoo bottles, not to mention wallpaper, towels, and other supplies. I wasn't going to pay for all the extras she wanted. Carolyn claimed I owed her for these things, but they stayed in her salon after I left. She owed me back my investment plus interest."

"At some point you filed for small claims, right?"

"You got it. I wouldn't let her steamroll me like that. I paid to open the shop same as her."

It looks like you reneged on your part of the deal, if you didn't contribute toward the overhead. Regardless, it appeared as though Carolyn had taken advantage of her friend's ignorance to seize control of the salon. "How did the case turn out?" Marla asked, trailing Peg back to her station.

"The judge, like, told her to pay me two thousand dollars. I felt that was grossly unfair, and even my mother said Carolyn got away with highway robbery. I think Carolyn ditched me because another player came along." Donning a rubber glove, Peg began applying coloring to her customer's roots. Marla waited patiently for another opening during the ensuing conversation between stylist and customer.

"You said Carolyn got involved with another player. How so? Did she acquire a silent partner?"

Peg shot her a sly glance. "All I know is, Atlas Boyd solved her money problems. I'm not sure they were actually partners in a business sense, if you know what I mean." She winked. "But she seemed to do a lot better after he came along."

"Who is this guy? Where can I find him?" Excited by this new lead, Marla couldn't wait to act on it.

"I dunno. He's some big-shot foreigner."

Her heart pounded. "Carolyn sponsored foreign students at the Sunrise Academy of Beauty. Do you think he was involved?"

"Who knows and who cares? Carolyn paid the price for what she did to me, and that's all that matters." Turning her back on Marla, the stylist proclaimed her dismissal.

"Because she was killed?" Marla persisted. "Or because she paid you two thousand dollars?"

"She died for her sins, you dolt."

"By whose hand?"

Peg whipped around. "You ask an awful lot of questions. I told the cops I had nothing to do with it, but I'm not going to cry over her grave. Like, that bitch stole my money, you know. She used the profits from our salon for personal gain without giving me any of the revenue. She got what she deserved."

Chapter Eleven

On the way home, Marla thought about her conversation with Peg Krueger. If Carolyn had been using salon profits for her own investments rather than putting them back into the business, that could account for her eventual decline. Had she used the money to buy Victorian jewelry, or to play bingo? Maybe she won enough cash at the casino to buy the baubles for herself. Marla needed to glean some idea about Carolyn's winnings from the gaming hall. That necessitated a return trip to the Indian bingo parlor and another chat with Rosemary Taylor. Besides having a key to Carolyn's place, Rosemary had known about the collection.

Carolyn had gotten cash flow from somewhere: first from her salon when it was profitable, a portion perhaps from bingo, then from a mysterious benefactor when her business faltered. Gripping the steering wheel and keeping her eyes on the road, Marla considered another alternative. Carolyn may have had a lover with generous pockets.

"Check out the man named Atlas Boyd," Brianna told her later that evening when Marla swung by Vail's house with take-out Chinese food. They sat in the kitchen eating from paper plates, and Marla had just filled in the teen on her recent progress.

"Peg seems to blame this guy for Carolyn's betrayal," Marla replied. "His name hasn't come up before, which makes me wonder why not."

Brianna gazed at her with serious brown eyes. "It's possible no one else knows about him. He could be history."

"I'll ask Claudia if she's met him. She's one of Carolyn's stylists," Marla explained. "If Boyd is a foreigner, he could be the one who helped Carolyn bring in those French girls."

"Then Peter McGraw might know about him. Daddy said the lawyer was involved with immigration stuff."

"True." Frowning thoughtfully, Marla bit into a steamed dumpling dipped in soy sauce.

"Daddy won't tell me about his latest case. I know he's afraid of scaring me since the girl was close to my age, but I heard about it in school. It's horrible, but I'm glad she wasn't anyone I knew."

Marla nearly gagged on her food. "So am I, but it's still frightening. I hope you always know to keep your doors locked and the alarm on when you're home by yourself, and to be aware of who's around when you get off the school bus."

"Like Daddy has told me a hundred times." Brianna thrust a forkful of lo mein noodles into her mouth.

From the way she chomped down, Marla could tell the girl was disturbed. Vail wouldn't be unaffected by this new case, either. It was too close to home. She only hoped it wouldn't keep him from pursuing Carolyn's killer.

"He told me about the hair," Brianna blurted, a noodle hanging down her chin. Avoiding Marla's eyes, she slurped it up.

"Oh." Wondering how to allay the teen's fears, Marla tasted her beef-with-broccoli dish. The crunchiness of the vegetable melded with the tender meat.

"I can't believe people made jewelry out of their dead relatives' hair," Brie continued. "That's so gross."

Marla heard her unspoken thoughts. Maybe someone was doing the same thing now, clipping pieces of hair from people he'd killed and keeping them as remembrances. But it didn't make sense. How could a dead fourteen-year-old girl be related to the murdered Carolyn? And where did Carolyn's missing collection fit in?

Vail strode through the door just before eight o'clock, and Marla didn't delay her departure. She still had things to do at home before retiring.

"Anything new?" she asked him after giving him a quick kiss in the front hallway. Brianna, organizing her backpack in her room, talked so loudly on the telephone that they could hear her.

"I'd rather leave my work at the station tonight." His smoky eyes regarded her with affection. "Thanks for keeping Brie company."

"No problem." She looked him over with concern. He didn't hide his fatigue too well. Lines around his eyes had deepened; his five o'clock shadow had grown darker; his shoulders sagged. And his rumpled suit needed a fresh pressing. Discontented with her brief greeting, he pulled her into his arms and kissed her soundly before nuzzling her neck. Although he was tempting her to stay, she knew he needed his rest.

Pushing him away, she spoke lightly. "Not tonight, honey. I've got to get home. Let's touch base tomorrow to exchange information. I saw Peg Krueger today, and she told me something interesting."

"Well, unless it's urgent, I'm too tired to act on it, anyway." He gave her a strained smile. "I wish you'd move in already. I hate you leaving like this."

"We'll talk about it," she promised. "Oh, there's one thing I wanted to mention. If we're going to, uh, be together, what are we going to do about holidays? I mean, Rosh Hashanah is this month. We usually have a big family dinner. Would you feel terribly awkward if I wanted you and Brianna to go?"

His gaze warmed. "Would your family mind?"

"They wouldn't have any say in it. My mother drags Roger to family events."

"He's Jewish."

"So? Some of my cousins have married goyim."

"I'll talk about it with Brie, okay?"

"We've never really discussed traditions and how we'll handle them," Marla said. "I've never met your family. We could run into barriers we're not expecting." Anxiety made her words pour out.

Placing his hands on her shoulders, he regarded her steadily. "All relationships have obstacles to overcome. We'll manage." His reassuring kiss melted her doubts, reminding her she didn't have to face things alone.

Vail's watchful eyes guarded her back as she strode outside toward her car. Crickets sang their nightly chorus, piercing the moisture-laden air. In the distant sky, a jagged streak of lightning exposed a mass of towering cumulus clouds.

That's nothing compared to the storm front that's going to hit when I suggest Dalton sell his house, she figured, dread sinking her stomach. It was one thing to consider which traditions of each other's they'd respect; it was another to ask him to shift his life completely by moving. She'd have to bring it up sooner or later, because she couldn't announce their engagement until they'd jumped this hurdle.

Dining with Brianna, she'd felt Pam's presence emanating from the angel figurines and painted plates in their glass-fronted kitchen cabinet. While she could tolerate the ticking grandfather clock, she wouldn't have chosen patterned fruit wallpaper or framed prints of wine and cheese. Never mind the claustrophobic feeling she got from the tiny window and garish fluorescent lighting. Imprinted with another woman's personality, the house would never suit her, no matter how many crystals she wore or bowls of water she put out to deflect negative energy.

"So when are you going to talk to him about it?" Tally said on the phone when Marla called her after she got home.

"Who knows? He's wrapped up in the case with this teenager. I don't want to add to his burdens right now."

"He's always going to have a case that draws his attention," Tally admonished. "Just as you leave work at the salon, he should leave his at the police station. It shouldn't interfere in your personal life."

"Oh, like your boutique doesn't come between you and Ken?"

"He has his job; I have mine."

"Maybe the pressure is what's keeping you from getting pregnant."

"That's what he says, and I've told him to take a hike. I'm not giving up what it took me so long to achieve. You know how that goes. Would you give up your salon to have a child?"

Marla laughed. "What, me get pregnant? Are you kidding?"

"You never know where life will take you. You're doing a bang-up job with Brianna. Maybe you'll want to have Dalton's baby some day."

"*Oy vey*, I can just imagine myself with a squirming infant. Better you than me," she said emphatically, considering all the things one had to worry about with a child. "Besides, I'd be a paranoid mother, scared of letting my kid do anything."

"You'd be a wonderful mother," Tally countered.

"I don't think so. My brother Michael can fulfill those family obligations, thank you."

"Ever since Tammy died, you've been striving to prove your worth. You've set yourself on a career track, become self-reliant, and given your time to prevent similar tragedies. If that's not enough to satisfy you, maybe bringing new life into the world is what you need to cleanse your soul."

"My soul needs more freedom, not less. I want to travel, maybe finish my college degree, expand my salon services. I'd rather be godmother to your baby. Is Ken really giving you a hard time?"

It was a long moment before Tally answered. "I'm beginning to feel he may have been happier with the stay-at-home type. It was okay for me to work before we wanted a family, but now his attitude has changed. His mother doesn't help the situation. She nags us for grandchildren."

"How does she feel about your shop?"

"She loves to bring her friends there and get a discount, but she's blaming me for not conceiving."

"And the fertility tests show nothing is wrong, if I recall. Are you feeling okay otherwise? I mean, you have no underlying health problems, right?"

"None that I'm aware of. You sound worried."

"Wilda the medium said someone close to me needs to see a doctor. I can't imagine who it is, although my mother's blood pressure has been bothering her, and my aunt's mental functions are deteriorating. Then I got anxious about you. Of course, Wilda could be spinning tales, but you never know."

"Well, don't be nervous on my account; I'm fine. When can I meet your psychic?"

"I'd rather you accompany me back to the bingo hall. I have more questions to ask Rosemary Taylor."

"How about if I give you a call when I have a free night?"

"That sounds like a plan. Meanwhile, I want to find out more about Atlas Boyd."

During a break in her routine on Tuesday, Marla ventured over to Hairstyle Heaven. Expecting to see Wilda at the front desk, she was surprised to find instead a strange young woman with a nose ring and tattoos covering her slim arms.

"That's ninety-eight dollars, please," the insipid brunette told a client. "Marcy said your hair was sixty-five dollars, with another fourteen for the anti-frizz product."

"What?" the middle-aged woman exclaimed. "Sixty-five plus fourteen equals seventy-nine dollars. Are you naturally math deficient, or are you trying to cheat me?"

"Let me see." Scribbling the numbers on a scrap of paper, the receptionist kept adding and crossing out figures. "Oh, all right, whatever."

After the irate customer left, the clerk gave Marla a loopy grin. "Hi, I'm Bunny. May I help you?"

Marla tore her gaze from the silver stud poking from the girl's nose. "I'm Marla Shore, owner of Cut 'N Dye Salon. Is Wilda here?"

"She won't be in today, miss. I'm the new temp she hired."

Spotting Claudia at her station, Marla waved. "If you don't mind, I'd like to have a word with Claudia. She asked for my help when the previous owner passed away, and I'd like to know if everything is okay."

Sticking a piece of chewing gum in her mouth, the girl nodded. Marla marched away, grateful she'd found Luis to man her front desk. She passed Lisette's station, smiling when she caught a snippet of dialogue.

"I've been thinking of getting my hair permed," a customer with stick-straight blond hair said. "But can I do highlights, too? And in what order?"

"*Oui*, madame. You should do the perm first, then add color a week later or more. Be aware that the bleach in highlights may straighten your curl."

Lisette, blowing out the woman's shoulder-length hair, nodded a greeting to Marla. "*Merci beaucoup* for your help, mademoiselle. Things are better now."

Not with that birdbrain up front. "May I suggest you girls collect your own money?" Marla said to Claudia over the drone of blowdryers, blaring radio music, and chatter. Business didn't seem to be hurting any. Rather than the notion displeasing her, she was glad the stylists were still able to earn a living despite their changed circumstances.

Claudia, checking her customer's hair-growth direction before doing a cut, glanced at her. "Madame Cleaver is pretty much letting us do our own thing, but Bunny is a joke." She pulled a comb out of her Barbicide jar, then proceeded to partition sections of hair. "*Mon dieu*, I am not sure what will become of us."

"What do you mean?"

"Carolyn Sutton is listed as our employer on our documents, but our situation has altered. I fear we will have to leave."

"Leave the salon, or leave the country?" Marla guessed.

Claudia shot her a wary look. "I am not supposed to talk about it."

"On whose orders?"

Claudia's mouth compressed. Picking up a pair of shears, she waved them in the air. "You have been very helpful, and you have our gratitude, but we do not care to jeopardize our position."

"Does this involve Peter McGraw, the attorney? I understand he does immigration work, plus he did Carolyn's will."

"*Non*, you do not understand." Turning her attention to her customer, Claudia blatantly ignored Marla while she snipped the woman's short gray hair.

Marla sauntered over to Jeanine, who she spotted smoking a cigarette by the open back door. Of course, they wouldn't be concerned about the air-conditioning bill now that Wilda was responsible for the overhead.

"Hi," she said to the hairdresser whose dramatic black hair contrasted sharply with her pale complexion. "I'm just checking on how things are going. Is everything okay with your visa status?"

The girl's brown eyes widened. "That is not for me to say, mademoiselle."

"Claudia seems concerned. She's afraid you'll be forced out. Is the attorney giving you trouble?" Marla wrinkled her nose as a choking ring of smoke permeated her nostrils. Stepping upwind, she resisted the urge to fan herself.

Jeanine didn't seem to notice her avoidance tactic. "Monsieur McGraw is on our side. It is the landlord who troubles us. He had a special relationship with our boss lady, you see? Without her here, he may decide to close the place."

"Dennis Thomson had something going with Carolyn?"

"He came to see her a lot lately. You can tell when a man and woman have secrets, *non?*"

Marla blinked. The landlord was a married man. Could he and Carolyn have been fooling around? Was that why she could afford the rent, because he made a special allowance in her case?

Maybe Carolyn hadn't needed to subsidize her payments through a benefactor, although that wouldn't account for those foreign students at the academy. Unless someone else had brought them in for other purposes.

"Jeanine," yelled Bunny from inside. "There is a person named Zelda Reiss asking for you on the phone. Can you take it? I've put her on hold."

A scowl lit Jeanine's face. "If that woman doesn't leave me alone, I will sue her myself." Scurrying inside, she threw her next comments over her shoulder at Marla who followed. "This customer rejoiced that poor Carolyn was gone."

"Oh my. Why was that?"

"She tried to default on her bill. Carolyn filed a charge in small claims court against her. Wait here."

Jeanine picked up the receiver. "I am sorry, madame, but just because Carolyn is absent does not mean your debt is erased. You still owe me for services rendered, and I doubt your appeal will overturn the judge's verdict. If we do not receive your check as ordered, I will call her myself to report your noncompliance."

Slamming down the phone, Jeanine turned to Marla to explain, but a delivery from Ace Beauty Company distracted her attention.

"Maybe I can smooth things over," Marla offered, using the diversion to coax Bunny into giving her the customer's contact information.

That accomplished, she reversed direction, intending to leave the shop, and collided into the solid chest of a large man whose slicked-back black hair sparked recognition. *Omigod, it's Grease Man from the hardware store*, she realized, swinging back to note his European tailored suit and stern expression.

"Monsieur Boyd," Claudia called, putting down her implements and rushing over.

"You're Atlas Boyd?" Marla gazed at him in astonishment.

His dark eyes scoured her. "And you are?"

"Marla Shore from Cut 'N Dye salon."

"*Mais oui*, Carolyn's competitor. Why are you here?"

Marla guessed he was French—from across the Atlantic, not Canada. "The girls asked for my help."

Claudia, her face twisted with alarm, said quickly, "We just needed some guidance until Madame Cleaver took over. Everything is under control now, monsieur. Please come with me. All our records are in order as you requested."

"He's an investor in foreign properties," Bunny told Marla as the pair strolled away. She waggled her eyebrows meaningfully. Having tweezed them into oblivion, they were drawn on her face like a caricature. "A good man to know, if you get my drift. Like, I hear he's loaded."

"Really?" Marla's answering grin quickly shut down. What authority did Boyd possess that he could demand to see the accounting records? Had he provided Carolyn with the funds she needed to set up operation in Palm Haven?

"Excuse me," she said, hurrying after him. "I'm sure you know there's an investigation under way into Carolyn's untimely demise. Have you spoken to Detective Vail?"

He turned slowly to face her. "I fail to see how that is any concern of yours." From the set lines by his mouth, the man looked as though he'd never smiled in his life.

"Even though Carolyn was not my friend, I was upset by her death," Marla said. "I'd like to see her case resolved."

"So would I."

When he said nothing else, continuing to scrutinize her as a manicurist might examine a hangnail, she blurted, "Her stylists came to me for assistance."

Claudia's eyes rounded. "Only because you were nearby and we felt lost without our patron. Now that Monsieur Boyd is—"

"I will be with you in a moment, Claudia," Boyd snapped.

Getting the hint, the stylist retreated to her station.

"Are you a hairdresser?" Marla asked him, unable to comprehend his connection.

"*Moi?*" His startled reaction was almost comical.

"Why else would the girls want your help?"

His expression clouded. "They know I have their best interests at heart."

"Why is that? How come they're willing to show you the books? Aside from your friendship with Carolyn, just what is your interest in this salon, Mr. Boyd?"

His fists clenched. "I do not believe you have any right to question me, mademoiselle. Come in here again and I will bring charges for obstruction of business."

"I doubt such a thing exists. Anyway, I thought Wilda Cleaver inherited this salon. Does she know you are here ordering her girls around?"

He stepped closer until they were face-to-face. She could smell his aftershave; it had a scent similar to expensive French perfume. "If I were you, I would be more concerned about those dear to me."

Her breath caught. "What do you mean?"

He waved a well-groomed hand. A large diamond solitaire flashed on his pinky finger. "Consider this a friendly warning. I've heard from a reliable source that a person close to you may require medical attention, perhaps even yourself. Carolyn displeased someone enough to get herself killed. Be careful, or your employees may be the next ones mourning their boss lady."

Chapter
Twelve

Too stunned by Atlas Boyd's words to respond, Marla stalked out of Hairstyle Heaven while muttering under her breath. The audacity of the man! He'd made a veiled threat against her, and it implied he'd been in communication with Wilda. How else would he know about the psychic's prediction?

She told Nicole about it while trimming her next customer's hair. "The man obviously has some hold over those girls. I'll have to tell Dalton about our conversation, but I don't want to bother him now. He's busy with a new case."

Nicole smiled knowingly. "He relies on your insights."

"I'd like to contact that customer Carolyn met in small claims court to see what she knows. A return visit to Mr. Thomson is also on order. Jeanine said he'd been seeing a lot of Carolyn lately. That could be how she was able to afford the rent."

Nicole's eyes widened. "You mean . . ."

"Exactly." Releasing another section of her customer's hair, Marla cut the ends at an angle.

"Have you listened to the weather report lately?" the customer piped in. The auburn-haired society matron had a charity luncheon the following day. "They say that storm is headed in our direction, and it's predicted to pick up speed as well as reach hurricane force by tonight."

"It's still too early to forecast landfall," Marla replied. "A high pressure ridge may yet turn it out to sea. Anyway, they say it may only get to be a Category One."

"Bottled water is already disappearing from the shelves. You'd better stock up on supplies before we have a storm watch."

"I'm not worried."

"You should be," Nicole interrupted. "We don't want to have any more power outages."

Marla gave her a shrewd glance. "Notice how the lights haven't gone out since Carolyn died?"

"Uh huh. Have you reviewed our hurricane plan with Jennifer and Luis? They may not know where you keep the batteries and such. Just in case."

"I should do that," Marla said, lifting another shank of hair and snipping with practiced skill. Like many Floridians, she had lived through many storms, but most of them caused little damage. She'd been too far north to be affected by Hurricane Andrew, the first really major storm to hit southeast Florida since she'd moved there. Getting too complacent was the greater danger. What would Aunt Polly do? Did programs exist for the frail elderly? She'd have to ask Anita.

Meanwhile, she made an appointment with Carolyn's former client, Zelda Reiss, who agreed to see her after work. They met at the Borders café on West Sunrise Boulevard near Sawgrass Mills Mall.

Nursing a mug of coffee, Marla regarded the woman seated across from her at the small table. Zelda's shoulder-length mahogany hair, with a healthy sheen that showed careful grooming, hung straight to her back. The ends were neatly trimmed, unlike her thick eyebrows. In need of shaping, they perched over entrancing eyes with brown irises blending into gray. The dichotomy in color seemed reflected in her clothing style. While she wore a wrinkled blue shorts set, her selection of jewelry showed particular attention. Marla especially liked the gold tiger with emerald eyes sparkling on a pendant around her neck.

"I appreciate your meeting with me," Marla began. "I'm from

the other salon in the same shopping center as Carolyn Sutton's establishment. The girls in there have asked for my help regarding management details, and I couldn't help overhear something about a problem you were having with Jeanine. I thought I might be able to help."

Zelda sipped her hot chocolate, then speared Marla with a glance. "I suppose Jeanine told you I didn't pay her for the extensions and hair weave that cost several hundred dollars. I was going to a party and wanted to do something different. She worked on me for hours but neglected the finishing touches."

After blowing on her steaming beverage, Marla drank carefully. She'd already burned her tongue once. "Why did you leave if Jeanine wasn't done?"

"You don't understand." Zelda grimaced. "I worked there, but I wasn't an employee."

"You're a hairdresser?"

"That's right. I rented my chair, but I left because Carolyn gave me no respect. She acted as though I owed her my life and said bad things about me to my customers. When I decided to move on, she claimed I deserted her. Like she came in one day, and my stuff was gone. What obligation did I have to her?"

"Did you tell her you were unhappy? I can imagine why she'd be upset if you left suddenly without giving her any inclination of how you felt." One of Marla's manicurists had departed abruptly, and she couldn't help feeling a sense of betrayal. It just wasn't professional to run away from an unpleasant situation without trying to resolve things first. Then again, she'd been miserably unhappy working for Carolyn herself, and nothing she'd done had changed the situation. Perhaps Zelda had run up against the same wall.

"I meant to work at my sister's place," Zelda continued, staring at ink marks scarring the table surface. "When my sister relocated, I asked Carolyn if I could come back and do some clients there. This was before she returned to Palm Haven, you understand. Carolyn wrongly assumed I planned to stay."

"So what led to your disagreement with Jeanine?"

"I asked for extensions for an upcoming holiday party. Jeanine said she'd do it, and it would cost six hundred fifty dollars. But Carolyn said they'd only charge me ninety dollars for the cost of the hair if I would advertise the salon. You know, go around and let people admire my hair and hand out her business cards."

"But you said Jeanine never finished the job."

Zelda nodded vigorously. "She did my extensions almost to the crown but left out the cover layer. I needed more hair on the top of my head."

"And how long did this take?"

"Several hours. Carolyn accused me of not keeping to my part of the bargain. I said I'd act as her model, but she expected me to continue working in the salon, and that was never my intention. So she charged me for the labor. I stopped payment on my credit card, and Carolyn filed suit to get the money she said I owed her."

"What did the judge say?"

"She awarded four hundred fifty dollars to Carolyn as fair cost of the services rendered. It's not fair; my hairdo wasn't finished. She has no right to that money."

"Doesn't Jeanine get it now? She's the one who did your hair. Or does she work on a commission basis?"

"I don't know what Carolyn's arrangement was with those other girls." Zelda leaned forward, elbow on the table. "If you ask me, something strange is going on there. I can't believe Carolyn left her salon to that voodoo lady. She was very superstitious, you know. Followed the woman's instructions to a tee. My attorney agreed there was something peculiar about Carolyn's financial affairs."

"Oh?"

"At first, I wondered if that guru had loaned Carolyn money to open the new salon, but when my lawyer checked into things, he learned Carolyn had some unexplained sources of income."

"Like a silent partner other than Wilda?"

"Not quite. Carolyn was the sole proprietor. I think she used the money to supplement her payments, you know, for rent and overhead expenses."

"She subsidized students at the Sunrise beauty academy."

Zelda jabbed a finger in the air. "Then she employed them when they graduated. I never understood why, but maybe it was her obligation in return for the funding."

"Hmm, you may have a point. Did you ever encounter Atlas Boyd? He speaks with an accent and seems to lord it over those French girls. I met him at Hairstyle Heaven this morning."

"I'd seen him once or twice, but not as frequently as Dennis Thomson, the landlord."

"I heard he came by her place often. Were Mr. Thomson and Carolyn having an affair?" Marla asked bluntly.

Zelda shrugged, returning her attention to the cup of hot chocolate. "If they were, it didn't affect me any. All I wanted was my hair done that day, and I got scalped. Four hundred fifty dollars, and Jeanine didn't even complete the job. Carolyn was a real bitch to work for, but then I don't have to tell you that, do I? She hated your guts, and I joined her blacklist when I left. If you're smart, you'll stay out of her affairs. Someone wanted her dead. Maybe it was another customer unhappy about her hair like me!"

"Do you really think that?"

Zelda gave a harsh laugh. "Talk to her sister. I met Linda Hall at a women's club meeting, and she recommended me to Carolyn. I don't know why, when there was no love lost between them. Two more diverse personalities, you've never seen. Linda's more the quiet sort, while Carolyn could talk up a storm."

"Linda told me Carolyn was jealous of her because she stayed home and raised a family, but Carolyn's friend Rosemary said it was the other way around. Linda was jealous of Carolyn, who owned a salon and had an independent career."

Zelda tilted her head. "I'd be more inclined to believe the friend. Linda seemed to be riding on Carolyn's coattails when she recommended her sister as a hairdresser. She must've been really pissed off when Carolyn connected with that psychic."

"Sometimes siblings don't get along as well as friends," Marla said, thinking of Anita and Polly.

"Yeah, well, I guess Carolyn pissed off a lot of people. That detective must have his hands full trying to determine who killed her."

Wondering if Vail or his deputies were making any progress on Carolyn's case, Marla swung by his house on the way home. He greeted her at the door with a welcoming smile and a hug.

"We're just starting dinner," he said, reluctant to disengage their embrace. She warmed to the affection in his eyes as he stood holding her. "Join us; we're having my famous lasagne."

"I was going to call but decided to stop over," she explained. She rubbed up against him, enjoying his spicy scent. Lifting her mouth, she invited a kiss. "How did Brianna do today at school?" she asked after he obliged in a manner that left her breathless.

"She's already complaining about having homework."

"I heard that," Brie snapped as they entered the kitchen arm-in-arm. "Hi, Marla. Whassup?"

"I have some news. I spoke to Zelda Reiss, one of Carolyn's clients. They had a disagreement that ended up in court."

Vail took a plate from a cabinet and ladled out a portion of lasagne dripping with tomato sauce. "I interviewed her," he commented. "She didn't tell me much I hadn't already found out. You?"

"I would agree that she didn't bear a grudge enough to commit murder," Marla commented. "I was hoping to learn something else from her that would shed new light on the investigation." She repeated the gist of their conversation, refusing his offer of beer but accepting a glass of merlot.

"Listen," Brianna said, pointing to the television while they claimed seats at the table.

"September is the most active month for tropical storms to form," the meteorologist on the news was saying. He pointed to a colorful map of the Atlantic and Caribbean basins. "On the average, we have three named storms in this month alone."

Marla's mind wandered. She'd heard this recitation every year and knew the categories by heart. Who wouldn't when even the supermarkets pushed hurricane guides every summer? Weather systems became tropical depressions when they rotated with wind speeds up to 39 mph. They got named as tropical storms when the circulation became more distinct, with wind speeds up to 74 mph. From experience, she understood these systems could bring heavy rains and gusty winds with local flooding. Once the wind speed reached 74 mph, the storm became a hurricane. Arlene looked as if she might surprise everyone. The circular clouds appeared to be aiming for Florida's east coast, and there was another disturbance right behind the first hurricane of the season.

"Arlene dropped several inches of rain on Barbados, where it uprooted trees and blew roofs off homes," the weatherman said. "It downed power lines in St. Vincent and will probably gain strength as it crosses open water."

Rattling off the latitude and longitude, the meteorologist segued into a recitation of hurricane preparedness. Marla always thought the newscasters loved hurricane season because it gave them something exciting to report. You heard talks of how to stock up on supplies ad nauseum. She'd rather think about all the questions to ask Vail regarding Carolyn's case.

"So tell me how your classes went today," she said to Brianna.

The girl gave her a pained look. "School sucks. I mean, it's good to see my friends again, but having all this work to do? Maybe there will be a hurricane warning so we can get a few days off. This is September first. It's the height of the monsoon season. Kids up north get snow days. We deserve storm days."

"No way; I don't need to lose the business at my salon. Besides, you were getting bored. Once your dance classes resume after Labor Day, you'll have plenty to keep you occupied. So, Dalton, what's new?"

He shrugged his massive shoulders. "I'm working with immigration to check into a few irregularities. There's some funny business going on between McGraw and those French girls, but that's not my sphere of expertise. I'm not sure what role Carolyn played, either."

"How about Atlas Boyd? He stormed into her salon this morning and demanded to see the bookkeeping records. It appears he's a foreign investor. Claudia couldn't move fast enough to oblige him. I wondered if he might have been Carolyn's silent partner, but Zelda assured me that Carolyn was sole proprietor of Hairstyle Heaven. Still, Zelda said Carolyn got income from somewhere. I understand she'd been seeing a lot of the landlord, if that means anything."

"Thomson showed me his invoices and receipts for rentals," Vail replied. "Sutton made her payments on time; he didn't give her any breaks from what I could tell."

Marla swallowed a mouthful of pasta with tangy sauce. "There goes my theory about them having an affair."

"Not necessarily. It's possible he keeps a second set of books, but I haven't been able to unearth anything yet."

"You mean he claimed to receive the full amount for her monthly rental, but maybe he didn't?"

"It happens. How many corporations keep crooked records? Why not a property manager who doesn't want his favoritism exposed?"

"Have you spoken to Thomson's wife? She might be suspicious about any shenanigans going on."

"She vouches for his fidelity, and I didn't want to start trouble by suggesting otherwise. The women did say Thomson's relationship with Carolyn went back to her first establishment."

"That could explain why he let her into the shopping center despite my protests, unless he accommodated her for another reason."

"Such as?"

"She had some kind of hold over him, like that chiropractor Rosemary mentioned. I should see Dr. Hennings again, find out what Carolyn discovered about him that he didn't like."

"Be careful. Snakes may hide under rocks you overturn." A frown creased his face. "Mrs. Thomson mentioned that her husband takes a lot of trips out of town to assess properties for his management company. I don't suppose Carolyn left her salon at those times, but I'll check."

"I can ask around if you let me know the dates." Marla glanced at Brianna, who was listening with a resigned expression. The teen was accustomed to their discussing murder cases over meals. If Marla moved in, perhaps she should set rules for dinner-time. Family discussions only, no business. Besides, hadn't Anita taught her not to disturb a man until he'd been fed? If she had *saichel*, she'd at least wait until Dalton finished eating before addressing sensitive topics. Speaking of her mother, they had to reschedule their barbecue.

"Next Monday is Labor Day. How about if we ask Anita and Sam for dinner then?" she said. "The holiday gives us a good excuse to have them over. My mother is dying to see your house." *Especially after I told her how much I hate it.* Despite Marla's intention of giving up the role of matchmaker, she had slipped into it again. But, she reasoned, having Sam present might mitigate Anita's reaction to Dalton's home. She could imagine her mother's disapproval already, especially when she saw Pam's angel figurines.

"That'll work." Reaching across the table, Vail patted her hand. "I wish you'd forget about fixing your mom with a date. She does well enough on her own."

"Sam is such as sweet man, and I think he's lonely. He hasn't called her, so he's probably too shy. If Ma likes him, she'll take it from there, and Roger will be gone until after the Jewish holidays. We don't have to worry about the competition at this point."

Wearing a fond grin, Vail shook his head. "I should lock you up. Then you wouldn't get into trouble."

"What trouble? I got Arnie and Jill together, didn't I? I'm just giving Ma alternate possibilities." *Like Ma pushes Roger's son, Barry, on me. All right, so I'm getting even. She'll come around when she sees Dalton in his domestic role.*

She smiled as she regarded Vail's food-splattered shirt. Poor guy; he needed a woman's guidance. It warmed her to the core that he'd chosen her. That Brianna had come to rely on her advice as well was only the tip of the iceberg. Marla needed them just as much as they needed her, and she was finally beginning to accept that fact.

Dalton must've seen something in her expression because his eyes darkened to a sultry slate. Her pulse accelerated, and she held his gaze until Brianna coughed.

"Earth to Daddy. If you're finished ogling Marla, you can help me with math."

Raising his hands, he laughed. "Not me, muffin. I don't do equations. Ask Marla. She does her own bookkeeping."

Oh, joy. Multitudes of evenings spent doing homework loomed in her future. But when she thought of the alternative, lonely nights where she could do what she pleased with no one to talk to except the dog, her answer came as a surprising affirmative.

"You get the dishes, and I'll help with homework," she told him. "Deal?"

"Did I ever tell you how you drive a hard bargain?" Shoving his chair back, he rose and crossed the room quickly to kiss her. Whistling, he grabbed their empty plates and proceeded to the dishwasher.

At home later that evening, Marla's thoughts focused so exclusively on Vail that at first she missed the sealed envelope on her front stoop. After collecting her mail at the cluster box, parking in her garage, and walking around to the front lawn to remove a palm frond that had fallen in a recent thunderstorm, she noticed the item by her door. Shaking it off to remove wet leaves, she stared at the typewritten address. Her name and street number were correct, but the lack of a stamp and return address alarmed her.

Grasping the envelope by the corner, she took it inside and dropped it on her desk. She didn't deal with it right away, instead letting Spooks into the backyard, removing the cell phone from her purse and plugging it into a charger, and plucking a sandwich bag from the pantry. Then she proceeded into the den, where she took a letter opener from her desk drawer, held the envelope with the plastic bag, and slit it open. A plain white paper fell onto her desk blotter. She stared at the stark typed words:

STOP ASKING QUESTIONS.

In the absence of clues as to who had sent the missive or why, Marla ventured a guess. Carolyn's killer topped the list, although Marla realized she might have stirred more than one hornet's nest. Certainly, return visits to most of the people she'd spoken to lately were in order to evaluate who might have perceived her inquiries as a threat, but time was getting short. The strengthening storm system could inhibit the investigation and disguise any number of foul deeds if it hit here. A fallen tree branch, or a blow to the head? A fire caused by downed power lines, or arson? Accident, or intent? Who, besides Dr. Hennings, had the knowledge or ability to kill a person by breaking their neck?

She hadn't discussed the critical factors with Vail. In addition to considering the murder technique, who else could have gotten into the meter room with a key? Anyone from the shopping center plus the landlord. How about alibis? Where were Mr. Thomson, the sister, and the psychic? Did the chiropractor see patients that day? Was Mr. McGraw in his office? And don't overlook disgruntled former employees or customers. Where were Zelda Reiss and Peg Krueger? Nor did she discount the mysterious Atlas Boyd. Vail hadn't said much about him. In fact, he hadn't told her nearly as much as she'd brought to the table. Next time she wouldn't be so easily distracted by his charm. Not if she wanted answers before Hurricane Arlene charged for the coastline with savage fury.

Her glance fell on the typed note on her desk. What if the approaching storm represented an ominous portent? What if Wilda's prediction hadn't been meant for one of Marla's friends or relatives? *What if it was meant for me?*

Chapter Thirteen

Work consumed Marla's attention for the rest of the week to the extent she was unable to follow up on anything she'd promised Vail. With Hurricane Arlene bearing down on them, she'd moved their barbecue to Sunday. Newscasters predicted the storm would hit by Tuesday unless an eastward high-pressure ridge forced it out to sea. This saving grace was expected to dissipate, having no effect on tropical storm Bret churning in the first gale's wake slowly toward the islands.

Tension mounted as hurricane supplies disappeared from the stores. Marla shopped early, making sure she had adequate bottled water, batteries, and canned foods. She decided she'd weather the storm at Vail's house with Spooks if it became necessary. Meanwhile, they'd wait on bringing in his patio furniture until a hurricane warning was posted.

Friday she dropped off a bag of groceries at Aunt Polly's apartment. The older lady scolded her for spending so much money and reassured Marla she'd be safe during a storm. At Anita's urging, Marla offered to help her sign up for evacuation assistance through a program available to the elderly.

"I can take care of myself," Polly snapped, flashing Marla a contemptuous look. "I'll bet Anita put you up to this, didn't she?" Polly shuffled into her living room wearing her customary ragged slippers and housecoat. "I don't know why she hates me so much. She says I shame her, but I don't do things when she orders me around. Is she that bossy to you?"

Marla swallowed. "My mother means well." Hoping Polly wouldn't notice, she advanced to the thermostat and turned on the cool air.

"I never see your father. Does he talk about me? Is he well?" Polly's rheumy eyes snagged hers. "Your mother keeps him from me, I know it. She's afraid he'll agree with me."

From the grave? I doubt it. "I'll take you to visit him. Our temple is holding a service at the cemetery next weekend."

"What?" Polly peered at her intently, her wrinkled face marred with more crevices than an iceberg. "You're going to serve me a cherry? I don't eat cherries, *bubula.*"

Marla rolled her eyes. "I give up," she muttered.

Accompanying Polly to the dining room table, she glanced at the papers strewn on its cloth-covered surface. Idly picking through them, she discovered empty envelopes from junk mail that Polly saved for recycling, expired grocery coupons, and an electric bill due two weeks ago. "Polly, have you paid this bill to FPL yet? And look, here's a second notice from your homeowner's insurance. You've missed the deadline for renewal."

Polly waved an imperious hand. "I'll get to them."

Things are only going to get worse. "I hope you'll allow me to help you. Where's your checkbook?"

Convincing Polly to accept her assistance took time, but Marla managed to fill out the checks and have her sign them. Then Marla readied them for the post office. "If we add my name to your checking account," she said, "I can come in periodically to help you with the bills." Not that she needed another chore, but Marla doubted Polly would accept aid from her mother. The alternative was to hire a caretaker, but they'd have to assess Polly's assets to see what the older woman could afford.

She discussed the situation with her brother, Michael, on the telephone the following day. "Can't you come down to keep watch on things?" Marla pleaded. "I have so little spare time."

"I'm a half hour away in Boca. You're closer," his firm voice stated. "If you wouldn't run around playing cops and robbers, you'd have more time for family."

"Gee, thanks, I needed to hear that."

"Leave the police work to your detective friend. Speaking of the fellow, it's clear you're stuck on him. When are you going to move forward in your relationship?"

Soon, bro, but you don't have to know that yet. "I've been burned before. I want to take things slowly this time."

"Go any slower and you'll have gray hair when you're rolling down the aisle."

"I thought of inviting him to our Rosh Hashanah dinner. Do you think the family would mind?"

"It's a good opportunity to introduce him to the rest of our cousins, at least the South Florida contingent. Would it make him uncomfortable?"

"I already approached the subject, and he's agreeable. If we're to be together, we'll have to respect each other's traditions. Learning about them is the first step."

"Ma would be horrified if you had a Christmas tree."

I'll deal with that when the time comes. "We'll work out some type of compromise. Anyway, Ma will be happy that I have someone to spend my life with."

"So it's that serious, huh? Have you made wedding plans? You could always honeymoon at our family reunion. Cynthia is planning a big bash in November for the entire extended family."

"Oh? I haven't heard anything about it."

"When's the last time you spoke to her? She's looking into some hotel that Aunt Polly recommended."

"Polly? What does she care? She can't even understand what you say half the time."

"She's the one who put the bee in Cynthia's bonnet."

"Well, that's interesting. I'll talk to Ma about it. In the mean-

time, give my love to Charlene and the kids. See you soon."
Marla hung up, puzzled over Polly taking the initiative regarding
a family reunion. It was true that she hadn't seen their distant relatives in many years, but why now?

More pressing concerns drew Marla's consideration on Sunday,
when she had to prepare for the barbecue at Vail's. Eager to get
on with the day's activities, she took her morning walk with
Spooks outside her town house. The poodle tugged her along,
stopping in front of Moss's place. Their elderly neighbor stood in
his driveway inspecting for damage from an earlier downpour. A
few black olive tree branches lay on the sodden ground.

His face brightened at their approach. "Hey, mate, I'd been
hoping to see you. Wanna read my latest poem?"

"Sure, Moss." She smiled at him fondly. Spooks chewed on
the grass while she waited for the retired carpenter to run inside
his house and retrieve his work of art. Taking the paper he offered, she read the words aloud:

A storm came to a town named Arthur,
Causing fright from floods and detours.
Stay inside, said the advisories,
Beware capricious winds and high seas,
Ride it out with a stout while you're indoors.

"I sure hope it doesn't come to this!" Marla replied, laughing.
"How is your poetry class?"

"Doing well, thanks." Moss shuffled his feet. "I submitted a
few poems to a magazine."

"That's great. You may have a new career ahead of you." After
inquiring about his reclusive wife, Marla moved on.

Spooks had gotten his feet wet on the dewy grass, and she
didn't want him to track dirt into Vail's house. She brought him
inside to dry off. By the time she'd showered and changed, the
poodle was ready for a quick brushing that restored his fluffy
coat.

*   *   *

"Doesn't he look cute," Brianna said, letting Marla and Spooks into their house when they arrived at one o'clock. Her face freshly scrubbed, the teen had a towel wrapped around her wet hair. Inside, Marla released the dog's leash, and he quickly bounded after Lucky, Vail's golden retriever.

"Want me to do your hair?" Marla offered, putting down her purse on a foyer table. "You can help me unload my car first. I thought I'd make my barley casserole for a side dish."

"Welcome, sweetcakes," Vail said, approaching from the kitchen. "I thought you were coming earlier." He'd tied an apron over his gunmetal gray shirt and black trousers. The colors brought out the silvery flecks in his eyes. His craggy face split into a grin as he surveyed her shorts outfit.

She warmed at his appreciative look. "I stopped at Macy's. They had a sale, so I bought you a present for when you entertain on the patio."

Vail cast his vote of approval for the French linen tablecloth and napkins, their vibrant colors contributing to a festive atmosphere along with citrus candles and blue-handled tableware. She grit her teeth when he brought out his late wife's treasured plates. One of these days, they'd have to have a serious discussion about household possessions.

"Everything Pam owned was either depressing antiques or *tchotchkes* with flowers," Marla complained to Anita when they found a moment alone, soon after her mother's arrival. "I can't stand it, especially those fruit pictures in the kitchen. You know what I think about still-life prints? If you're still looking at them after a few minutes, you need to get a life."

Ignoring Anita's chuckle, Marla gave full vent to her resentment. "It's not that I don't respect the value of these things to Dalton, but I can't live with them. They belong to another woman's world."

Anita tilted her head. "You'll have to tell him how you feel, but only if you decide a permanent move is in order."

"We're talking about it." She didn't have time to say more because the doorbell rang, and Sam arrived.

Anita gave a cry of surprised pleasure, and Marla greeted him happily. Smiling shyly, Sam handed her a bottle of cabernet. "I-I appreciate the invitation," he said. "It's not often that I get out to socialize."

"Come on, now," Marla's mother crooned, "I find that hard to believe. Surely a handsome gent like yourself can find plenty of ladies willing to show you the town."

Sam grinned. "Maybe so, but not all of them display your zest for life."

Taking the cue, Anita wrapped her arm in his and drew him toward the kitchen. Marla didn't hear her response because they disappeared outside to the patio, while she remained in the kitchen to check on her casserole. She'd doubled the recipe for the barley, wild rice, and mushroom dish. It would go well with their steaks and asparagus. Checking the timer on the microwave, she saw it had about five more minutes to go.

"What do they want to drink?" Vail asked, putting the finishing touches on the salad.

Marla admired his tall form as he cut grape tomatoes in half before adding them to the wooden bowl. Stan had never liked to cook, regarding the kitchen as a woman's domain. Nor had her ex-spouse helped with domestic chores the way Vail did. The detective almost seemed to find such tasks a release from the ugliness he viewed every day in his job.

"I didn't ask," she replied. "Maybe I should bring out the lemonade."

"Go ahead. I'm going to start the steaks."

Carrying a pitcher frosty with condensation, Marla headed out to the patio. Without screening or a pool, it still would have been a pleasant backyard oasis if his orange trees hadn't been destroyed. As she placed the lemonade on the outdoor counter, the germ of an idea sprang to mind. Maybe she could tempt him to move if she found an area where citrus trees still stood.

Anita appeared to be having an amiable conversation with Sam when she approached. "What can I get you to drink?" Marla offered. "We have wine, beer, or lemonade."

"I'll take the lemonade, thanks." Anita took blood pressure medication that she didn't like to mix with alcoholic beverages. Sam requested a beer. "Sam was just telling me about his business up North. Did you know he was in the garment industry? He lived in Brooklyn not far from where cousin Yakov moved."

"I thought you had retired from the building business," Marla said, certain that's what he'd told her.

His face flushed. "I switched when there was a downswing and joined my brother, who was a builder."

"And you built houses in New Jersey?" He'd given her the impression that he'd resided in the Garden State with his late wife.

"That's right."

"What was the name of your development company?"

"Oh, er, Brickman and Associates," he said, staring at the ground. Marla followed his glance. Vail had replaced the original Chattahoochee surface with bricks. His orange trees would have provided shade, but now the flooring reflected the afternoon heat.

"I wonder if you put up any homes in Montclair. I love those mansions on Upper Mountain Avenue. We used to visit an uncle who lived in Caldwell, so we crossed through there on our way." Marla watched for his reaction. From the way he shifted his gaze, she sensed his discomfort. Maybe he hadn't done as well in his business as he liked people to believe.

"I-I'm not familiar with that area. We worked in a different section of the state," he said. "But that's water under the bridge now. I made myself a bundle so I could retire to Florida."

"It's too bad your wife couldn't come with you," Anita said sympathetically. "I understand how she'd want to stay up North to be near your son. And then she got sick. Such a shame."

Son? Sam hadn't said anything to Marla about having children. Before she could question him, he'd taken Anita's hand. "What made you move to Florida?" he asked her mother in a gentle tone.

"Like everyone else, we couldn't stand the cold winters anymore. Besides, I have a lot of relatives down here."

"I'm sure they were glad to have you join them. Such a radiant flower would only wither in the snow."

Give me a break, Marla thought. She turned away, wondering where Sam's shyness had gone. He didn't seem to need any help getting into her mother's good graces. In the kitchen, she got him a beer from the refrigerator. Pausing by the stove, she put the bottle down to stir the cooked mushrooms into her casserole. Dalton, having put the meat on the grill, returned to dish out their salads.

Marla considered telling him about the note she'd received at home earlier in the week, but she had decided to keep quiet about it. No sense in alarming him. He'd only warn her off the case, and she wanted to continue her interviews. So she bit back her confession and told him instead about her conversation with Sam. His alert expression piqued her interest, but then Brianna waltzed into the kitchen, interrupting them.

"When are we going to eat? I'm hungry."

"Did you finish your homework?" Vail demanded.

Her ponytail swishing, the teen tugged on her tube top. "Not quite. Kathy and I were talking about what we're going to wear tomorrow."

"If you spent as much time on your schoolwork as you do on the telephone, you'd get straight As," Vail said, looking to Marla for support.

She grinned in response. "Get used to it. The telephone will probably be attached to her ear until she graduates high school."

"When will you get me my own cell phone?" Brianna whined. "Everyone else has one."

"Like who?" Marla retorted, recognizing the manipulative tactic as one she'd employed.

"Come on, Marla. Daddy got you a cell phone for your birthday so he could reach you easily."

"You don't go out on your own," Vail said, wagging his finger at her. "Enough on this subject. Here, take these salads outside. Did you say hello to Mrs. Shorstein and Mr. Levy?"

Brie jutted her lower lip. "Marla's mother said I could call her

Anita." A wicked gleam entered her eyes. "Or maybe I should ask if she can be my Bubba. Is that the right Jewish word?"

Marla, taking a sip of wine from the glass she'd poured herself, choked. "Isn't it a little early for that? And what about your other grandparents? Don't you ever visit them?"

"My folks live in Maine," Vail said quietly. "They have a more homogeneous population there than we do in South Florida. I'm afraid their attitude can be rather provincial. Pam's parents come from Michigan. We haven't seen them since the funeral."

"They wanted me to come live with them," Brianna confessed. "Nana felt Daddy's job . . . well, she thought I'd be better off being raised in a more stable environment."

"Nonsense. Your father loves you, and that's all that matters." Obviously, there was considerable tension in the relationship with both families. Thank goodness they lived elsewhere. As another thought surfaced, she gulped her merlot. She'd been so concerned about her own family's reaction to a mixed marriage that she hadn't considered Vail's side. How would his relatives feel about a Jewish bride? For that matter, what denomination of Christian was he? They'd avoided discussing religion because it hadn't inhibited their relationship. But as they took the next step together, it would play a bigger role.

"Can I help?" Anita said, breaking their tableau. "What an adorable kitchen," she gushed, entering. "Dalton, dearest, you haven't given me the grand tour. Why, what quaint wallpaper. I haven't seen this style since the sixties. Is your house really that old?"

Blood rushed to Marla's face. Couldn't Ma be more subtle? "How about if we eat first, and then Dalton can show you around?" she suggested.

"It's okay," Vail contradicted, giving her a pointed stare. "You can show Anita and Sam the house while Brie and I set out the food."

Handing her mother the glass of lemonade, Marla nodded. "I'll just bring Sam his beer, and then—"

"No, let me." Vail's sharp words brought her pause.

"All right," she agreed slowly. He had something up his sleeve, but she couldn't imagine what it might be. Retrieving Sam, she began her tour in the living room. By the time they'd done the bedrooms and family room, Vail had laid out the meal.

While they ate, conversation centered on the weather and the vagaries of Florida living. When they needed drink refills, Marla stood, reaching for Sam's empty bottle and Anita's glass.

"Leave them," Vail ordered, standing so abruptly that he nearly knocked his chair back. "I'll get new ones." He returned shortly with a new beer bottle and glass of frothy lemonade. After placing them on the table, he topped off Marla's wine. "How are the steaks?"

"Just right," Sam said appreciatively while chewing. The old guy seem to be having a jolly good time, judging from the way he was chowing down his food. Maybe he'd just missed home cooking.

Refusing their offer to help clear the table after they'd demolished a key lime pie, Vail directed Brianna to show Anita and Sam his efforts to grow tomatoes on the side of the house. As soon as they disappeared from sight, he charged into the kitchen. Marla had already begun stacking their dishes, but she stopped to stare wide-eyed as he returned with gloved hands to stick the empty beer bottles into separate plastic bags.

"What are you doing?" she hissed, following him back into the kitchen, where he hid the bags under the sink.

He tossed his disposable latex gloves into the trash. "Marla, have you ever thought that Sam had access to a key for the meter room? That he was on the premises the day Carolyn died? And that some of the things he says are contradictory?"

"I don't believe it." Tilting her head, she glared at him. "You've collected those bottles to check his fingerprints. Is that why you let me invite him? You suspect he may be the murderer?" She'd never heard of anything so insane. Maybe Sam lied a bit about his background, but he was probably just trying to impress her mother.

Vail closed the distance between them, placing his hands on

her shoulders. "Look, I know you like the guy, but it isn't safe to fix your mother up with strangers. You don't know that much about Sam. I went along with the invitation so I could sound him out."

A wave of guilt struck her. "I suppose you're going to say I should have minded my own business, as usual. Ma is happy with Roger, and I shouldn't have let my own dislike of him interfere. Okay, I'll warn Ma off where Sam is concerned, but he's probably just a lonely widower looking for companionship."

She kissed the stern detective on the lips. "You wouldn't know someone else like that, would you?"

Chapter Fourteen

"As long as you're checking things for prints, add this to your collection." Marla handed him the plastic bagged envelope from her purse.

Vail's eyebrows crowded together as he scanned the contents of the note inside. Replacing the paper carefully in the envelope and returning it to the plastic bag, he dropped it under the sink along with the beer bottles. "When did you get this?" he said in a tight voice, facing her.

Marla swallowed. "Earlier this week. I forgot about it until now." His look of disbelief prompted her to confess. "All right, so I didn't mention it before because I knew you'd get upset." Relating the details, she added, "I'll ask my neighbors if they've noticed anyone snooping around."

"It's too late now. Your inquiries are making someone nervous. I think you'd be wise to curb your interest in this case and leave it to me." His expression softened. "I know I asked for your help, but not if it puts you in danger. You don't owe anything to Carolyn Sutton."

"According to Wilda, Carolyn wants me to solve her murder. When I do, Carolyn will tell me which one of my relatives needs to see a doctor."

"Who has to see a doctor?" Anita said, entering the kitchen.

Marla whirled on her. "I don't know. What about you?"

"Oh, I'm fine. Just a bit tired these days." Her keen gaze shifted from Marla to Vail. "Marla, would you be a dear and get the sweater from my car? Here's the key."

Suspicious of her mother's sudden request, Marla complied nonetheless. Outdoors, she glanced apprehensively at palm fronds swaying in a stiff breeze. The smell of impending rain tinged the air. Just what they needed, more storms. Puddles still remained from the last cloudburst, meaning the ground was saturated. Even if the approaching hurricane veered out to sea, downpours would fringe its tail, increasing flood conditions.

A white rocket shot past, followed by a golden arrow barking up its own storm. Oh no. She'd left the front door open, and the dogs had escaped. "Spooks!" she yelled, sticking Ma's keys into her pocket. Running in sandals on a rain-slick street wouldn't normally be her choice, but she had no alternative as she charged after the moving targets. "Lucky, come here!"

Spooks took the lead, dashing from a fire hydrant to a stop sign and on to a mahogany tree, where he peed against the trunk. Lucky, tail wagging fiercely, bounded up to sniff the poodle's derriere.

Marla, segueing into stealth mode, advanced steadily. "Spooks, come," she called in a singsong tone to coax him. "I'll let you visit Rita when we get home," she promised.

Spooks lifted his aristocratic snout in her direction. He recognized the name of her neighbor Goat's black poodle. With a disdainful shake, he dismissed the allure of that promise and charged off across the street to wind in and out of people's yards. She thought she had him cornered when he stopped to poop, but Lucky veered in the opposite direction, directly into the path of an oncoming car.

Marla shrieked.

The driver slammed on the brakes, tires squealing.

Lucky scooted past with a few inches to spare.

Her heart racing, Marla turned back to find Spooks missing. The near accident with Vail's dog had left her knees weak and her body trembling. Why didn't the man come out to see what was taking her so long? Twirling around, she spotted Spooks by the side of Vail's house, nibbling on his prize tomatoes.

"Naughty dog," she scolded, rushing forward with her arms outstretched. Swooping him into her embrace, she grimaced as his wet feet spread dirt and leaves on her clothes. His face, sodden with crushed tomato pulp, glared at hers with puppy-eyed resentment. Holding his squirming, muddy body, she headed for the house. One down, one to go.

She needn't have worried. Once her playmate was inside, Lucky docilely trotted toward the front door. Shutting them both inside, Marla completed the errand for which she'd paid such a high price. Paw prints marred her shorts, necessitating a trip later on to the cleaners and at least a five-dollar tab.

After a quick trip to the bathroom to scrub the dirt off her skin, Marla hunted for Vail to confess her mishap. No wonder he hadn't come chasing after her. He sat outside on the patio engaged in an intense discussion with her mother, confirming Marla's impression that Anita's demand had been a ploy. Yikes, was Ma asking him what his intentions were? Embarrassment warred with resignation. They might as well let Anita in on their unofficial announcement if she didn't already know.

Sam had occupied himself by quizzing Brianna about her school activities and schedule. Marla had noticed him admiring the teen and couldn't fault Brianna's manners in front of company. It made her proud to see how much the girl had mellowed since they'd first met.

"You'll consider what I've said?" Anita asked Vail upon Marla's approach.

"Definitely," he replied in a firm tone. His pewter gaze caught Marla, bringing a flush to her face. "We're talking about you."

"No kidding." She tossed the sweater to her mother. "Anything I should know about?"

"I told Ma we were thinking of getting married."

Ma? Since when did you get so familiar? "Oh."

Anita's eyebrows soared. "Don't worry, I won't say a word. It's not official anyway until you get a ring." Her face broke into a smile. "Just don't make me wait too long." Rising, she strode to Marla and hugged her, whispering into her ear, "I want you to be happy."

Stepping back, Marla regarded her mother warily. "Would it be okay if Dalton and Brianna join us for Rosh Hashanah dinner? It would be a good way for him to meet more of the family." *And for him to taste our different culture,* she added silently.

Anita's expression brightened. "Delightful idea. We don't have a police officer among us," she told Vail. "You'll be the first. Our relatives are doctors, accountants, lawyers. As a detective, I bet you'll get all sorts of interesting questions."

Now you're ready to brag about him, when before you told me hooking up with a policeman would lead to heartache? Marla curbed her sharp retort, addressing Vail instead. "Sorry to tell you this, but the dogs got out and messed up your tomato plants. I'll pay to replace them if necessary."

Vail waved the offer away. "Don't worry about it."

"Hey, want to catch the weather report?" Sam asked, weaving in their direction. "My place is near a lake, and I may have to secure my boat if the winds get any stronger."

"You have a boat?" Marla glanced at his arms, which weren't frail like the typical old man's but rather sinewy from a lifetime of physical labor. He must have hammered a few nails into those homes he built, she surmised.

"Just an old rowboat," he stated casually.

"Where do you live? Lakefront property is always more expensive." She could have bitten her tongue after the words flew out, but Sam didn't appear perturbed.

He lifted a hand in dismissal. "It's not one of those artificial lakes. I got a good price for substantial acreage."

"Is that so? In which development?"

His eyes narrowed. "I don't think you'd know the name. It's not in Palm Haven."

"Marla, can you take me to ballet on Tuesday? Daddy has to work late," Brianna said from behind.

Marla swung around, annoyed at the interruption just when she was getting Sam to talk. "Your class might be canceled if we have a hurricane warning. Why don't you call me in the afternoon?"

Sam gave Brianna's ponytail an affectionate yank. "This one will break a lot of hearts when she gets older. I can see it coming." He gazed down into the teen's eyes. "Someone ought to teach her how to behave toward a man."

"She's a little too young for that," Marla said, shouldering him aside and putting her arm around the girl. "Don't you have homework to finish?"

Brianna pouted. "I have to make a phone call first."

"Don't clog the line," Vail warned her, passing by with an armload full of dirty table linens.

Anita, following on his heels, wagged her finger. "You may want to consider adding a second phone number. When Marla was her age, she talked nonstop. She'd wake up with a hoarse voice every morning."

"Really?" Vail threw Marla an amused glance.

"Yeah, and now I don't have time to say two words on the telephone."

They congregated in the kitchen, while Sam veered into the family room to watch the weather channel. "Ma, maybe it wasn't such a good idea to get you and Sam together. We don't know enough about him," Marla cautioned her mother in a low tone. "If you like being with Roger, then I won't interfere. Your happiness is what's important."

Anita kissed her cheek. "Thanks, *bubula*, but I think I can make up my own mind. I like Roger, but it doesn't hurt to keep my options open. You, on the other hand, will disappoint his son when you announce your engagement. Do it soon, so you don't keep Barry dangling."

"I never led him on. He's just a friend."

"That's not the relationship he wants. Heed my advice."

When she got home later, Marla remembered Vail's advice to bow out of Carolyn's case rather than risk endangering herself.

Opening the garage-door entrance to her house, she deactivated the alarm before following Spooks inside. Emptiness yawned before her in contrast to the lively activity at Vail's place. Rather than appreciating the solitude, she missed Vail's company. Not his exhortation to absent herself from any further involvement in Carolyn's affairs, though. She had a few loose ends to tie up on her own.

Monday morning brought nasty weather, so it was just as well she was forced to change her plans. A phone call to Wilda dashed her hopes of visiting the medium that day; Wilda's machine answered. Nor was Wilda at Hairstyle Heaven. The salon was closed for Labor Day, and Marla didn't know how else to reach the psychic. What's more, the holiday prevented her from revisiting Dennis Thomson and the chiropractor as she'd hoped to do. But at least she didn't have to worry about the hurricane destroying the rest of her workweek. True to the forecasts, a high-pressure ridge turned the maelstrom out to sea, though it left South Florida with outlying patches of storm cells.

A nagging need to do more research on Carolyn's obsession led Marla to the computer this morning. Fascinated by the subject of Victorian mourning customs, she read how widows from that era had to wear black attire with a "weeping veil" of black crepe during the first stage, which was one year plus one day. Queen Victoria decreed that only black jewelry could be worn during this deep-grieving period. Popular materials for the jewelry included black enamel, onyx, black glass, vulcanite, and jet, a type of fossilized coal that came from Whitby, England, where it washed up on shore.

In the second mourning period, which lasted for nine months more, widows lifted their veils back over their head. Half-mourning came next for another three to six months, during which women employed more elaborate fabrics as trim for their clothing.

During these second and half-mourning periods, jewelry made from human hair, gold, and gutta-percha adorned the ladies. Gutta-percha, a natural latex obtained from evergreen trees in Asia, was the first known plastic material ever used for costume jewelry.

Hair art became popular during this time. As far back as the Egyptian age, pharaohs and queens had exchanged balls made from hair as tokens of everlasting love. Now hair became regarded as a symbol of life, and the fashion of incorporating it into jewelry spread throughout Europe. Weaving hair from a loved one into knot designs for a brooch was the most popular practice, but rings, bracelets, earrings, watch fobs, and necklaces with hair all became common during the latter portion of the century. In England, mourning pieces included semiprecious stones in gold settings. Garnets were particularly well regarded. Marla discovered that much of this antique jewelry was selling today for significant prices.

When did Carolyn start collecting the stuff? Marla wondered. *Did it make her feel more worthy because she owned these valuables? How did she pay for them? From her bingo earnings? Or were they gifts from a lover?*

Frowning over her keyboard, Marla pondered how to find more information. Picking up the phone, she dialed Tally's number at home. Ken told her Tally was working at the boutique doing inventory. He didn't sound pleased.

"Any chance of us getting to a bingo game within the next few days?" Marla said after dialing the shop number.

"I'm too swamped," Tally replied in a weary voice. "I have my new winter line coming in this week. Maybe you'll stop by and choose some outfits before I put them on the racks."

Marla tamped down her disappointment; she'd have to visit the casino alone. "Let me know when the clothes arrive. I liked that brick red blazer in your catalog." She paused. "How are things between you and Ken?"

"So-so. He's still nagging me to cut my hours. It's not such a bad idea. I wish I could find decent help to give me some relief."

"I'm in the same boat. I don't trust anyone to handle things when I go away for more than a few days."

"You have Nicole. She does a good job."

"True, but I've never left her in charge longer than four days, and that's usually when I've gone to a hair show. Gosh, I wonder if Dalton will want to go on a honeymoon. It's something we haven't discussed, but then again, he's always busier than I am." Too late, she realized she'd let the cat out of the bag. "Whoops, I didn't say that."

"You sneak! Has he proposed?" Tally squealed.

"Well, yes, although we're not telling anyone yet. I mean, I haven't exactly accepted. We've looked for a ring, but, you know, I want to make sure I'm doing the right thing before we make a formal announcement."

"Marla, I'm so happy for you. Holy smokes, we'll have to celebrate. I'll plan a party. This is too exciting."

"Hey, wait. It's unofficial, okay?"

"Brianna must be thrilled."

"We haven't told her. Look, just keep it to yourself for now, all right? You can tell Ken, but that's all. In case one of us changes our mind." She wouldn't have a chance to back out once her friends and relatives had mentally tied the knot.

"That won't happen. You're meant for each other. Opposites attract, don't you know?"

Marla heard a click on the receiver. "I've got to go; I'm getting another call. Look, if you get a night off this week, contact me. Rosemary Taylor knew about Carolyn's collectibles, plus she had a key to Carolyn's place. I'd like to ask her if she ever ran into our landlord there."

Pushing the FLASH button, Marla answered her other call. Speak of the devil, Rosemary's voice squeaked from the other end of the line.

"Marla Shore? It's Rosemary Taylor, Carolyn Sutton's friend. Remember? You met me at the bingo parlor? You said I should call you if I remembered anything important. Well, I did."

"Go on," Marla said, gripping the handset tightly.

"I recognized that person who's watching me. I saw him leaving Carolyn's apartment once. She'd mentioned they had a hobby in common, and she wanted to show off her collection."

"Her antique jewelry?"

"That's right." Rosemary's voice crackled with urgency. "He must be working for them. I told you they were on to me. Then I saw that article in the newspaper, and it got me to thinking. What if she was one of us? I mean, hired to snoop them out like I was? They did away with her, and now I'm next."

"Whoa, Rosemary, you've lost me."

"You read about that girl who was killed?"

"I thought you were investigating the tribe," Marla answered. Rosemary's ramblings were confusing her more than ever.

"Yes, but don't you see? This thing is about to break wide open, and I'm in the middle of it. He knows what Carolyn told me. Hair today, gone tomorrow. Get it?" Her delusional cackle raised goose bumps on Marla's flesh.

"You're not making sense," she said in a soothing tone. "What did Carolyn tell you?"

"She used cash from her salon to play bingo, then she took her winnings and bought herself baubles," Rosemary said, sucking in a raspy breath. "Foolish twit. Why didn't that voodoo lady warn her against buying stuff belonging to dead people?"

"Did Wilda know about her antique jewelry?"

"No, just me and . . . one other."

"Carolyn's boyfriend?"

"Carolyn used men; she didn't date them. She should have known about him, though. I'm surprised that psychic didn't foresee what was coming. Maybe Wilda works for them. I can smell a phony a mile away, and I'll tell you that woman never told Carolyn anything she didn't already know for herself."

Marla gritted her teeth in frustration. This conversation was dancing in circles, hinting at important data but never quite exposing it. How could she get Rosemary to focus her thought processes? "Who were Carolyn's so-called male friends?" she tried, aware of the edge of desperation creeping into her voice.

"You already know some of them. That's why I called. If he's onto me, you may be in danger, too. He's seen us together."

"Can you give me a name?"

"The details aren't important. You have to—what's that noise?" Her tone sharpened. "There's nobody in the next room, but I hear . . . Hello?"

"Rosemary, wait." Marla's heart thudded in her chest when she heard the clunk of the receiver, a few seconds of silence, then a distant cry.

Listening intently, she caught a faint rhythm of breathing at the other end. Her blood chilled when she realized someone had lifted the telephone. Then a click came, followed by the dial tone.

With trembling fingers, Marla pushed the FLASH button and punched the code for Vail's cell phone. His deep, masculine tone responded, reassuring her.

"Do you know where Rosemary Taylor lives? She's Carolyn's bingo partner," Marla reminded him. "I think she's in trouble." Quickly, she repeated the gist of their conversation.

"Stay home and lock your doors. I'll send a patrol car to Taylor's place."

"Call me," she requested before cutting their connection.

Several hours passed while she waited for Vail to get back to her. After tidying her house, she reheated leftovers for dinner but ended up gnawing on her fingernails and sipping coffee. A soft knock on her door around eight o'clock brought her flying to the foyer along with Spooks who barked excitedly.

"It's me," Vail said unnecessarily when she spied him through the peephole.

Turning off her alarm, she opened the door. His grim expression floored her.

"Rosemary?" she croaked.

Stepping inside, he nodded. "You were right, she was in trouble. Someone got to her before we did."

Marla's hand flew to her mouth. "Omigod."

"I need you to repeat everything she said in her telephone conversation to you."

Her feet frozen to the ground, Marla stared at him. "She knew someone was coming for her. I should have called you right away. Instead, I-I tried to get more information from her."

"Why do you always think everything is your fault?" Vail's strong hands clasped her shoulders. "Get a grip, Marla. I need your help."

His haggard face told her how tired he must be. "Yes, of course. Have you eaten dinner? Oh dear, Brianna is home alone again, isn't she? I'm sorry, it's thoughtless of me. I should have gone over there."

"You do enough already; Brie is safe. It's you who worries me." Trailing her into the kitchen, he sank into a chair at the table. "I'm starved," he admitted, scraping stiff fingers through his hair.

Marla prepared a plate of leftover brisket with macaroni and cheese and heated it in the microwave, handing the dish to him along with a bowl of prepackaged salad.

Working in the kitchen made her feel better. She didn't want to learn the details of what he'd found at Rosemary's place. That was the stuff of nightmares. In her mind, the dead woman's words flashed like a cattle brand: *If he's on to me, you may be in danger, too.*

Chapter
Fifteen

Marla found it difficult to focus on work Tuesday morning; her thoughts kept returning to events from the night before. A sense of urgency swelled within her. As though she'd acquired Wilda's psychic powers, she sensed bad vibes in her future.

"There must be a correlation between the killer's behavior and Carolyn's hair jewelry," she said to Nicole during a break. "Rosemary said she saw a man leaving Carolyn's apartment who shared an interest in the same hobby. Maybe he makes jewelry out of the hair he collects from his victims. Serial killers often take souvenirs." Was that what they were dealing with here? She'd assumed Carolyn had been murdered by someone with a personal vendetta, but maybe this wasn't the case.

"At least you know the killer is male," Nicole replied, sipping a Diet Coke at the next station. "That eliminates Wilda and Carolyn's sister. Have you asked Claudia about the immigration attorney and that other man, Atlas Boyd? You said he knew about Wilda's prediction."

"I'll stop by Hairstyle Heaven today to see what else turns up. I still want to find out why Mr. Thomson frequented Carolyn's salon, but he won't be back in his office until tomorrow. His wife said he takes a lot of business trips."

"So?"

"Maybe he does more than survey land deals on his jaunts."

Nicole gave her a doe-eyed look. "Speaking of trips, I thought you meant to go to Cassadaga."

"I haven't had time. Sunday, Ma came over to Dalton's house for a barbecue. We invited Sam, but now I'm not so certain that was a good idea. I really don't know much about him, even though he seems all right."

"Surely you're not suspecting that nice old man from the hardware store?"

"Looks can be deceiving."

Nicole folded her arms across her chest. "Oh, come on. What about that chiropractor? If anyone would know how to snap a neck, he'd be the one. Did you find out what Carolyn had on the guy?"

"Not yet. I have to make another appointment." She paused. "Someone left a warning letter at my doorstep. My inquiries are stirring up trouble, but I can't decide where to look first."

Nicole fixed her with a level stare. "Carolyn's salon must hold her secrets. If anyone can search behind the scene, you're the one."

As soon as Marla had a respite in her schedule, she hustled over to Hairstyle Heaven. Fortunately, Wilda manned the front desk. Marla winced at the sight of her. The psychic's outfit would be great for a séance, but it didn't seem appropriate for a salon. Her flowing caftan, with silver stars and moons sprinkled against a navy background, matched the turban on her head. Silver drop earrings clinked at her ears.

Wilda's face brightened at Marla's entrance. "I knew you'd come in today. Carolyn indicated that you're doing well. You're getting closer to her murderer."

Marla stopped by the waist-high counter. "Oh? What else did she tell you?"

"Your attention is needed urgently. Danger is in the air." Wilda's gaze flickered to the staff.

Marla struggled to interpret her words. Did she mean danger

threatened her here? Scanning the operators, Marla noted Claudia's absence. "Where is Claudia? I hoped to ask her how things were going."

"She'll be back tomorrow. She's taken a few days off."

A thought struck Marla, but it seemed too coincidental. "Dennis Thomson is out of his office until tomorrow. I wanted to see if Claudia knew why he visited the salon so often. Now I'm wondering if he came to see Carolyn at all."

Wilda gave her a sly smile that lent her wrinkled face the expression of a fox tracking prey. "Interesting observation." Closing her eyes, Wilda appeared to ignore the whirring blow-dryers, chatter of customers, and radio music as she swayed slowly back and forth. A red-haired woman breezed through the door, stopped by the front desk, and tapped her foot impatiently. "Excuse me?" the lady said, scraping her acrylic nails along the countertop.

Wilda didn't budge, so Marla interceded. "I believe she's communicating with those who have gone beyond. May I help you?"

A pair of gray eyes surveyed Marla with disdain. "I have an appointment with Jeanine. And you are?"

"Marla Shore from Cut 'N Dye salon down the strip. I'll tell Jeanine you're here." *Great way to run a business, Wilda. Tune out to talk to the dead when you have a live customer in front of you. You'll increase your customer base if you offer readings at the same time as a blowout.*

"Jeanine, your three o'clock is waiting up front. Should I tell her to get shampooed?" Marla queried the ebony-haired stylist who hung out the open rear door smoking a cigarette.

"*Oui, merci.*" Jeanine dropped her stub to the ground and stamped it out. "This person who is in charge, she is not altogether with us, if you know what I mean." Her accented voice lowered. "Monsieur Boyd has made her an offer. We are hoping she accepts. It would secure our place here."

Marla stepped partially outside. "What kind of offer?"

"To buy the business. It is not the way his plan was supposed to work, but he says this will be better."

"I see." What plan? How could she find out more? "I never fully understood his role," she said carefully.

"You don't need to know. It could be dangerous. If Carolyn—how you say, ticked him off?—he may have been the one who, well, I have said enough." She thrust her pale face close to Marla's and expelled a breath of nicotine-tinged air. "I have to thank you for speaking to Zelda. She sent me a check."

"I'm so glad. Now you both can move on from that incident."

Shuffling her aside, Jeanine signaled for her customer to get washed. "Maybe our boss lady will tell you what she plans. Some of us may leave if she stays in charge, especially if she moves our location to Miami. Monsieur Boyd is not happy with this arrangement, but Claudia is even angrier." Along the way, Jeanine paused to straighten a rack of magazines.

Marla trailed her indoors, aware that she had to return to her own salon in a few minutes. "Claudia isn't here today."

"She misses too many days. Because you helped me, mademoiselle, I will tell you something. Carolyn threatened to fire Claudia. She didn't like the way Claudia spoke to customers. My friend would tell people about how we're struggling to make a living in this country, and they gave her money. Carolyn accused her of being unprofessional, but Monsieur Boyd insisted Claudia remain."

"What influence does Atlas Boyd have over this salon?" Marla demanded. His name seemed to pop up everywhere.

"Ask Madame." Jeanine beckoned to the redheaded customer weaving in their direction, her hair dripping with moisture, and said, "I must go now. Thank you for your concern."

"No problem." Marla retreated toward the front desk, where Wilda smiled at her benignly. "I see you've come out of your trance. Did you get another message from Carolyn?"

"I did, darling." Wilda's eyes widened. "She said to tell you one of her friends is a thief. I keep seeing the same image in my mind: a necklace with a pendant that looks to be quite old."

"An item from her collection?" At Wilda's blank look, Marla explained. "Carolyn collected Victorian mourning jewelry. Remember how her sister, Linda Hall, was supposed to inherit some valuables, but no one could find them? Rosemary Taylor believed Carolyn's killer might have stolen the jewelry."

"Rosemary is the lady who played bingo with Carolyn at that Indian place, yes?" With a cry of pain, Wilda squeezed her eyes shut. "I sense her presence. That means . . ."

"Rosemary is dead. Murdered."

"Sweet saints."

"Getting any signals from her?" Marla asked, biting back her cynicism.

Wilda's lids flew open. "Don't discount the power of Spirit, my dear. You're susceptible to negative energy. It surrounds you, more menacing than the monsoon that almost wreaked havoc along the coast. You cannot escape it unless you take the precautions I suggested."

Yeah, right. Putting out a bowl of water will absorb bad vibes and keep me from ending up like Carolyn and Rosemary. Not so, pal. The only way to get rid of evil spirits is to expose them in this life. "What are your plans for the salon?" Marla said, changing tactics. "I noticed Bunny isn't here today. Did you dismiss your new receptionist?"

"She's part-time." Wilda spread her hands. "This isn't really what I wanted. I appreciate what Carolyn did for me. She was a good friend, despite what you believe. But this plane of existence is too grounded for me. Let me tell you a story. I had a man knock on my door once. He was beside himself with anxiety, constantly fidgeting and not knowing what could be wrong. From his aura, I could see where his energy was blocked. Stuck in a rut, he desired change but lacked courage to make the leap. After I cleared his channels, his renewed surge of energy gave him the guts to go after what he wanted."

"And this relates to things how?" Marla glanced at her watch, impatient to move on. She didn't have time for Wilda's long-winded tales.

"Having to take care of these mundane tasks obstructs my chakras. It's not for me." Her sharp gaze lanced Marla. "You, on the other hand, it suits quite well. You see the inner beauty in people, and your skill translates that into style. This place would be wasted on Carolyn's sister, whose narrow view obscures her vision. Mr. Boyd has his own agenda. That's why I'm thinking of making you my beneficiary."

"What?"

"I either need to get rid of the place or move it closer to my home. I can't keep commuting like this."

"Jeanine said Atlas Boyd made you an offer."

"Mark my words, that man is more than just a foreign investor. He has a peculiar interest in these French girls, but that's not my problem. I have to follow Carolyn's wishes."

"Carolyn would jump out of her grave if you handed me the salon. Anyway, it's in the same shopping strip as my place, and I'm not sure I'd even want another responsibility. What did you tell Boyd about me? He seemed to be aware of Carolyn's message."

"I mentioned that you had a vested interest in seeing Carolyn's murder solved, and why."

That would account for his menacing remarks, Marla thought. Pursing her lips, she pounced on another theory. "What about Claudia? Do you think she had any designs on Hairstyle Heaven? Maybe she expected more from Carolyn and got angry when she was overlooked."

"You mentioned that Claudia is gone the same time as our landlord. This may be significant," Wilda remarked, raising an eyebrow. "The girl speaks highly of him and is impressed by his war stories. I don't see how that sniveling idiot can impress anyone, but Claudia may be looking for a sugar daddy since her sponsor is dead." Wilda's eyes glazed. "Oh my."

"What's wrong?" Marla asked with a note of alarm. Claudia's absence didn't herald anything more sinister, did it?

"I just realized . . . Dennis Thomson had been in the Marines. Not that you can tell from the current shape he's in, but he would have had combat experience."

All right! Besides the chiropractor, here was another suspect who probably knew how to break someone's neck.

"Go now, Marla. You're needed elsewhere. Hurry."

Giving Wilda one last glance, Marla scurried from the salon. *Maybe hauntings were for real,* she mused as she entered Cut 'N Dye with a sigh of relief. The contrast between her brightly lit establishment and Carolyn's was like the difference between a level-one and level-ten hair color: night and day.

Welcome warmth rushed over her as Luis smiled from behind the receptionist's desk and waiting customers called out greetings. Scents of finishing spray mingled with the faint chemical tinge ever present in the filtered air. Feeling relief at being back at her own place, Marla pushed aside Wilda's warnings and focused her skills on the next client's hair.

Marla wasn't expecting Vail to show up. He'd been scheduled to work late, and she had promised to take Brianna to dance class. So when he burst into her salon with Brianna in tow at five o'clock, she felt a chill wind breeze past. Perhaps he'd let in Carolyn's ghost, she thought, licking her lips nervously.

Brianna didn't look well; the girl's complexion paled as though she'd seen the walking dead. "What's the matter?" Marla demanded, aware this wasn't a social visit.

"Brie had a scary incident," Vail said in a brusque tone. "Can we talk privately?"

"I'm just finishing up. Give me a minute." Spraying her last customer, she surveyed her work with satisfaction.

"My sister wanted me to ask how long she has to wait to go swimming after having her hair highlighted?" the customer said.

Unfastening the woman's cape, Marla replied, "Ideally, she should wait seventy-two hours after highlights, but she can swim right away with precautions. After she comes out of the pool, tell her to rinse her hair with clear water and apply a conditioner."

Ten minutes later, Marla had put away her supplies, swiped her counter clean, and turned off the power to her outlets. Nicole and Jennifer were working late; they could lock up. Snatching her purse from a drawer, she signaled to the waiting duo. "I'm ready. Wanna go to Arnie's for a bite to eat?"

"No." Vail's mouth was set in a grim line as he took her arm and steered her toward the door. Brianna shuffled behind them, unusually quiet. She'd slung her knapsack over one shoulder and carried her ballet bag.

Outside, the summer sun burned the pavement with heat. It had yet to descend enough to cool the humid air.

"Brie will go home with you until it's time for class. I want you to walk her inside. Don't let her go unaccompanied."

He halted, clenching his fists at his sides in an uncharacteristic gesture that made Marla want to offer comfort, especially when she saw the worry in his eyes.

"Someone accosted Brie on her way home from the school bus. A man in a black sedan. He wore a ski mask, pointed a gun at her, ordered her to get in his car. She did the smart thing and ran. Unfortunately, no one else witnessed it, so we don't have more details."

"Lord save me. Oh, you poor child." Putting an arm around the girl's shoulders, Marla drew her close. The teen seemed so fragile and vulnerable that Marla's protective instincts swung into play. The ferocity of her own feelings surprised her. "I'm so sorry. You must have been terrified. Thank God you didn't get in the car."

"He knew my name."

Hairs prickled on Marla's nape. "Was it anyone you recognized?"

The girl shook her head, ponytail swinging. "He looked as though he were medium-height, with black hair sticking out from the mask. All I could see was the gun pointed at me."

"Of course." She turned to Vail. "Can't you track the vehicle?"

"No luck. That other girl who was killed . . . she went to the same school. I'm checking into people who work there."

Marla hugged Brianna, then released her grip. "I'll take care of her. She won't be alone."

Vail cleared his throat. "Keep your cell phone on," he said gruffly, "in case I need to reach you. And make sure you don't park in any dark corners."

"I'll watch my back and Brianna's, too. You get on with your work. Don't worry about us."

The detective escorted them to Marla's Toyota. He stood in the parking lot, consternation twisting his features as he observed them driving away. Marla clutched the steering wheel, feeling a flood of warmth at the trust he'd placed in her. He'd given her his most precious possession, showing his faith that she'd keep his daughter safe.

"I don't feel well," Brianna said when they reached Marla's town house. "I'd rather skip dance class today."

"You had a scare, honey. I don't blame you for being frightened, but you shouldn't let it restrict your activities."

Spooks barked on the other side of the garage door. Inserting her key in the lock, Marla pushed open the entry and quickly punched in the alarm code.

"No one took Lucky out," Brianna said, throwing her bags on the tile floor.

"Dalton will have to worry about your dog." Spooks yipped excitedly, sniffing Brianna's ankles. "See, he smells your golden retriever." Stooping, Marla scratched the poodle behind his ears and told him, "Come on, I'll let you into the backyard."

While Brianna sagged into a chair at the kitchen table, Marla laid her purse on a counter, let the dog out, and quickly rifled through the mail she'd picked up at the cluster box. More bills; nothing that couldn't wait. After washing her hands, she turned her attention to Brianna.

"Can I get you something to drink?" she asked the girl, peering at her more closely in the bright interior light. Brie's skin looked flushed, her eyes glassy.

"I really don't want to go to dance class tonight. I have homework due tomorrow, and my head hurts."

"Are you sure that man didn't touch you?" Maybe Brie felt too uncomfortable telling her dad everything.

"It has nothing to do with him. I wasn't feeling well earlier."

Alarm frissoned through her. Perhaps more had occurred than

Brianna could confess aloud, and the trauma was manifesting it-self in other symptoms. She dispelled that notion as soon as she pressed the back of her hand against Brianna's forehead. Her skin felt burning hot.

"Uh oh, I think you really are sick. Wait here. I'll get a ther-mometer." Since she'd played nurse's aide at Miriam Pearl's house, Marla had invested in a digital oral thermometer. It read 102.8 degrees after Brianna stuck it under her tongue.

Panicking, Marla phoned Vail who wearily told her to give the girl some aspirin. If that didn't work, she could call their doctor. A cool sponge bath would help to bring the fever down.

"I don't know how to deal with this," Marla said in a frantic tone. "Can't you leave yet? Your daughter needs you." *And so do I.*

"You can handle it. Call me in an hour and let me know how she is."

Plopping down the receiver, Marla rushed into the bathroom to fumble in her medicine cabinet for a bottle of Advil. Was the thirteen-year-old considered a child or an adult? Scanning the dosage directions, Marla decided to give her two tablets right away.

"Do you have a sore throat? Is your nose stuffy?" she asked Brianna, setting the two pills in front of her along with a glass of tap water.

"I just have a headache." Brianna swallowed the tablets then gazed at Marla with listless eyes. "Where can I lie down?"

"In the guest bedroom." Marla's three-bedroom town house included her master suite, home office, and guest room plus the kitchen, laundry, family room, and rarely used formal dining area. She loved its spaciousness and the fact that it was single-story, so she didn't have to climb stairs.

Settling Brianna onto the queen-size pullout sleep sofa, she hovered over the bed like a nervous nanny. Now what? "Do you feel like eating dinner? Or shall I get you a Coke?"

"Just the drink," Brie said in a feeble voice. "My stomach feels upset."

Oh, great. Marla pushed an empty wastebasket to the side of

the bed in case Brianna threw up. What was wrong with her? Did she have an ordinary virus, or something worse?

Michael didn't make her feel better when she called her brother for advice. He and Charlene had two young children. They'd know all about childhood illnesses.

"Could be meningitis," he offered. "Or mono. Kids get that a lot when they share drinks and such."

"Gee, thanks. What else should I worry about?"

"Jacob is having hip pain. He shouldn't be experiencing a joint problem when he's only five. We're taking him to the doctor tomorrow."

"I'm sorry to hear that. How do you manage when both of you work?" Michael's job as a financial adviser kept him glued to Wall Street reports, and Charlene couldn't just take leave from her elementary school at any moment.

"No problem. We call a sitter when one of our kids gets sick; otherwise we work appointments into our schedules."

"Well, I don't know any baby-sitters, and I can't take off from work when I run a salon and have clients scheduled. Maybe I'll call Ma and see if she can come over."

"I spoke to her this morning. She's changing her blood-pressure medicine and needs to adjust to the new regimen, so I wouldn't bother her if I were you."

"You're not much help!"

"This is what it's like when you have children. Get used to it. Taking on a teenager is an even bigger burden."

"Brianna is a sweetheart. She acts like a tough cookie sometimes, but inside she's just a needy child." Marla spoke in a low tone from her telephone in the study. "Do you think her fever will be gone by tomorrow?"

"Who knows? If it's a virus, it may last up to five days. Temperature is always higher in the evening, so check it the same time each day. It should respond to the Advil, but you can put a cool washcloth on her forehead."

"I'll do that, and good luck with Jacob. Let me know what the doctor says."

Marla hung up, dwelling on the number of people she knew who were ill. For which one of them had Carolyn's warning been intended? Or had it been aimed at herself?

One thing was certain: as soon as Marla had a free day, she'd head for Cassadaga to consult a certified medium. Another reading might help to dissipate the cloud of anxiety that enveloped her.

Chapter Sixteen

"I don't know if I'm ready to take on the burden of raising a child," Marla said to Tally on the road to Cassadaga. Sunday morning found them on the turnpike heading north. It had been her first free day after Brianna's illness, which had turned out to be an upper respiratory infection.

For the rest of the week, Marla had been stuck between taking care of clients in the salon and rushing out to tend the teenager at Vail's house. At least one good thing had resulted: the virus that had kept Brianna home had given the child time to recover from the trauma of the attempted abduction. She was a resilient kid, and Marla admired her fortitude. Brie had been scared but had learned a valuable lesson in caution.

"You can expect more of the same if you marry Dalton," Tally remarked.

"I worried myself sick over that girl. This is precisely why I didn't want to have children. I can't handle it on a full-time basis. Raising kids takes too much from life," Marla said, gripping the steering wheel.

They had passed the Fort Pierce rest stop at ten o'clock. That meant they should arrive at the spiritualist camp in time for lunch. Marla peered out the window at rows of orange trees laden with green fruit. Would she ever be able to take enough days off for a real vacation?

"That's a selfish attitude," Tally replied.

"So? I worked hard to establish my salon and build my business. I can't stay home with Brianna, and I'm afraid Dalton would expect me to fall into that role."

"He's not like Ken. The detective respects your ambition. It's one of the reasons he was attracted to you in the first place."

"A lot of men change when you marry them. Look at your husband. Ken encouraged you to open the dress shop, but now he wants you to remain home and breed babies. They're all alike."

"Have you talked to Dalton about it?"

Marla shook her head, soft strands of hair brushing her face. "Dalton will have the same response you did and say I'm being selfish. Maybe I am, but I want more from life than taking care of children, watching them leave the nest, and constantly worrying about their health and safety."

"It's a big responsibility," Tally acknowledged in a wistful tone that made Marla glance at her. With her lithe body encased in a tank top and shorts, Tally looked ready for a jaunt to the beach. How would her friend feel after having several kids when she couldn't fit into a size eight anymore?

"Are you prepared to stay home with your brood when they get sick?" Marla shot at her.

"I can always hire a nanny. But if I decide to go that route, I'll definitely need a manager. You should take more time off too, Marla, if only to give yourself a break. I've seen those brochures of Tahiti in your purse. Are they just pipe dreams, or do you really want to go?"

Marla grimaced as the dart hit home. She'd hardly traveled anywhere except with her parents in her younger days, and she yearned for adventures abroad. Sometimes you had to put off the things you wanted until you developed the means to get there.

"I'm working on it," she said vaguely. "In the meantime, I hope to ask around to see if anyone in the psychic community has heard of Wilda Cleaver. I'm still not buying into her fortune-telling."

"What about your nephew? You said he'd been ill."

"Jacob had a mild joint inflammation treated with rest and children's aspirin. He'd fallen off their swing set; that's how he got hurt. Ma is feeling better, too, so I'm not sure who Carolyn's supposed message was meant for. I'm more worried about the man who tried to accost Brianna than any of our ailments."

"You'll see what the psychics say at Cassadaga. What do you know about the place? I've never been there, although I always wanted to go." Shifting in her seat, Tally raised an inquiring eyebrow.

Marla sniffed her friend's favorite Poison perfume. It scented the dry air-conditioned interior. "A man named George Colby founded the settlement in the late 1800s," she said. "He grew up in Minnesota, where his dead uncle sent a message through a medium that George would establish a spiritual center in the South. He developed the ability to communicate with spirits himself and traveled around giving séances."

"No kidding? My deceased relatives don't give me any good investment advice."

Marla chuckled. "Listen to this. His spirit guide directed him to go to Florida and obtain a patch of government land that the spirits had selected for their camp. Colby filed a homestead claim, part of which he deeded in 1895 to the Southern Cassadaga Spiritualist Camp Meeting Association. That's the town's formal title. It's listed in the National Register of Historic Places."

"Holy smokes. So the spirits ordained where this camp should take root."

"Actually, I think people wanted a place to escape from the cold weather." Marla's lips twisted cynically. "Most of the settlers came from up North. Residents pay a yearly rental fee to the association for use of the land. We'll be staying at the Cassadaga Hotel."

"I hope we can see the auditorium. My drumming-circle guide

said the vibrations in its séance room are strong due to the ectoplasm produced by mediums over the years."

"Ectoplasm? Isn't that a made-up term from the *Ghostbusters* film?"

Tally threw her a narrowed glance. "It's for real, Marla. Ectoplasm is electromagnetic energy that emanates from a medium's body. Wrapped around a spirit, it lets you view the entity."

"So you can see ghosts?" Marla scoffed. "Oh, joy. Just what I want to meet: Carolyn's spook admonishing me to find her killer. Give me a break."

A frown creased Tally's brow; she took this stuff seriously. "If you don't believe in psychic powers, why are you here?"

"To ask about Wilda Cleaver and see if anyone knows her. To get another reading and compare it to her predictions. I'm not totally closed to the possibility of extrasensory events," she added, considering the fact that she needed an ally, and Tally might be more helpful if she felt Marla could accept metaphysical phenomena, "but I'd like confirmation."

When they reached Orlando, Marla took I-4 east until they reached Deltona. Shortly thereafter she spotted a sign for Blue Spring State Park and Cassadaga. Turning off at Exit 114, they came to a traffic light, where she turned left. *If I had natural psychic tendencies*, Marla thought, *I wouldn't need a map. Instinct would lead me in the proper direction.*

Approximately a half mile farther, she made a right onto Dr. Martin Luther King Jr. Beltway. Following Tally's instructions, she hung right next, turning on County Road 4139. Scenes from old Florida unfolded as she drove along a narrow two-lane wooded road through hilly terrain. Welcoming the change from blistering hot South Florida, Marla felt her muscles relax and her mind ease. She didn't see any people as they passed a house labeled SPIRITUAL GARDENS and entered downtown Cassadaga.

"It sure is dead around here," she quipped. "Wow, look at that sign. It says we're coming to a congested area. They must mean that intersection with all of five buildings." Pressing on the brake, Marla checked out the village bookstore on the right and the hotel on the opposite corner. Other public buildings beckoned her interest, but she figured she'd explore them later. Across the street, Marla parked in a gravel lot in front of the hotel. Traffic was nonexistent; she wondered if residents were as wraithlike as the ghosts summoned in séances.

Emerging from the Camry, she smoothed her rumpled tan capri pants. Insects swarmed past her nose, drawn by a sweet honey scent pervading the humid air. Her envious glance surveyed Tally, who appeared none the worse for wear from their four-hour drive. Marla always felt practical when she compared herself to Tally's svelte looks. It served her well during investigations. While men gawked at the tall blonde, Marla steered their conversation in the direction she needed to go.

"Quaint hotel," Tally commented, fanning herself. "My guidebook says it was built originally in 1927 and renovated in the 1990s, so I hope that means it has central air-conditioning. Did you ask when you made our reservation? It's so hot; we'll have to go somewhere else if it isn't cool inside."

"Don't worry; I'm sure they have modern amenities." Marla's doubtful gaze swept the two-story building with a cream facade and red awnings. A sign said, FOR A READING APPOINTMENT, INQUIRE AT THE FRONT DESK. While a light breeze stirred wisps of her hair, she listened to the twitter of birds and the occasional rumble of a car cruising past.

Her pumps crunched on gravel as she approached the ivy-covered building. A couple of middle-aged women sat on the front porch playing cards. One of them glanced up when Marla and Tally pushed open the screen door and climbed the steps. The lady's plump face showed a heavy application of makeup. Into Marla's head popped an image of a woman swathed in silk and seated around a crystal ball. *If she's one of the mediums the hotel offers, I'll pass.* Apparently the north porch invited smokers, because ashtrays sat on the scattered tables. Marla hoped that meant the interior was a smoke-free environment.

Inside a cool rush of air-conditioning brought welcome relief to her heated skin. Orchestral music played quietly in the background while ceiling fans twirled overhead with Victorian-style lights. Green velvet upholstered chairs and polished wood tables wore lace runners. On a cocktail table in front of the sofa, a red candle squatted in a circle of fake red roses and baby's breath. Marla had never liked artificial flowers; they reminded her of death. She took in the potted plants placed at strategic locations around the lobby, which, she admitted to herself, exuded a certain charm.

"I love this place," Tally cried, studying a lamp with crystals dangling from an old-fashioned shade. A bar decorated with painted landscapes lent to the time-warp atmosphere. "I'll have to take photos tonight. Did you know that when you use a digital camera in the dark and balls of light show up in the pictures, those may be spirits? They're called orbs."

"*May be* is the proper term," Marla retorted.

Restroom doors painted black and a creaky staircase rising to the second level made her wonder if there were phantoms inhabiting the hotel. A sign announcing an evening ghost tour gave her the answer. Tally might want to move in. Her friend reveled in this stuff.

"You can sign up for readings with one of our mediums," a desk clerk said in the gift shop. After registering and securing their single room key—a real key and not a modern card—Marla had inquired about seeing a spiritualist. "Or else visit the bookstore across the street. In the back room is a bulletin board listing the certified mediums and healers who are available today. You call them to make an appointment; there's a phone provided. Be sure to pick up a copy of the program booklet while you're there. It'll let you know what's going on tonight."

"Thank you." After accepting a free copy of *Horizons*, a newsletter containing spiritual insights and local advertisements, she proceeded upstairs with Tally to deposit their luggage. Their suite turned out to be two bedrooms with the wall removed between them and the beds essentially foot to foot. A window air-cooling unit provided relief from the heat. It looked to be a fun night, Marla thought, glancing at the few amenities. No telephone, no television. Not much in the way of furnishings except for a huge wardrobe that could easily hide a dead body, a dresser with a bouquet of silk flowers that looked wilted, and a radio alarm clock, the only sign of modern civilization. *You're supposed to seek inner peace here,* she reminded herself with a wry twist to her lips, *not the delights of the technological age.*

"Let's get something to eat," she said after refreshing herself in the single bathroom. Lacking a stall shower, the facilities consisted of a toilet and a tub framed by maroon drapes. A pedestal sink stood in the bedroom.

"This is so cool," Tally crooned as they descended the carpeted staircase. Marla suppressed her unenthusiastic response. When they entered the Lost in Time Café, her mood lightened at the sight of other guests chatting happily in a bright, inviting dining room. A waitress wearing a black vest over a white blouse and black slacks brought the menus and took their drink orders. Resisting the urge to order a glass of wine, Marla got an iced tea to go with her mushroom swissburger. Lacy white curtains flanked the windows, while silk plants and paintings combined with the cozy decor to maintain the feeling of having been transitioned back in time.

Fortified with food, they headed outdoors to the bookstore across the street. Remodeled through the years, the single-story structure boasted a faded yellow exterior and low-slung roof. Reaching the front porch, Marla pushed open the door and stepped inside. The pleasant scent of incense drifted her way. Cruising the interior, she looked askance at books on topics ranging from astrology to the afterlife. Jewelry gleamed in display cases. Trying not to appear too clueless, Marla peered at pairs of metal balls in boxes, stones painted with symbols, and other strange items the purpose of which she hadn't an inkling about. Clearly, she was out of her element here, although Tally squealed with delight as she browsed the contents.

This may suit you, but I'm getting the willies. The only spooks I want to know is my dog, and he's safely in the kennel.

Leaving her friend behind, she meandered into the next room, which held the bulletin board listing available mediums. Scanning the roster, Marla wasn't struck by any intuitive guidance as to which one to pick. A natural inclination to choose a woman came to mind; otherwise, it was a crapshoot. Mustering her nerve, she picked up the phone and arbitrarily dialed one of the numbers.

A throaty female voice answered. "Hello?"

Marla wondered if the psychic had known she was going to call. "Hi, is this Reverend Hazel Sherman? I'm interested in getting a reading. Can you please give me more information?" She felt like an idiot, not quite knowing what to say.

"Is this your first visit to town, dear?"

The woman's voice poured over her like warm honey. "Yes, it is. I'm not really sure how to go about this."

"It's all right, I have an appointment available at three o'clock. Would that be suitable?"

Marla glanced at her watch. An hour to spare. "That's fine." She cleared her throat. "How much do you charge, and will you take a check?"

"It's forty dollars for a half hour. A check will do."

"Okay. Where do I go? I'm calling from the bookstore."

"Take a right turn at Stevens Street, continue along until you get to Lake Street. Hang another right." Hazel gave her house number. "I'm just opposite the park."

Marla hung up, then wiped her sweaty palms on her coral polo shirt. Hopefully, she'd made a good choice and her interview with the spiritualist would prove illuminating.

"I have some time to spare before my reading," she told Tally, who was examining an amethyst pendant. "I'll talk to people to see if anyone has heard of Wilda."

"Did you know you can ask the crystal questions and it will give you an answer? It has to be a yes-or-no answer," Tally said, her expression serious.

"Is that right? Why don't you ask if Wilda's prediction is true?"

When Tally dangled the crystal as though to comply, Marla grasped her wrist. "Just kidding. Do you want to come with me?"

"No, do you see that place across the street? The Spiritualist Psychic Therapy center? It says they have mediums on duty. I'd rather go in there than call a stranger on the telephone. We'll compare notes later."

Parting from her friend, Marla headed outside and across the street to the Purple Rose gift shop, where crystals, tarot cards, and dream-catchers were sold along with readings for thirty dollars apiece. When she mentioned Wilda's name, the proprietor gave her a strange look along with a firm denial. The closest she came to an affirmation was in the post office, where a clerk informed her, in a hushed tone, that Wilda had once been a resident of Cassadaga.

Marla glanced behind her, wondering why he kept giving furtive glimpses toward the door. This was the tiniest post office she'd ever been in, consisting of rows of rental boxes lining the wall and a single sales counter.

"So is Wilda known as a certified medium?" Marla said.

"Oh, she's known, all right," replied the thin young man. "Folks around here have long memories."

"What does that mean?"

The postal clerk leaned forward. "It means if you're smart, you'll steer clear of her."

A startled expression crossed his face when another customer entered. Marla debated waiting until the woman left, but then Tally stuck her face in the door, gesturing wildly.

Reluctantly, Marla gave up her place in front of the counter. "What is it?" she asked her friend.

Tally's eyes were lit with excitement. "Look at this." She waved her copy of *Horizons*. "They're having a Sweat Lodge Ceremony tonight."

"And that is?"

"It's awesome, Marla. You'll like it."

Envisioning herself sweating inside some hot, close building with a bunch of believers, Marla shook her head. "No, thanks. Maybe I can find a healing program. I need to calm my nerves. Let me see the schedule."

Classes on meditation, feng shui, past-life regression, transfiguration, and animal spirits might appeal to Tally, but not her. Or maybe she'd give that last one a try. Then she could communicate with Spooks after he was gone.

"I have to head over toward my psychic's house. We'll hook up later," Marla said to Tally, taking her leave.

Outside, she squinted in the bright sunlight. She could probably walk the distance and would be glad for the opportunity to observe the town. Passing by the bookstore, she continued along Stevens Street to a small meditation garden. Two wooden benches, painted faded red, sat on a concrete slab overlooking a gushing fountain where water squirted from a gold statue of a goddess. Her ears picked up the hum of an air-conditioning unit competing with birdsong and crickets. Occasionally, a car rumbled past, but traffic remained light.

Across the street stood Brigham Hall, an impressive two-story white house with a sign out front advertising metaphysics. Since the sidewalk ran along that side of the street, Marla crossed over. Chimes hung on the front porch, screened at ground level. Planters decorated the steps, ferns and another greenery spilling out. The sweet scent of jasmine filled her nostrils. She noticed purple morning glories and other flowering plants decorating the residences as she strolled along the pavement.

Some of these homeowners need to remember they are still alive, Marla thought, surveying the peeling paint, plastic-covered windows, tin roofs, dented doors, and overgrown weeds. The neighborhood gave her the impression the inhabitants communed more with spirits than reality. Either they were extremely unmaterialistic, or else they didn't make enough money offering psychic counseling to cover basic living expenses. *You'd think they would maintain their property for safety's sake, if nothing else.*

She halted in front of Colby Memorial Temple, where a sign

said, GET IN TOUCH WITH LOVED ONES WHO HAVE PASSED TO SPIRIT. On the left, a pavilion labeled Caesar Forman Healing Center posted its hours on a closed door.

Marla followed the Reverend Hazel Sherman's instructions and found Seneca Park, with a pond glistening in the near distance. At the end of Stevens Street, a house rose on a hill like the Haunted Mansion at Walt Disney World. Getting the creeps from the deserted road and dilapidated houses, Marla trudged up Lake Street toward the address Hazel had given her.

A gray cat scooted in front of her when she arrived at the quaint blue cottage on a quiet side street. Sweating and thirsty, Marla licked dry lips as she knocked on the door.

Her eyes widened when the door swung open and an attractive brunette smiled at her. "Please come in," the woman said, standing aside. She wore an apricot blouse, white pedal pushers, and tennis shoes. Marla couldn't have been more surprised at her appearance. She'd expected an older, heavier-set woman in flowing garments. The image probably came from movies with gypsy fortune-tellers, but then again, Wilda favored caftans.

Marla got a quick glimpse of an appealing living room before she was led into an office.

"I'm set up here to do a tape recording, if you would like one," the Reverend Sherman said, indicating Marla should take a seat opposite her desk chair. Cradling her purse in her lap, Marla complied, studying the papers strewn over the desk and the computer with its screensaver in motion. What, no crystal ball? An edge of disappointment teased her.

"Yes, I'd love to have a backup tape," she replied, wishing for a cold can of Coke instead.

The other woman seated herself, then regarded Marla with a friendly expression. She looked to be in her forties, Marla surmised, noting a wedding ring on her finger. "It helps if I hold something that belongs to you," Hazel said with a smile.

"Oh." Fumbling in her handbag, Marla withdrew her sunglass case. "Will this work?"

"That's fine." Hazel took the case, turning it in her hands while staring forward. A long pause ensued, then she began speaking rapidly. "There's a change of residence coming up around you before one year from today, and the change of residence is very positive. It's kind of like a local change and not a long-distance change. You're also in the process, before the end of this year, of doing more stuff as far as relationship is concerned. You need to make some relationship changes around you. Both people are kind of like very independent of each other, and now you're in the process where you want to cement things together."

Is that how I feel about Dalton? Marla asked herself. What about a change of residence? Did that mean she'd finally move in with him?

"You've had, like, bad things happen to you in the past, and for a long time you blamed yourself, but you were able to put them behind you and move on," Hazel continued. "It's made you a stronger person, and, don't take this wrong, but you still tend to get into, like, self-imposed guilt trips. You'll be making some major changes to rid yourself of this anchor weighing you down."

Marla swallowed. The psychic's words hit close to the mark.

"You also need to do something about a career aspect, and that's coming to you within the next few months. You're getting your self-esteem back, and you're not so scared to make changes. Before this, you were frozen in one spot, and that's totally unlike you. You used to be a person, like, you'd make up your mind to do something and come hell or high water, you would do it. But lately, I don't know, you're just stuck. You don't give yourself enough credit to go forward. You've been, like, in a limbo stage for a while, and you have to make some major changes to get out of the limbo stage and move on. Some opportunities have come up around you"—Hazel caught Marla's gaze with her own—"but you didn't take these opportunities. You had to get your heart and your self-esteem to where you needed to be, so you can move yourself into a good place. You've avoided any kind of change for a while, and now change is, like, very, very positive for you."

That could apply to anyone. "Are you referring to my business or my personal life?" Marla asked with a note of skepticism.

Hazel gave a small smile. "That's for you to decide. You have a natural, God-given talent. I mean, God gives everyone a talent, but you've kind of been, um, walking away from yours for the past couple of years. He's given you a message, and your talent is even stronger. You can't walk away from it anymore. You're creating your own destiny. Not everything is going to be a cakewalk in life. You can be your own worst enemy, and it's, like, you have to change that. You want to get to a point where you can accept yourself."

What? Marla realized she'd had problems accepting herself over past misdeeds, but she had gotten over that, hadn't she? Or was this holding her back from committing to a lasting relationship with Dalton? Could it also be keeping her behind the salon chair when she had the potential—yes, and the talent—for doing more?

"There is someone unsettled around you," Hazel intoned. "You have to finish the task you've set yourself to help that person, but then you should put more energy into yourself. You're doing too many things for other people."

You sound like my mother, although she's the one who talked me into helping Aunt Polly. Or did Hazel mean Carolyn? Marla's task, according to Wilda, involved solving her rival's murder. She fidgeted in her seat, uncomfortable with how accurately the medium was reading her. What happened to the ghostly visitations she'd anticipated? This wasn't how she'd expected the session to go. She'd thought Hazel would be in contact with a spirit from the world beyond.

"You're also going to be involved in, like, taking care of or mentoring a child, but this child is not your child," Hazel said. "It's not something you have to do, but you volunteer to do it."

You're right, Marla thought, envisioning Brianna.

Hazel's face sobered. "You're going to take a trip, and it involves family issues. Something bad is coming up around this trip. Not for you; your health is good. But someone else . . . there may be a death before the end of the year."

Chapter
Seventeen

Marla's spine stiffened. "I consulted a medium at home, Wilda Cleaver, who said someone close to me may be ill. She claimed that a late friend sent this message. Now you're telling me someone in my family's going to die?" Her pulse throbbed in her throat.

Hazel raised a hand. "There's something bad coming up around this trip you're going to take, and it involves a family member. I can't see exact details. It's just a feeling I get."

So Wilda was on the level. Yet Marla's skepticism kicked in. "Could a dead person really send such a warning?"

"It's possible."

"Can you contact the spirit to ask who gets sick?"

"It doesn't happen that way."

"Why didn't Carolyn send her message directly to me?"

"You have the gift, if you listen to your intuition. Did this person cross over recently?" At Marla's nod, she said, "You may start seeing things going on around you that are associated with your friend, little signs, and you'll know those are signs she's giving you. When a person passes away, there's a time frame where you won't have dreams, you won't have anything. It's kind of like they're going through an orientation process, and it's different for each individual when they cross over. But once that's done, you'll see a lot of signs, many things happening. But it's you, too. You have to get rid of your self-imposed pressure first."

Hazel fingered the eyeglass case in her lap. "Do you have a brother? You have an emotional aspect around him. It's been brewing for a while, and you need to resolve the issue. There's still a lot of water underneath the bridge, and you, like, have to let go of the past."

Marla bit her lower lip. Hadn't she fully reconciled with Michael regarding old history between them?

"He has some health issues coming up around him in the next six to eight months. Does he have a heart problem or chest pain or something? Is he a very stressed-out person? Either he's doing it to himself or . . . Nothing bad is going to happen; I just see this coming up around him."

Holy highlights, Marla wondered if Michael was the family member who needed medical aid.

"Your father's been a very strong presence nearby you for the past two years. He's moving around your brother now, because your brother is experiencing some kind of, like, tremendous, I would say, emotional difficulties that he's, um, created for himself. It's producing a snowball effect, and so he's having to make some major changes in his lifestyle, I want to say this year."

Marla leaned forward. Truthfully, despite her mother's admonitions, she rarely called Michael. Living in Boca Raton with his wife and two children, he seemed to have the perfect family. Was Hazel hinting at undercurrents Marla hadn't detected? Guilt rushed through her for not paying more attention.

"I don't know if he's overextended himself or something," the psychic said, "but a lot of it has to do with his finances. He's kind of gone off the edge, and now he's in the process where he's getting himself back to a conservative place."

Hazel cleared her throat. "For some reason, before your dad passed away, he had some unresolved issues concerning your brother. Your dad wanted to take steps to resolve it, but your brother couldn't go in that direction. Maybe he thought he was going to have more time, and he didn't, and I think that's, like, a major burden around him. Your dad is worried whether your brother can get past that, because it's weighing him down. He can't emotionally beat himself up about it anymore. Your father has accepted everything, and your brother has to move on."

What unresolved issues? Marla would have to ask Michael if any of this applied. She'd had her own problems with her brother, but that was something different.

"Your dad is very happy where he is," Hazel continued, her eyes glazed. "He looks forward to the day when he can meet you again. Meanwhile, he wants you to go forward. He knows that no matter what, you bounce back, you can make it. Also, he feels bad because you're putting a lot of your energy into someone else. He wants to tell you not to worry about that person and to start doing more for yourself. You have some family business you're going to finish, and that's good, because it will take the emotional headache off you."

Did this mean one of her cousins would share the burden in caring for Aunt Polly? That would certainly relieve an extra responsibility she didn't need.

"Is anyone in the legal field, or something to do with the law?" Hazel asked, startling her. "Some kind of family issue is coming up for them. It's nothing bad, but it may cause problems. They'll have to deal with it."

Oh no. The psychic must mean Dalton Vail.

"There's something around you that involves a piece of property that'll help you out with the financial aspects. In the past year, there's been a lot of unexpected high expenses around you, but it's, like, whatever it is you've spent money on, things are coming back around you."

That could be the rental property I bought from Stan. "When did you get started doing this?" Marla asked in unabashed awe.

"Oh, probably close to twenty-five years ago."

"How did you know it was your calling?"

"My intuition . . . I pick up on people all the time, things going around, and dreams."

"Did you go for training?"

"I went to classes in parapsychology and meditation, but everybody has their own way of doing it."

"How do you sense this stuff?"

"Sometimes it's symbols, sometimes words or colors."

"What about negative energy and all those crystals and talismans other people talk about?"

"You don't need that. What's in your heart is what counts. Rocks, candles, and incense won't do anything for you. If it helps you relax, that's fine, but you shouldn't put all your hopes, dreams, and wishes into a rock, candle, or crystal. If you look at everything in life, God's hand is everywhere. You have to have faith; it keeps you going. There most definitely is an afterlife. You'll understand one day."

The medium's eyelids fluttered. "Right now, you're obsessed with completing your task. You feel the need to pursue justice. Learning the truth will bring you peace."

A chill captured Marla all the way to her toes. She'd pronounced similar words as part of her bat mitzvah speech: *Justice, justice, shall you pursue.* How could they form on Hazel's lips?

"Treat yourself as fairly as you treat others," the medium went on. "Accept who you are, and you'll find the power within you to move forward. Above all, don't give up. The truth is just around the horizon."

Then let's find it. "How about Wilda Cleaver, does her name ring a bell? I imagine a lot of you practitioners know each other."

"Sorry, I never heard of her, but that doesn't mean anything. You have to let intuition guide you in choosing someone."

Suspending any further inquiries, Marla paid her bill and left. Her head reeled with all the revelations. How much of it was valid? So many insights seemed accurate that Marla was inclined to believe Hazel. Then again, how many people could rightfully be told they needed to make changes in their life?

"You won't believe the things I heard at my reading," Marla said to Tally in the hotel lobby about fifteen minutes later. She'd found the blonde poring over a stack of New Age books. "Did you buy all of those?"

"These are great topics. How did your session go? Hey, listen to this article. It says you should do a life-purpose inventory to discover your special mission. Ignore any negative self-talk, and eliminate the clutter in your life. That will help you create a solid foundation for daily living."

"No kidding. Like who doesn't know that? It's common sense."

Tally pursed her lips. "It's the first step toward discovering your higher purpose."

"Good, you clean out your closet to dispose of clutter, and I'll find Carolyn's killer." She paused. "The medium mentioned some words similar to my bat mitzvah speech," she confessed. "The section I read provided for a judicial system during the old days. There's no way Hazel could have known my Torah portion unless she received a message from my father."

"Start at the beginning, Marla."

"Let's go upstairs. I don't want anyone else to hear us."

At the second level, Marla unlocked their door and entered the room. Tossing her purse onto her bed, she flopped down beside it, then proceeded to relate everything to Tally.

"Tell me more about your speech," Tally said when she'd finished.

"Back in biblical times, the Torah provided laws. One of them was that no one should be found guilty unless two or more witnesses provided evidence. Innocent until proven guilty, right? If an appointed judge had trouble making a decision, he was referred to a higher authority, like our Supreme Court. But in my speech, I said that not all God intended has come to pass. Witnesses make mistakes. Juries don't always judge fairly. Often criminals are released and become a threat to society. As individuals, we can't always affect these issues, so we have to focus on treating others with fairness. This is how we move closer to God."

"So what's the relevance?"

"Hazel said if I treat myself as fairly as I treat others, I'll accept myself, and I can move on." Examining her fingernails, Marla noticed where her polish needed repair.

Tally eyed her. "She may have a point. Hazel also mentioned relationship changes, and it's time you decided where you're heading with Dalton."

"Maybe my purpose in life is to seek justice, and that's why I help him with his cases."

"Nonsense. You've always felt guilty about Tammy's death, and that's been your driving force. Now it's time to put the past behind you and go forward. Dalton needs you, and so does Brianna. You should listen to the psychic's advice. Maybe the unsettled soul Hazel told you about isn't Carolyn; it's you."

"I'm more inclined to worry about one of my relatives falling ill during an upcoming trip."

"That still gives you some time to discover who's sick." Pacing the room, Tally glanced at her. "What would Wilda gain by urging you to find Carolyn's killer?"

"How should I know?" Marla tilted her head. "Tell me about your session. Who did you see?"

A knock on the door startled them both. Marla opened it to see the desk clerk holding a sealed envelope.

"This message was delivered for you."

"Thanks." Waiting until the woman left, she tore it open. "I have information about Wilda Cleaver," Marla read to Tally. "Meet me tonight at ten o'clock by the picnic table at Lake Colby Park. Come alone." Marla stared at her friend. "We're finally hitting pay dirt."

Tally's alarmed blue eyes regarded hers. "It could be a trick. I'll go with you."

"No, I'd better do this by myself. I have my cell phone. If I don't call you by ten-fifteen, you can get help."

Following the directions in the note, Marla turned right from the main hotel entrance toward an intersection where she could either turn left onto Marion Street or go straight downhill toward the park, which was bound to be deserted this time of night. Having decided to walk the short distance, she brushed a mosquito off her neck as she trudged down the decline, watching her footing with the help of a flashlight from her glove compartment. At the bottom, a dirt road looped around the lake. Her light source pinpointed a lone picnic table under a shady canopy.

Advancing a few hundred feet, Marla halted when a sticklike figure emerged from the shadows. Moonlight illuminated the features of the postal clerk she'd encountered earlier that day. His grinning expression didn't indicate a threat, so Marla moved toward him cautiously.

"I'm glad you decided to share some information," she began, feeling a crawling sensation on her arm. Suppressing a shudder, she brushed away whatever insect had landed there to taste her flesh.

"I couldn't talk to you where anyone else could hear," he said with a nervous tick on his thin face. "I'm not one of them, so their code of silence doesn't affect me. I think you should know that Wilda Cleaver is a thief."

Marla's heartbeat accelerated. "Really?"

"She belonged to the spiritual camp once. When she lived here, Wilda set up a phony psychic hot line and duped thousands of victims, sending collection letters to those who didn't pay for her services. The association expelled her. She was an embarrassment, a blemish on their reputation."

Wow, she'd stumbled upon a gold mine of disclosure. "Are you saying that Wilda does not have any true psychic power? Everything she says is false?"

His eyes hinted at old wounds. "I'm not qualified to make that judgment, but I wouldn't trust her, and I certainly wouldn't give her any money. She claimed to have studied with a shaman in Brazil, but that's garbage. Wilda is a butcher's daughter from the Bronx."

Withdrawing a folded envelope from his pocket, he offered it to her. "Here, I made copies for you. You'll find more information in there."

"I owe you, friend."

"Doug Rosenfeld. I just hope this has been helpful."

"More than you know. Thanks a bunch." Stumbling up the road, Marla resisted the urge to tear open the envelope right away. Knowing Wilda was a fake eased concerns about her family, at least until she remembered Hazel's pronouncements.

"Maybe Wilda fleeced a lot of people and got kicked out of camp, but she still may be a viable medium," Tally told her while they readied for bed in their room. "What's in that envelope?"

Dressed in her cotton nightshirt, Marla sat beside a round table covered with a lacy cloth and pulled out a pile of folded papers from the crinkled envelope. "They're all about Wilda."

Standing, Tally pulled a brush through her long hair. "What do they say?"

Marla scanned the materials, mostly copies of news clippings. "She ran a two-dollars-and-fifty-cents-per-minute psychic hotline, with nearly four million people calling who were charged an average of fifty bucks. She tried to collect millions in overdue charges."

"How did she get away with this?"

Marla choked back a cry of incredulity. "Wilda put on a phony accent, called herself Sequina the Seer, and claimed she'd been trained by Brazilian shamans. She also earned money from television advertising and a Web site." Marla shuffled through the articles, filtering more details. "Consumer complaints started the investigation. Once the members of this community learned the extent of her activities, they kicked her out.

"Hey, this is interesting. Wilda wasn't acting alone." She glanced up. "Be careful with that brush or you'll damage your ends."

"Yes, madame hairdresser." Tally set her brush down on the dresser. "Should we barricade the door?" she asked, her silk pajamas rustling as she pointed toward it. "Ghosts may pass through walls, but people use doors."

"I don't believe it's necessary. People who come here are look-

ing for spiritual fulfillment, not thievery. These mediums probably help folks just by listening and providing a sympathetic ear,
don't you think? Anyone who's lost a loved one wants reassur-
ance they'll meet again some day, so the psychics help with grief
counseling."

"Not to mention healing. It's really what you believe in that
counts," Tally said to Marla's surprise.

"In that regard, you can interpret the medium's advice any
way you want. They don't give clear details because it might influence your actions." She folded her legs Indian-style on the
bed. "Back to Wilda's origins. A Fort Lauderdale company hired
her, pursued collections in her name, financed TV spots and an
Internet site. The Federal Trade Commission entered the picture after several thousand consumer complaints. They accused
the firm of making false promises of free psychic readings, de-
ceptive billing practices, and abusive telemarketing techniques."

Tally's gaze reflected puzzlement. "Did they sue Wilda, or just
the company that used her as a front?"

"The FTC just went after Titan Resources. They reached a
settlement with the company, which canceled any outstanding
bills and paid a fine. Meanwhile the state attorney general's office filed suit against the firm plus Wilda. She ended up getting
the case dismissed against her, claiming she was a victim as well.
She wasn't aware of all the activities the company propagated in
her name."

"Bullshit. She probably knew everything that was going on."

"I'll bet." Marla mused over the pages. "I wonder who defended her. I can probably look up newspaper archives on my
computer when we get home. This must have all happened before she moved South. From what Dalton told me, Wilda appears
to run a respected business now."

By the time they returned home on Monday, Marla was so
eager to share her news with Dalton that she stopped by the police station after dropping Tally off. At two o'clock, she'd ex-

pected to find him in his office, but the front-desk receptionist told her he was out. Dialing his cell phone number, she blurted her news as soon as he answered.

"Whoa, hold on," he said, "I can't talk now. Will you be free for dinner later?"

"Yes, that works for me. Is everything okay with Brianna? Shall I pick up something to eat?"

"We're all right. Why don't we come to your house? I'm sure you have enough to do. Chicken or Chinese food?"

His thoughtfulness made warmth coil through her. "How about a stir-fry from the Chicken Kitchen?"

"You got it. I'm glad you're back safely. We'll discuss what you've dug up when I see you."

After Marla retrieved Spooks from the kennel, she drove home, unpacked, then called her mother. Briefly, she recounted her experience with the psychic, leaving out the parts about her brother and any upcoming family ailments. "Do you really think Daddy was communicating with me?"

"I'd like to think so."

"So where does that leave me in Carolyn's case? If Wilda is pulling my leg, I don't have to be involved."

Anita clicked her tongue. "Your father advised you to follow the path to justice. Perhaps there was a portion of truth in what Wilda said."

Exasperated, Marla raised a hand. "I give up. I might as well chase this thing through to the end."

"How did Tally make out? Are her problems with Ken smoothed over?"

"Not exactly." Marla squirmed on her study chair. "Tally's reading with a psychic told her that troubled waters are ahead. She'll have to make some important decisions to go after what she really wants."

"Seems like we all have decisions to make regarding relationships. I have a date with Sam this weekend."

"You're kidding. He asked you out?"

"He finally got up the nerve. I kind of like the guy. He's a lot quieter than Roger, but he has a sort of boyish charm."

Marla wouldn't describe Sam Levy that way, but perhaps he showed a different side to her mother. "Well, let me know where you're going so I can keep tabs on you."

Anita laughed. "Don't you have our roles reversed?"

"That happens when you get older."

"Have you checked on Aunt Polly since you've been back?"

"No, I'll visit her soon. She's letting her bills slide, and I want to get my name on her checking account so I can help pay them."

"See if you can convince her to get some decent clothes. With Dalton and his daughter coming for Rosh Hashanah, I'd hate to be shamed by my own sister."

"I'll try, but she's stubborn. How are Michael's kids? Are they doing okay?"

"You call him, *bubula*. He's your brother."

Marla agreed and signed off. Delaying the obligatory call until later, she phoned the chiropractor's office to schedule an appointment. Then she finally took a break to refresh herself, stuff down some chopped liver on Ritz crackers, and consult the computer for background information on Wilda Cleaver.

By the time Dalton came with Brianna at six-thirty, she had more information on the Fort Lauderdale company that had hired Wilda to play the part of Sequina the Seer. Hopping back and forth with excitement, she greeted them at the door and ushered them into the kitchen. Vail gave her a quick kiss before depositing a large paper bag on the counter. Brianna bent over to pet Spooks, leaping at her ankles.

"Did you know Wilda Cleaver lived in Cassadaga, where she got involved in a telemarketing scheme?" Marla began.

Vail's hot gaze passed over her while his mouth curved in a lazy grin. "She ripped off thousands of customers with a phony psychic hot line, calling herself Sequina the Seer and charging two-fifty a minute."

"You rat. Why didn't you tell me about her background?" Marla clamped a hand on her hip.

"I didn't want to influence your impressions. Besides, she seems to have come clean. Her clients rave about her in a manner that suggests she has some real talent."

Marla pointed to the copied articles scattered on the table. "A man who works in the post office gave me those. Wilda isn't welcome at the spiritual camp." She helped him unpack their meals, her mouth watering at the aroma of garlic and onions.

"I'd hoped you would find out something new," Vail admitted.

"Titan Resources was the company that collected unpaid bills from Wilda's unsuspecting customers. They sponsored Sequina the Seer's television commercials and Web site." Marla laid out silverware, then put a two-liter bottle of ginger ale on the table along with glasses filled with ice. "The word Titan reminded me of something I'd seen in Peter McGraw's office. I forgot about it until now. On his desk was an envelope with *Iapetus* written across it. The lawyer saw me looking at the note and snatched it away. Guess what Iapetus means?"

With a bemused look, Dalton played along. "What?"

"Iapetus was one of the titans in Greek mythology and the father of Atlas. Don't you see? This could mean there's a connection between Peter McGraw and the European, Atlas Boyd."

Too buoyed to eat, Marla watched Vail dig into his chicken and vegetables. Brianna ignored them both, chatting on her dad's cell phone while she picked at her food.

"An attorney from Peter McGraw's firm defended Wilda against the state," Vail remarked, chewing with gusto. "McGraw owned a stake in Titan Resources. Assuming he's the link to Atlas Boyd, how did Carolyn get involved?"

"Through Wilda, dork-face," Brianna chipped in. The girl must be adept at multitasking, Marla reflected, if she could listen to two conversations at once. "Let's work this out," she said. "When Wilda lived in Cassadaga, she was approached by Peter McGraw, who offered her the chance to make much more money than she could bring in as a genuine medium. The postal clerk told me she grew up in the Bronx. As a butcher's daughter, Wilda may have craved a more affluent lifestyle. She might even have regarded McGraw's opportunity as ordained by the spirits."

"Why take her? He could've established someone else in that role." Vail regarded her from under his heavy brows.

"You have to admit Wilda has a certain flamboyant style. Moreover, there may be a statement of truth in what she tells people." Falling silent, Marla lifted a forkful of buttery brown rice to her mouth.

"Oh? I'm surprised to hear you say that."

"In Cassadaga I consulted a psychic who told me a lot about myself. I'm not sure how to interpret her reading, or if her advice is valid, but she seemed to share Wilda's premonition about one of my family members. Anyway, I have a theory."

"Go on."

Marla glanced between father and daughter. It brightened her kitchen to have them both present. "My guess is McGraw hooked Wilda, who later became friends with Carolyn. Maybe Wilda mentioned to him that Carolyn was looking for investors."

"Enter Atlas Boyd, a financier with money to spend in this country. Carolyn begins sponsoring French students at the beauty academy, who are later employed in her salon. I've suspected that much," Vail let on, "but I don't see what's in it for Boyd."

"Couldn't you get any more information on him?"

"I'm waiting to hear back from the guys in Immigration. Seeing as how Peter McGraw's practice includes that aspect, I smell a skunk. Seems to me they may all be wrapped up in some scheme together."

"I can ask Claudia. Jeanine told me Carolyn was about to fire her. I meant to get back to her last week, but things piled up on me. I'd also like to see if her absences coincide with our land-lord's business trips."

"Sorry if I messed up your schedule," Brianna mumbled.

Marla touched her arm. "Oh no, honey, I wasn't complaining about you. You know you're more important to me than any of this stuff." That was true, she realized in surprise. Her glance caught Vail's, and she felt her insides turn to mush. Nothing else mattered when a child's well-being was threatened. "I'll talk to Claudia tomorrow. Maybe she can tell me if Carolyn's friend Rosemary ever showed up in the salon. Rosemary captured the killer's attention somehow. For all her rambling, I think the bingo player knew what was going down."

Chapter
Eighteen

Marla slipped into Hairstyle Heaven on Wednesday afternoon, having found little spare time the day before between work, taking Spooks for a grooming, and stocking up on groceries under the threat of another tropical storm. Squalls erupted with frequency during September, but thankfully none of them had yet hit home with hurricane force.

"Yo, Marla," said Bunny, chewing on a piece of gum. The vapid receptionist, rifling through a *Salon News* magazine, gave her a cursory glance.

Marla's gaze flickered beyond the front desk to the stations lined up like tanks on parade. Claudia waved from where she was doing foils on a yuppie patron. Jeanine, shaving a man's nape, offered an acknowledging nod. Other operators hovered around their occupied chairs, applying coloring agents, moussing and spraying, and curling with hot irons. An unwanted image burgeoned in her mind: Wilda signing over the place to her. She'd expand her business to offer spa services and turn this into a center for massages, facials, and more. Affluent clients were always asking Marla where they could get a good herbal wrap. Think of the possibilities for broadening her horizons.

Think of the rent. Extra electric bills. Staffing problems. Added bookkeeping. Yikes. She'd stick to styling and sleuthing.

Leaning across the counter, Marla lowered her voice to speak to Bunny. "I need your help," she said. "Do you have a record of Claudia's schedule? I'd like to get a sense of her days off. In case she decides to move on, you know, I may offer her a job. But I don't want to step on Wilda's toes, so please don't say anything yet."

Bunny gave her a conspiratorial wink, especially when Marla slid her a twenty-dollar bill in her closed palm. "It'll take me a few minutes. How far back do you want to go?"

"The past couple of months will work. I'll say hello to the girls in the meantime."

Inquiring about their well-being, Marla determined that things were running smoothly, and that Wilda had even begun taking care of inventory. A wave of disappointment washed over her. She had truly hoped Wilda might move the location for the establishment. Fear struck her that Wilda still might sell it to Atlas Boyd, but when she mentioned that possibility to Claudia, the stylist negated that idea.

"Madame does not trust Monsieur Boyd. She said something about his stars being out of alignment, whatever that means. I cannot say what her plans are for us."

"I'll talk to her and see what I can learn," Marla promised. *I'll also find out why she insisted I must find Carolyn's killer. Is it to throw suspicion off herself? Could this have been a plot with her former employer to gain control over the salon?*

Armed with the list Bunny had given her, Marla hustled back to her own place. Before her three o'clock appointment arrived, she dialed Vail's cell phone. "I'd like to see if Claudia's days off correspond with our landlord's out-of-town trips. I got her schedule. Would you be able to look into it? I doubt Mr. Thomson would give me that information, nor do I want to show up at his house and ask his wife. You could do it as part of your investigation if I fax it to you."

"All right," his gruff voice answered, "but I can't promise I'll get to it today."

Frowning, Marla studied a clump of dust on the storeroom floor. She should talk to the cleaning staff about doing a better job in there.

Cleaning staff! Why hadn't she thought of that before?

"I'll send you a copy," she told Vail before cutting him off. Her fingers shaking with excitement, she punched the number for a janitorial service that was used by most of the stores in the shopping strip and had taken over cleaning duties for Carolyn's salon.

"Hello," Julio answered with a heavy Hispanic accent.

"Hi, it's Marla Shore from Cut 'N Dye salon." She hesitated, wondering how to phrase her query. "I was thinking about that poor woman who died from the other beauty shop and what I could do to help her staff. When you cleaned Hairstyle Heaven, maybe you found things that weren't easy to identify. You know, since I'm from a salon and all, I could tell what's still useful."

She heard Julio's thoughtful sigh. "Anything important would have gone to the cops or the woman's sister, senorita."

"What about unimportant stuff? I suppose you threw out the trash. And besides, the police probably examined it."

"Just one moment. I will contact Perez. He does their place."

Marla tapped her fingers on the counter while she waited. Finally, Julio's voice came back on line.

"There is one bag left. I should call the authorities."

"They probably looked through everything before letting you into the place," Marla said quickly. "Can I pick it up?" Maybe Vail had overlooked something that hadn't held significance at the time. Her heart thudded. Things were finally starting to gel. Once this case was behind them, she and Vail could focus on their relationship.

Marla finished her last customer in record time, but it was too late. Julio's office had closed. No matter; she'd stop by his workplace in the morning. Fulfilling her family obligations by visiting Aunt Polly, Marla convinced the elderly woman to set aside a date when they could go to the bank together to add Marla's name on her checking account. Then Marla helped Polly fill out the application form for hurricane evacuation. Satisfied that her aunt had enough food in the refrigerator and no more unpaid bills lying around, Marla left.

Storm reports gripped her attention on the news that evening. Another system was churning toward the northeast and was expected to gather strength over open water. Drat, Marla didn't want any delays now that they were getting close. Vail hadn't spoken much about the investigation into Rosemary's death. Maybe he didn't want to reveal his findings until he connected the evidence to Carolyn's case. What about the fingerprints he'd hoped to gain from Sam's glass at their barbecue? Nothing must have come of it, or he'd have told her. Nevertheless, Marla called her mother anyway to inquire about their date.

"We're going to brunch on Sunday, and then Sam wants to show me his house on the lake," Anita said in her soothing tone. "He invited you along, but I declined. You have enough to do on your days off, although it was thoughtful of him."

"Yes, it was. Did he say where he lives?"

"Not exactly, just that it's east, and he's worried about the weather. He joked that I may have to help him put up storm shutters."

"You'll have to cancel if it gets that bad." A cascade of thunder sounded, followed by the splatter of rainfall on the roof. "This isn't a good time to be near the coast."

"Stop worrying, *bubula*. That's my job."

Not anymore. "By the way, did you ever ask your friends about Dr. Hennings?" Marla had contemplated the various reasons why Carolyn might have had a hold on him. Could she have caught the chiropractor at income tax evasion? Prescription fraud? Faulty billing practices? Or something more personal, like he didn't want patients to learn he was gay?

"Well, yes, now that you mention it," Anita replied. "Two people I know had gone to Dr. Hennings for back problems. Their Medicare statements listed treatments they'd never had."

"That's great, Ma. I'll talk to you later." Now she had a bit of leverage she could use as a bluff.

Thursday morning, she stopped by the janitorial service to pick up the bag from Julio and drove on to the doctor's office, where she had an early appointment.

As she entered the waiting room, Marla considered what to say. After her gaze swept the empty seats, she zoomed in on the receptionist. Voices drifted from an examination room: Dr. Hennings and a patient. She might have only a few minutes to question the girl behind the front desk.

"Hi, I'm Marla Shore. I have a nine o'clock appointment. Gee, the doctor must come in early if he's already seeing someone. You know, I couldn't remember when I was here last. I believe I was here on . . ." She mentioned the date Carolyn died.

The clerk made pleasant small talk while shuffling through their appointment calendar. "Here we go." Her finger ran down the entries. "I don't see your name. Are you sure this is the right day?"

Marla peered at the upside-down writing. "It appears Dr. Hennings was fully booked that Tuesday. I guess he doesn't get many breaks, huh?" she said, smiling encouragingly. "Does he even leave for lunch?"

The girl's mouth set in a thin line. "Dr. Hennings won't leave the clinic when our schedule is full. If I recall, that day was so busy with walk-ins that he didn't have time for meals." Her eyes glittered. "Is there a particular reason why you want to know?"

"I'm just such a ditz-brain; I don't remember my own schedule half the time. It doesn't matter." Waving her hand airily, Marla paced the room until her name was called, about ten minutes later.

She trotted after Dr. Hennings into an examination room, where he nudged the door shut and turned to face her. "So. What brings you back, Marla?"

"My neck is bothering me again."

"I see," he said, although his tone expressed disbelief.

While he palpated her vertebrae, Marla spoke in a casual voice. "It's so sad about Carolyn. Do you know she confided in her friend Rosemary, who told me about their conversation? And now poor Rosemary is dead."

His hands held her head, then he twisted with a crack. Marla cried out at the jolt.

"I thought Carolyn wasn't that close with her bingo pal."

"Oh? How do you know they played bingo together?"

"Carolyn told me things, too. Like how much you aggravated her." Wrapping his arms around her from behind, he jerked her spine with another loud pop.

Reeling, Marla tried to concentrate. "Rosemary indicated you felt the same about Carolyn," she said, turning to face him. "Was it because she found out about your scheme?"

"I don't know what you're talking about."

"Ever heard of Medicare fraud? It's rampant in South Florida with all the senior citizens. Probably many of them don't even read their statements to see if Medicare paid for treatments they never got. Doctors pad bills for tests and procedures all the time and hope that patients will file claim forms without checking them."

"No doubt that's true, but so what?"

"I've met several of your former patients who've said your charges were unjustified. Carolyn had proof, didn't she?"

"You're guessing." He scowled but didn't move toward her.

"Carolyn took advantage of people. I'm figuring she wanted to get paid to keep quiet, but you should know she kept records of every payment."

"Even if you're right, her bank receipts won't point to me; I pay certain debts in cash."

Maybe you got tired of paying. Carolyn died from a broken neck. With your expertise, that method would be a snap for you. Marla glanced toward the treatment-room door that had drifted partially open. She heard voices coming from the reception area. Stepping nearer the exit, she said, "The authorities are looking into the background of everyone who knew Carolyn."

His jaw twitched. "What's your point?"

"She was murdered. Don't you want to see her killer brought to justice?"

"I didn't do it. That's all the cops care about."

"Oh, so you're not worried about what they might find?"

"You mean how Carolyn discovered my creative billing techniques?" He shrugged as though it were inconsequential. "I could afford to pay her off. She even started referring patients to me."

"That sounds like something Carolyn would do. How did she catch on?" Marla's voice held praise, as though she admired her rival's chutzpah.

He glanced away. "I billed her insurer for certain extra procedures. Carolyn came to me instead of notifying her insurance company."

"I see." Marla remembered a case on the news involving an orthopedic surgeon who bilked insurers for services he didn't perform. He gave massages that he reported as prescribed neuromuscular therapy. Some of the massages had an additional therapeutic benefit, mainly the doctor's, who took advantage of his female patients.

Dr. Hennings gripped her arm. "While I was relieved by Carolyn's death because she couldn't threaten my practice any further, her loss saddened me. I wouldn't have harmed her."

The sincerity in his eyes convinced Marla. "Detective Vail isn't interested in chasing down insurance fraud," she said, shaking him off, "but he will want to hear about Carolyn's activities. Can you think of anyone else she might have roped the same way?"

At his negative answer, she took her leave, feeling she had achieved closure in terms of the chiropractor's relationship with Carolyn. If the police wanted to follow up on his illegal activities, that was their prerogative.

Reaching her car, Marla took a peek inside the trash bag in her trunk and gave a snort of dismay. Nothing but old *Modern Salon* magazines. No wonder the cops passed up on them. Climbing into the Toyota, she glanced at the clock. Another half hour remained before her first customer. Claudia was supposed to be back at work, and Mr. Thomson should be in his office. Figuring Vail hadn't had a chance yet to look into the latter's activities, she decided to swing by his office.

"Hello, Marla," the landlord said, greeting her from behind his desk. His drawn eyebrows indicated he wasn't happy to see her. "It's too early for you to be bringing the October rent."

"I'm not here about my salon." Sinking into a seat, she spoke rapidly before he could chase her out. "I was wondering if you knew what's going to happen with Carolyn's place. I spoke to Wilda, and she was considering moving its location closer to Miami. One of the girls told me that Atlas Boyd made her an offer, but she turned him down."

Thomson's eyes narrowed. "If you're so interested, why don't you ask Miz Cleaver yourself?"

"I just thought you might have heard something. Did you know Wilda had a previous business association with Peter McGraw? He's the attorney who handled Carolyn's estate, and I also gathered he helped bring in the French girls who staff her shop."

"Funny you should mention that." Folding his hands on the desk, Thomson leaned forward. "I just got a call from some officials who said those people extended their limits in this country. Something about their visas being fraudulently obtained. I said I didn't know anything about it." Sweat beaded his brow. "Is this your way of causing me trouble?"

"Excuse me?" Marla sat up straight. "You're the one who let Carolyn into the shopping strip, knowing the competition would hurt me. I don't know why you dislike me so much. You almost ran me out of here by accepting Stan's offer when he tried to outbid my lease. He'd aligned himself with Carolyn then, but when my former husband failed to derail me, you let Carolyn in anyway. How much did she bribe you?"

Thomson wouldn't meet her penetrating gaze. "She didn't have the money."

"No? Then who did? Or were you seduced into agreement?"

He clenched his fists. "I knew this would get me in hot water. If only Alice would stop comparing me to her brother."

"What?"

"My wife. All she does is tell me how great Eric looks because he dyes his hair and works out at a health club. Like she's not happy with me the way I am." He glared at her. "Why else do you think I started seeing Carolyn?"

"You tell me." She'd never glimpsed this view of her landlord before. He rarely talked about his family.

Pointing to his white dress shirt, he said, "I have a dandruff problem. It's embarrassing, and Carolyn was helping me with treatments. When Mr. Boyd offered me a generous down payment for her to occupy our vacant space, I couldn't refuse. She was lucky to have found someone to back her. Carolyn wasn't the ogre you make her out to be."

"We had our personal differences, but that doesn't get around the fact that you knew having two salons in the same location would be harmful to me. I run a good business, and I've always been on time with rental payments. Doesn't customer loyalty mean anything to you?"

He shrugged. "Having a high occupancy rate means more to the developers."

"All right, then," Marla said spitefully. "What about Claudia?"

He gave her a startled look. "What about her?"

"If she's one of those illegal visa holders, you'll have to end your affair, won't you?" When his mouth gaped, she added, "I asked Detective Vail to check the dates of your out-of-town business trips against Claudia's days off. I thought there might be a correlation."

His skin paled. "Alice can't find out. You'll tell the detective not to talk to her, won't you?"

Marla smirked. "It might be too late, but I'll try, especially if you make an effort to move Carolyn's salon away from here." Truthfully, she'd already gotten used to the place, and it no longer impacted her business. With Carolyn's nasty pranks ended, Marla had become busier than ever.

Rising, she smoothed her skirt. "One more thing. Do you think Claudia had anything to do with Carolyn's death? A little birdie told me Carolyn planned to fire her."

Thomson stood, his full height not much above Marla's five feet six inches. "Claudia's guilty of many things, but not killing her boss."

"Is that because you did it?"

"Huh?"

"Wilda told me you had combat experience in the Marines. You'd know how to get rid of someone silently."

"Don't be absurd."

"Did you murder her because she discovered your affair with Claudia? Or were you afraid of being implicated regarding the immigrants she employed without proper documentation?"

"Maybe you should pose the same questions to Atlas Boyd."

"That man certainly throws his weight around the salon. His influence over Carolyn must have been considerable."

"Perhaps she intended to pull out from whatever agreement they had, and he didn't like that idea," Thomson suggested.

"You may have a point." The European seemed the type who expected obedience from his underlings. How would he have felt if he financed Carolyn, then she turned her back on him?

Rounding his desk, Thomson stopped in front of her. "Look, I'm sorry we haven't always gotten along. You're right in that you've been a good tenant. You'll keep quiet to Alice, and I'll see what I can do for you in return, okay?"

"I don't blackmail people, Mr. Thomson. I'll share what I know with Detective Vail, but I can't see any reason to involve your wife."

Returning to her establishment, Marla got caught up in her duties until closing. As she was leaving, she spied Sam hurrying toward her along the pavement.

"Hey, Marla," the wiry fellow said, ruffling his silvery hair with one hand. "I've been meaning to stop by and say hello. Your mom tells me you won't be able to join us this weekend."

"No, I'm sorry, I have too much to do."

"How about Brianna? Would she like some relief from her homework?"

Marla gave him an odd look. What made him think the teenager would prefer the company of an older couple to her friends? "I'll ask, but I wouldn't count on it. Ma said you're taking her to see your house. I don't remember where you said you lived."

Sam grinned, waving a hand. "It's a private community." He watched a pair of young women drive past. "Check with the kid, will you? She'd have a good time. I've a boat on the lake."

"Sure. But where . . . ?" Her skirt whipped about her legs. "It's rather breezy, isn't it?" she asked, distracted by the gusty weather.

"That hurricane is heading directly for the coast," Sam warned, concern dimming his pale blue eyes. "Did you hear it's been up-graded to a Category Two? They say it may get here early next week unless it picks up speed. Best keep an eye on the news."

Marla hadn't heard anything about the latest storm, having been preoccupied with the murder investigation. She preferred to keep an eye on Brianna, so she detoured to Vail's house, realizing her anxiety over the girl bordered on paranoia. Either she was becoming too much like Dalton, or her latent psychic powers had awakened.

A sense of impending disaster twisted her gut, and it didn't herald the approaching gale.

Chapter
Nineteen

After performing her usual mundane chores at home, Marla sat eating a bowl of borscht and rye bread with butter in front of the television. Annoyed with all the commercials on the news station, she'd just switched to the weather channel when the phone rang.

"Thanks for checking on Brie," Vail said on the other end, his deep, resonant voice curling her toes with pleasure. "You wouldn't have to keep coming over if we were together."

"I know. We need to talk about it."

She'd already decided that she could never live in his house on a permanent basis. It just didn't suit her personality, and it held too many memories from his past.

"Rosh Hashanah is coming up. Do you think we could discuss things before I meet your family?" he said. "I'd like to know where we stand before you introduce me."

She heard the resolve in his voice and swallowed. "Of course. This weekend?"

"Can't. I'll be tied up working on these cases."

"Oh." Would their lives always be disrupted by his work? Her own job necessitated a regular schedule; she could count on the same days off each week. His erratic pattern meant Brianna couldn't rely on him, either. *If it doesn't bother Brie, it shouldn't bother me,* Marla concluded. They'd find ways to get around his irregular work habits.

"Have you learned anything new?" she asked, diverting his attention from their personal differences.

"Nothing I can talk about, except the net is closing. What are your plans for the next few days?"

While his inquiry might have annoyed her early in their relationship, now she knew he asked out of concern for her welfare. "I'll be working Friday and Saturday, but I kept my evenings free for you. Since you're busy, I might call one of my girlfriends and make plans for tomorrow night." She hesitated, hoping to avoid being tied down. "What about Brianna?"

"She has a skating party and a movie date. Her friend's mother will be driving."

"Ma has a date with Sam this weekend."

"You might advise her to stay home." A heavy silence. "You know, with the weather and all."

"Is there something you'd like to tell me?"

"I want to keep my women safe until this is over."

His women. She weighed her response. "Unless you can be more specific, I don't see any reason for us to hide in a cave. Oh, I almost forgot. I saw Dr. Hennings today. Are you aware he cheats Medicare by making false claims?"

"That's someone else's department, but, yes, he's under investigation."

"Instinct tells me he didn't kill Carolyn. He was too forthright discussing his situation with me. So who does that leave?"

"Plenty of people," Vail murmured.

"I spoke to my landlord. Mr. Thomson had a motive if Carolyn threatened to expose his affair to his wife, but he pointed the finger at Atlas Boyd."

"I didn't get a chance to check Thomson's schedule against Claudia's yet."

"It may not be necessary. I'm interested in how Boyd's name keeps popping up. He made an offer to Wilda for the salon. Have you found out anything more about him?"

"Yep. I'm finding out a lot about McGraw, Boyd, and the victim. I suspect Rosemary got killed because she knew too much. But then there's—"

"Who?"

"Can't say. Just watch the company you keep. I'll be in touch." He rang off, leaving her with the conclusion that he withheld important information.

Marla got a break on Saturday when Wilda phoned her at the salon. Dumping a pile of wet towels in the dryer, she hustled to the extension in the back storeroom.

"I heard from an old friend that you've been nosing around Cassadaga asking about me," Wilda said in a high-pitched tone. "You'll be sorry. You should be paying more attention to Carolyn's business. Now that you've opened a door to the negative energy, it surrounds you. Trouble waits in the shadows."

Staring at tubes of coloring agents lining the shelves, Marla gripped the receiver. "Is that a threat?"

"No dear, it's a warning. I'm sensing bad vibes around you."

"You ran a phony psychic hotline in Cassadaga. Why should I believe anything you say when you were stealing people's money?"

"I paid the price, or the fine, I should say. And I learned a valuable lesson, too," Wilda added. "My talents were exploited by nasty people. I was too young to know differently, and I got caught up with greed. Everyone makes mistakes."

"Yes, they do," Marla replied quietly. The shame of her own past still haunted her.

"Despite the danger, you must carry on. Walking the path of truth can be dangerous, but stay your course. Just be careful."

Forewarned was forearmed. What was Wilda trying in some oblique way to tell her? Did she suspect her former associate, the attorney? Was she too afraid to name him personally? Or did she still feel an inappropriate sense of loyalty?

All questions, no answers. Marla approached her next customer, a simple blow-out, with theories tumbling through her mind. Maybe she could work it out later. She hadn't made any plans for that night, not with the weather threatening to deteriorate. She'd tried to get hold of Anita to advise her to postpone her date, but Ma didn't answer the phone. Nor could Marla contact Sam; he had the weekend off. Hopefully, they'd be smart enough to watch the news and get in touch with each other.

Worry gnawed at her when she glanced outside. The afternoon sky appeared flat as a straightened strand of bleached hair. Rather than the usual summer blue with scattered clouds of fluff, the sky had a peculiar cloudless tint, as though the storm fermenting out to sea had sucked all the moisture from the air while it built up energy to become an avenging monster.

Meanwhile, another tropical depression had formed just east of the Lesser Antilles. If only the paths of these tempests weren't so unpredictable. The one after Bret, forecast to hit the southeast coast, ended up being downgraded from a Category Four to a Category Two hurricane that struck Louisiana.

Similarly, Hurricane Dennis continued to gain strength on its northwest path straight for the Keys. Meteorologists expected a pattern that would keep it from turning away. The storm should be about two hundred miles off Florida by Monday, and although it barely made hurricane status now, Dennis could end up with winds in excess of ninety miles per hour. That still wouldn't make it a Category Two, but it was enough to cause flooding and minimal damage. Marla worried about her mother visiting Sam's house, in case he lived near the shore. The South Florida Water Management District had already lowered water levels in canals, and residents might be advised to evacuate low-lying areas. Why didn't she know his address?

Television reports showed supermarket shelves going bare of bottled water, batteries, and canned goods. Marla checked her supplies, including dog food, then phoned Anita again. The phone kept ringing, ringing.

Should she go over there? Her mother could be anywhere, shopping, or out with a friend. She'd chastise Marla for getting alarmed over nothing. *And she'll be right. I can always get hold of her in the morning.*

But when morning came, the news was even more sobering. The *Sun-Sentinel* front page showed an enormous circular orange swirl in the Atlantic Ocean with the headline, "Dennis Bears Down on Southeast Florida Coast." Now the storm was predicted to hit on Monday with winds in excess of 110 mph. That would make it a Category Three; tonight would see blustery squalls as the first storms rolled in, then it would only get worse. Television news stations presented running commentary regarding hurricane preparedness.

Marla's lip curled. It figured the monsoon season would bring one headed this way that shared her landlord's given name.

Knowing Anita woke up early, Marla dialed her number at nine o'clock on Sunday. She hung onto the line, clutching the receiver while waiting for her mother to pick up. *Come on, answer the damn phone.*

Oh, heck. She'd have to drive by Anita's place after all. Having dressed, eaten, and walked Spooks, she grabbed her purse and keys and rushed out the door. Hesitating, she remembered the trash bag in her trunk. At least she could remove that load.

Dumping the pile of magazines on her kitchen table, she noticed the issues weren't too old. She kept her new ones in the salon; maybe she'd look at these later. Then again, maybe not. They'd belonged to Carolyn and might transmit the dead woman's negative energy. *Be mindful of Wilda's words*, she told herself. *Don't tempt fate.*

A crumpled article fell out from between some pages, and she grasped it just as the telephone shrilled.

Her knees buckled when she heard her mother's voice on the other end. "Ma? Where are you? I've been trying since yesterday to get hold of you." Glancing at the Caller ID, she noted it wasn't her mother's name. The person listed was Sam Cleaver. Cleaver?

"I'm at Sam's place," Anita said in a strained tone. "It's lovely here; he suggested I invite you and Brianna to join us."

"Didn't you hear the weather report? You need to come home." A sense of urgency shook her. "I'll get you. Give me the address."

"Sam said he'll meet you."

Wind rattled the window panes. "What for? I can drive there." Her ears picked up the sound of a gasp. "Ma, are you okay?"

"She's fine," Sam replied. "We're having some trouble with the phone line. I'll call you back."

Chewing her lower lip, Marla waited for his return call. When it didn't come right away, she glanced at the paper in her hand. Good heavens, it was an old newspaper article describing a brutal murder up north. Some teenage girl had been abducted and killed in New Jersey. Marla recognized Carolyn's handwritten scrawl across the top: *Ask Sam if this is near where he lived.*

Why Sam? And how had Carolyn obtained this piece?

Rifling through the other magazines, she failed to come across anything else exciting. Still, this was enough to make her scoot out the door in search of her mother. The White Pages had yielded an address for Samuel Cleaver. That didn't mesh with Sam Levy, but Marla would ask him about it in person.

Lifting her cell phone, Marla intended to call Vail, but service was down. Must be the storm causing trouble already. To the east, a huge bank of angry gray clouds roiled forward. That pinkish tinge in the sky didn't bode well. How did that proverb go? *Red sky in the morning is a sailor's sure warning; red sky at night is the sailor's delight.* She hoped to make it before the rain. Slapping the cellular device into its charger, Marla cursed herself for not having called Vail before she left the house. That would've been the smart thing to do. Now she raced against time to reach Anita when he could have sent a squad car.

But why should he? Just because her breath caught with panic didn't mean she was onto something. Vail still suspected Peter McGraw or Atlas Boyd of being involved in Carolyn's murder. He had considered Sam at one point, but the detective hadn't said another word about it. Anyway, why would Sam want to harm her mother? He wanted to date her. Unless it was a ruse to get Marla, and through Marla, to lure Brianna. If he had a predilection for such things. If he was the child killer described in that worn article.

Nah, she was letting her imagination run away again. Logic kicked in. Sam was just trying to impress her mother.

Thirty minutes later plus two wrong turns and a dirt road, Marla decided she'd better impress upon him the need to evacuate his location. South of Dania, his address presented a target too close to the shoreline. Her Camry bumped down a clamshell driveway flanked by live oaks and seagrape trees. At a circular swath in front of the address, she jolted to a halt behind a black Honda. Dead leaves glossy with moisture blanketed the hood.

Thunder pealed in the distance as she emerged. Heaviness hung in the air, not a leaf stirring, the plants respiring quietly as they waited. A spicy scent tickled her nose. It mingled with the earthy aroma of decay.

Her nape prickled at the isolation. Dark water glinted beyond a grove of gnarled mangroves at the far end of the yard where a lake bordered the lone cottage. Above, the harsh brightness of the sky had given way to a sickly yellow glow. Crickets sang at a louder pitch than normal, as though they knew something ominous blew on the breeze. The stillness pierced her, especially as she noted there weren't any signs of her mother's presence. Sam must have picked Anita up in his car, if she was here.

She turned toward the single-story house whose windows stared at her like vacant eyes. It appeared to be built from coral rock, with a shingle roof and step-up front porch. When her knock failed to summon a reply, she twisted the doorknob. It opened easily.

Having locked her purse in the Toyota, Marla dropped the car keys into one of her jeans pockets and gripped her Swiss Army knife in her right hand. It gave her a measure of comfort as she proceeded inside.

"Sam? Is anyone home?" she called out, a tremor in her voice. "Ma, are you here?"

She stepped into a small foyer, her heart beating alarmingly fast. A quick glance showed her a living room straight ahead, bedrooms to the right, and a kitchen forward to the left. There might be a family room in the back facing the lake. This was like no home she'd imagined Sam inhabiting, however. Her image of the nice old man included a neat abode with sentimental mementos from his past.

She found mementos, all right, but they weren't the kind she'd expected.

Her stomach lurched as she stooped over the photographs strewn on the unmade bed in the master bedroom. They showed teenage girls in various poses mixed in with articles detailing gruesome murders. Her numbed mind made the connection that her startled gaze refused to acknowledge.

Souvenir locks of hair, carefully labeled in plastic bags, were stapled to the photographs. All of the girls were nudes, with an unfocused quality to their eyes.

Slapping a hand to her mouth to hold down the queasy contents of her stomach, Marla whirled around as a footfall sounded behind her.

Sam faced her, his lanky frame and silver hair no longer disarming her. Marla's heart leapt into her throat. She couldn't speak. Even though she held the closed pocket knife in her fist, her body froze.

"I'm glad you came, my dear," Sam said, blocking the doorway. "I've been wanting to show you my collection."

"Y-your collection?"

"You were so interested in Carolyn's treasures, I'd hoped to show you mine. That's how we connected, you know. Carolyn told me about her hair jewelry. I couldn't help mentioning that I kept hair as well. Fascinating custom, keeping remembrances of the dead by saving locks of hair."

"Is that why you got rid of Carolyn, because she knew too much about you?"

"I was showing her a couple of my pieces, and an old news article fell out. It must've gotten stuck to the plastic wrap. The conniving bitch latched onto it and learned more about me than I cared for her to know."

"So you lured her to the meter room?"

Wetting his lips like a slobbering wolf, he nodded. "I had the key from the hardware store. She thought I meant to pay her. Dumb fool. After I finished with her, I switched off your electricity, hoping you'd be blamed when you showed up at the scene. It didn't work that way because the police detective was soft on you."

"And Rosemary?"

"She saw me coming out of Carolyn's apartment. I knew they were friends. Carolyn may have told her about me. Then she started talking to you. All the trails lead to you, don't they?" He wrung his hands, an anticipatory gleam in his eyes.

"What about Wilda Cleaver? Weren't you afraid Carolyn told her psychic adviser about you, also? Carolyn was closer to her than Rosemary."

Something flickered behind his expression. "Wilda wouldn't expose me."

Marla considered mentioning the dead woman's message but decided against it. Wilda had her own reasons for involving Marla.

"Did you steal Carolyn's hair jewelry?" she asked, stalling for time.

He advanced closer. "I'd made an impression of her house key, so it was easy to get a copy. After she went to work that morning, I slipped inside her apartment and helped myself to what I could find. Then I reported for duty at the hardware store and called Carolyn to meet me out back. Wrong move on her part to threaten me. She should have kept her mouth shut, but she couldn't pass up the opportunity to blackmail me."

Apparently, Carolyn had reached into several pockets. Her rival had been ruthless when it came to acquiring income.

"I gave her a payment all right, one she deserved. Now it's your turn." His lean form blocked her escape route.

Feeling like a trapped animal, Marla kept her eyes fastened on his. "Where's my mother?"

"Oh, she's secure for now. When the storm hits, it'll be different."

"Why take her? Why not come after me directly?"

"Anita was my bait to get you here. I really want you to call your lovely friend, Brianna, and tell her I'm on my way to pick her up. Let her think she's joining you for the day." He laughed, a nightmarish cackle. "In a way, she will be."

Marla's blood iced. "Brianna. So your plan *was* to use me as a lure to bring her here. Did you try to get her the other day in your car? A masked man accosted her after school."

"She didn't recognize me in my disguise, did she? I should have waited until I had you. The girl is smart but she's soft on her daddy's girlfriend. Maybe I'll tie you up and do you both to-gether."

He gave an evil leer, and Marla shut from her mind the images that pressed to the surface.

"No one is going out with the storm coming," she said, trying to reason with him. "This place could be flooded. We need to evacuate."

"There's a telephone, Marla. Make the call."

"You're sick. You molest children and then murder them. Detective Vail knows. I told him I was coming."

"He doesn't know anything. I was never caught. I moved to Florida before things got too hot."

Marla edged sideways, aiming for the door. "Did you really live in New Jersey like you said?"

"Nope. I wasn't a building developer, either." He grinned, a hollow effect with his frigid eyes. "I worked at a slaughterhouse in the Midwest before moving to the Bronx. My brother had a butcher shop in the Jewish section. When I went to work for him, I took on the name Levy. Figured it would make me less con-spicuous."

He held up his hands. "You should see how I used to break the necks of chickens."

Her heart raced when Carolyn's prostrate form came to mind, her head bent at a peculiar angle.

She glanced out the window. Swollen clouds scurried across the blackening sky like runaway locomotives. Even the edge of a hurricane delivered torrential downpours. If she succeeded in getting away from Sam, she might get stuck here once the rain began. Her gaze swung back to the only other occupant of the room. Drawing her arms behind her body, she opened the Swiss Army knife. It wasn't much, but any weapon was better than none.

"Are you going to make that call or not?" Sam demanded, his tone lacking any inflection.

"Why?" Marla asked, curiosity compelling her. "Why did you kill those girls?"

"Because they hurt people," he said. "They don't care how much damage they inflict. They're mean and cruel, leaving us guys out in the cold, not realizing how the scars they leave can last forever. They deserve punishment."

He must have been rejected by a young woman and he'd never recovered. Marla could remember times she'd been callous to men who'd courted her, but it was only because she'd had a lot to learn about relationships. It wasn't intentional, just a sign of immaturity.

"I haven't done anything to you," she reminded him.

"You're just the same as all the rest, dangling that detective by his nose while you have a good time. I'll make you pay for your meanness."

"Let my mother go," Marla pleaded. "Where did you put her?" She slid a notch toward the doorway, hands still behind her.

A gust of wind shook the house. "I'll take you to Anita." Baring his teeth, he reached for her.

"I'll find her myself, you bastard."

When he lunged at her, Marla slashed him with the knife. He jerked back, yowling with pain. It gave her the moment she needed to charge for the door. Which way to go? He'd said Anita was all right for now, but she wouldn't be once the storm hit. That indicated Ma must be outside.

Bits of shell formed a lumpy surface underfoot as Marla trotted around the structure's exterior, calling for her mother. Leaving without her was not an option. Presuming Sam to be wounded, she paused to listen for a response. A chameleon altered its brown color to green as it slid from branch to grass, then back to brown again as it scooted up a tree. She stared at a squirrel poised on a branch. Slowly, it turned to face the south, as if the creature knew something she didn't.

Bird calls altered their range. Instead of individual warbling sounds, Marla discerned a single cry, birds in unison wailing with a sharp, edgy sound. Then suddenly it ended, and silence fell. The yellow sky darkened into copper. And then the wind gusts strengthened.

Pine trees swayed; oak leaves rustled. The second gust blew stronger, producing an eerie whistling through the branches. The third one brought rain, cascading in sheets, driven by the wind.

Splattering onto her head and shoulders, the downpour quickly soaked her. The day had grown so dark as to imitate night. She heard, rather than saw, Sam crashing down the front steps. Now what? He must have hidden Anita in the woods or by the lake. Either way, Ma would be at risk exposed to the elements. Droplets cascaded down her face as she trod carefully along the path in her canvas shoes. At least the noise of the pelting rainfall drowned out her progress.

The lack of a response from her mother worried her. Rather than search for her blindly, she changed tactics. Sam would head directly for Anita, knowing that was Marla's goal. Doubling back, she crouched beside a pile of lumber watching his wiry frame trudge past. Unfortunately, she hadn't hurt him nearly bad enough. He cradled his elbow, so she'd probably only nicked his arm. Too bad. Marla had learned to defend herself to the fullest extent possible.

She veered toward the lake, her shoes crunching over dead pine needles and skirting fallen palm fronds. Her ears picked up nothing but the roar of the wind. Swaying against the pull of the storm, she dodged just in time to avoid being hit by a flying coconut. She felt chilled, but it wasn't due to the drop in temperature. Her thumping heart told her she raced against time, needing to beat the forces of nature as well as a murderer—with nothing in her hands except a penknife. That wouldn't do much damage unless she caught him by surprise, and he'd be expecting her.

A thump from behind made her scream, but her startled cry was obliterated by a shriek of wind. Rain slashed sideways, blinding her. Then she saw the fallen tree limb that had caused the noise. Trees bent wildly in the howling wind, its pressure pounding her ears. Twigs, leaves, moss, and birds' nests flew about in the turbulence. Something hit the side of the house, and a window shattered. Still the wind strengthened.

Marla could no longer distinguish the lake. A mass of water swirled and churned in front of her, diminishing visibility to zero. By following the path, she came to a dock extending over the water. Sam stood at its edge, waiting for her, an evil grin distorting his gaunt face.

Hair lashing at her eyes, Marla scanned the scene before her frantically for her mother. "Ma! Where are you?" Good God, he hadn't drowned her, had he?

Sam pointed downward toward the sloshing lake, its level rising with each surge brought on by the gale. With shuffling steps, Marla edged closer. Peering over the side, she spotted a rowboat tossing on the erratic current. No one was inside. Feeling the blood drain from her face, she lifted her eyes to meet Sam's cold glare.

"My mother?" she croaked.

"Tied to a post." He ignored the rivulets that dripped down his weathered skin. "The water is already up to her chest, but that's not the only danger. Do what I tell you, and I'll let her go."

"What's that?"

"Come closer. Take off your clothes."

She could still run, reach her car. But by the time she summoned help, it would be too late for her mother.

Her gaze darted to the deck; the splintery wood offered no handholds. Nor were there any fallen branches that she could use to defend herself.

The boat. If it had oars . . .

With a running leap, she flung herself past Sam and over the edge of the dock. Landing in the water, she quickly surfaced and grasped the edge of the rocking boat. Adrenaline gave her the boost she needed to drag herself into the water-laden vessel. Steadying herself with one hand, she pocketed the tiny knife she'd been holding in a death grip and released the oar from its restraints.

She spied her mother's bound form wriggling against a post under the dock just as a heavy thud threatened to submerge the boat. Gripping the oar, Marla whirled around. Sam's clutching hands reached for her. Ducking, she swung the oar, aiming low for his stomach. But he crouched at the same time, and the oar connected with his forehead. With a muttered cry, he fell backward into the water.

Her arms shaking, Marla threw down the oar and turned toward Anita, whose wide eyes stared at her above a swath of tape covering her mouth. Marla leaned over, balancing herself while she gently tore off the gag. It wasn't easy to stay upright when the vessel surged with each swell.

While Anita worked her lips to regain feeling, Marla slipped into the water. Taller than the older woman, she half-swam, half-bounced off the sludgy bottom to get close enough. Using her pocketknife, she sawed at the cords binding Anita's wrists behind the post. Semi-submerged, she spit out the murky liquid as it entered her mouth in strengthening spurts. Something brushed her leg, and she gritted her teeth. *I can have an attack of nerves later. Now is not the time to think of the snakes and alligators that live here.*

"Marla, I didn't want you to come," Anita said, her voice raspy. Her slender body trembled violently. "Who knew? About Sam, I mean."

"I wanted to tell you to stay home today, but I couldn't reach you. He must have picked you up early."

Anita spoke from between chattering teeth. "He insisted on bringing me here. I should have guessed there was something wrong with him. He looked at every young girl we passed."

Marla shivered. "It's my fault. I set you up together."

"So? I fell for his act. Don't blame yourself." Her face drawn, she drew in a shaky breath.

"Hang on, Ma. I'm almost done."

"Look out!"

Sam lunged at her from the water. "You bitch . . ." A blast of wind-driven rain stole the rest of his words.

Marla gasped, instinctively grabbing the oar floating nearby. The torrential onslaught blurred her vision as she struck out wildly and impacted something with a *thwack*.

His eyes rolling up, Sam toppled into the writhing waters. Without wasting time, Marla untied the last of her mother's bindings.

"Quick, we have to get to shore." As she pushed her mother toward the tangle of mangroves edging the lake, an ominous thrashing sounded from behind. Aware that blood attracted predators, Marla scrambled toward higher ground.

She didn't want to think about what was happening back there. She didn't want to think at all. Not about nearly losing her mother, about almost becoming a victim herself, or the stash of photographs inside Sam's house.

They still had to get out of there before flooding obscured the road. Ducking a log that hurtled through the air, she crawled onto the sandy bank. Her mother collapsed beside her among gnarled roots. Rain pummeled them, and wind roared in their water-soaked ears.

"It's okay," Marla said, grasping Anita's cold fingertips. "We just have to reach my car."

Summoning reserves of energy, she forced herself to her feet. Not much farther to go.

Chapter Twenty

Rosh Hashanah dinner brought out the best and brightest of Marla's relatives. Vail had already met cousins Cynthia and Bruce at a Taste of the World charity function last December, but she'd never introduced him to her brother Michael and his wife Charlene, cousins Julia and Alan, or any of their kids. More cousins came out of the woodwork to celebrate the Jewish New Year, making a total of thirty around the rectangular table in a private room at Weston Hills Country Club.

Dalton, looking impressively handsome in a tailored navy suit, sat quietly observing the happy chatter during most of their meal. Through the chicken soup with matzo balls, the gefilte fish—which he turned down politely—and the roast brisket with potato latkes and vegetables, he'd muttered brief asides to Marla on his right. Brianna flanked her on the other side, while Anita sandwiched Vail on his left.

Vail idled his time by stroking Marla's thigh under the table. It had the disconcerting effect of making her yearn for time alone with him.

"So, Marla," said Julia in her usual disdainful tone. "I understand you solved another murder case. It appears your salon doesn't keep you busy enough. Or your boyfriend." She snickered.

Vail stiffened, but Marla placed a calming hand on his arm. "I'm happiest when I'm multitasking," she crooned. "And what occupies you these days?" Married to Alan, an accountant, Julia hadn't worked a day since she'd married.

"I see my personal trainer three days a week. It's totally exhausting." Her hand fluttered limply in the air. "I barely have time for my art history class."

Have you tried makeup lessons? Marla asked silently, noting Julia's lipstick blurred at the edges. "I get my exercise chasing killers who prey on innocent victims."

"I don't know why you keep risking yourself," said Cynthia, giving her a knowing glance, "but you're awfully good at sleuthing. Maybe Dalton should deputize you."

"Cool idea," Brianna inserted, her dark eyes dancing playfully. The teen wore her hair in her usual ponytail, making her look younger than her thirteen years.

"Over my dead body," Vail muttered.

Titters of nervous laughter floated through the room. Everyone seemed on edge with strangers in their midst, especially a police officer. Most of Marla's relatives were white-collar professionals; the idea of toting a gun was as far removed from their lives as a platinum tint from an ebony rinse. They'd never understand the raw sensuality that Dalton exuded or how it affected her. Quiet authority radiated from his broad shoulders, confident posture, and arrogant grin. While his commanding presence made others uncomfortable, it stirred Marla in female regions that didn't need to be named.

Vail still seemed put out by her recent adventure. She'd finally gotten through to him from Sam's telephone, and he'd arrived with a couple of squad cars. Marla and her mother had made it home before the hurricane hit full force, although it had ended up targeting the Keys so that Fort Lauderdale only got brushed by its outer edge. That had been enough to cause wind damage, flooding, and downed power lines. Now, a week later, most of the debris had been cleared up—except for Dalton's anger, which still simmered beneath the surface when he spoke of her close call with Sam.

Marla hadn't even mentioned Sam's demand for her to call Brianna. She'd merely pointed out that Sam had flirted with her mother to get closer to Marla, hoping to learn what she or the detective had discovered about him. Eventually, the results on Sam's fingerprints had returned with a positive match. It linked him to the killings up North.

"My sister almost ended up dead," Aunt Polly remarked in her frail voice. "That's what she gets for gallivanting around with different men. It isn't seemly at her age."

"You're just jealous," Anita said crossly.

"Tell us again how this all started," Cynthia said, fascination mixed with longing in her gaze. Marla had always thought Cynthia had everything: a rich husband, a magnificent mansion, and two children. She'd learned looks could be deceiving. Together, she and Cynthia had defeated another murderer, one bent on destroying Ocean Guard, Cynthia's favorite charity, and the adventure had sparked new life in her cousin. Cynthia looked now as if she yearned for another such experience.

"Wilda Cleaver, the dead woman's spiritual adviser, told me Carolyn sent me a message from beyond the grave. She couldn't rest until I uncovered her killer."

Marla's gaze met each one of her relatives' prying eyes. She hadn't told them Wilda's other prediction, that someone close to her was ill. Was it Polly, who looked thinner each time Marla saw her? Anita, whose high blood pressure needed medication for control? One of her cousins, or her brother's children? Or none of them?

"Wilda turned out to have a blemished past," Dalton said quietly, playing with his wineglass. Clearly, he felt less comfortable conducting social conversations than discussing crime. "She'd been sucked into a scam orchestrated by a Fort Lauderdale attorney, Peter McGraw. Using a company called Titan Resources as a front, they bamboozled gullible victims out of millions of dollars. It involved her soothsayer talents."

"Tell them about Atlas Boyd," Marla said.

"Boyd is a foreign investor who owns a chain of French salons. He wanted to expand his business into this country, so he contacted McGraw, whose practice includes immigration law."

"Wait a minute," Anita said, breaking off a piece of challah bread. "How did Carolyn get connected to this lawyer?"

"Through Wilda. She'd stayed in touch with McGraw after their scheme broke up. When he mentioned needing a contact with access to salons, Wilda told him about her new client. Carolyn had consulted her for a reading and became a regular customer. McGraw acted as a link between Carolyn and Boyd."

"Atlas Boyd wanted to establish franchises in this country," Marla explained. "He sent in his girls as students to the beauty academy and paid their tuition. In return for subsidizing Carolyn's move to Palm Haven and a monthly stipend, she promised to employ them after their graduation."

"Boyd hoped to add certain standards of quality to his franchises by importing French staff," Vail added. "The man had grandiose plans, but he went about them the wrong way. McGraw obtained visas intended for senior executives from multinational firms. Obviously, hairstylists and colorists don't qualify."

"What will happen now?" Cynthia asked.

"Atlas Boyd and Peter McGraw will be charged with immigration fraud in federal court. Boyd faces fines, while McGraw could go to prison."

"Atlas Boyd made Wilda an offer for Carolyn's salon," Brianna prompted. "Marla, aren't you going to share your news?"

She beamed with pride. "Wilda doesn't want anything else to do with Hairstyle Heaven. Claudia, Jeanine, and the rest are returning to France. Not only did their visa applications claim they were taking positions that didn't exist, but they also falsified their expected salary. They made substantially less. None of them chose to remain, given the chance to reapply."

"And?" Brianna said, poking her arm.

"And so Wilda offered me the salon."

"What?" Vail half-rose from his seat. "You didn't tell me that."

She studied his face, searching for his reaction. "I'm not sure what I'll do yet. I've been thinking of adding spa services to my salon menu, and this might give me the opportunity. But I don't know if I can afford to maintain two establishments, let alone find the additional staffing. Plus I'm concerned about the extra time I'd need for bookkeeping and so forth. I've been hoping to cut back my hours, not add to them."

His expression gentled, and he gave her a quick kiss in full view of her gaping relatives. "It's your decision, sweetcakes. You know I'll support whatever you choose."

Her bones melted. "What did I do to deserve you?" Letting her gaze sweep her wealthy, idle cousins, she added, "It's tough to find a man who respects a woman's success," her acerbic tone indicating what she thought of their leisurely lifestyle. She looked back at Vail fondly.

"Hey, wanna give me a job as shampoo assistant?" Brianna said, laughter in her young voice.

"Not yet, honey," Marla responded, dragging her gaze from Vail to give her an affectionate squeeze.

From across the table, her brother cleared his throat. "How did this psychic lady end up inheriting a salon?"

Marla glanced at him sitting beside his wife, Charlene, and their two children. She was just as guilty of snobbery as her cousins by not calling him more often. Maybe there was a reason for her avoidance, she thought, remembering the reading in Cassadaga. How much did she really know about her brother's life now, and how much did she want to get involved? She'd have to rectify her inattention in the future to avoid becoming like Polly and Anita. Or Carolyn and her sister, Linda. Besides, if the predictions were right, Michael might need someone to confide in.

"Carolyn felt closer to Wilda than she did to her own sister," she said. "I guess my rival never learned about Wilda's notoriety, or else she didn't care. Nor did any of us suspect Wilda was related to Sam. When I spoke to her this past week, she confessed that's why she involved me in solving the murder. Wilda suspected Sam, but she couldn't go to the police. You see, Sam was her uncle. He moved down here to escape from his crimes up North. He had no intention of resuming his evil deeds until Carolyn found out about him. That triggered his need to kill again."

Anita put a hand to her heart. "Oh my. To think that I believed his shy act."

Marla could relate to this; she'd nearly fallen for Wilda's act. Then again, maybe it hadn't been merely a ploy on the medium's part to ensure Marla's cooperation, but had actually been true. Now that her killer had been exposed, Carolyn's soul could rest. Should Marla still be concerned about a family member? She shrugged aside her fears. When she'd asked Wilda for more details, the psychic had said she couldn't be more specific. Carolyn had moved on and she no longer sensed her. Marla concluded that it was likely everything Wilda had said had just been part of her act to lure Marla onboard.

"What else did you learn about Sam?" Anita addressed Vail after the waiter served dessert and coffee.

While they helped themselves to honey cake, Vail leaned forward. "From my investigation, I pieced together the sequence of events," he said, his voice somber. He couldn't interview the criminal. Sam's remains had been recovered from the lake.

"Sam Cleaver, alias Sam Levy, admired a hair ornament Carolyn was wearing, so she told him about her collection of hair jewelry," Vail explained. "She brought samples to the hardware store and told him there were more where those came from."

"That was the man who worked in the same shopping center as Marla's salon?" Michael's eyes widened in horror. "Mother, you didn't tell me."

Anita dismissed him with a tilt of her head, her attention focused on the detective. "Go ahead, Dalton. I want to hear the details of his evil. It just appalls me how he deceived people."

Vail grasped his coffee cup. "Sam took out a few locks of hair he'd saved in plastic bags labeled with girls' names. He said he'd like to learn how to make them into jewelry. Carolyn invited him over to her place to show him more pieces. But when she teased him about clipping his girlfriends' hair, he got nervous. Maybe he'd revealed too much about himself.

"Still, he envied her collection. Carolyn mentioned that her friend Rosemary was the only other person who knew about it, although Rosemary didn't know its hiding place. Rosemary, who baby-sat her plants on occasion, had a key to her apartment, and so did Wilda. Sam, fascinated by death rituals, couldn't stay away. He brought over some jewelry-making supplies and one of his hair trophies. Working with the hair made him anticipate another kill."

"How gruesome." Julia shuddered. "Can't we change the subject?"

Alan patted her hand reassuringly. "She's right. Today we're supposed to be celebrating the new year. We don't want to hear bad things."

"Shush, sonny," Aunt Polly interceded. "I haven't heard such a good story in years."

That's because you don't go anywhere, Marla thought to herself. "Tell them the rest," she ordered Vail, "or they'll plague me for details."

He gave her a smile that warmed her all the way to her toes. "All right. One time, Rosemary came over just as Sam left Carolyn's apartment. He wondered what Carolyn had told Rosemary about him. But he forgot about her friend when Carolyn found something he'd inadvertently left behind: a torn clipping about the murdered girl whose lock of hair he'd shown her. She blackmailed him, and he killed her. Then he became afraid Rosemary would remember his visit. Disguising himself, he spotted her with Marla at the bingo hall. Rosemary became a security risk and had to go. He couldn't stop once he was on a binge. He murdered that young girl a couple of weeks ago."

His pointed glare at Marla told her his conclusion: *you would have been next.*

"Most of Carolyn's antique jewelry was recovered from Sam's house," Marla added. "Her sister got a nice nest egg. Anyway, it's over now." She gave Vail a demure grin in an attempt to lighten his mood.

"You got that right." He lifted a dish of sliced apples. "Didn't you say we eat apples with honey on this holiday to ensure a year of sweetness?"

"So we do." Her eyes met his, her gaze questioning.

Was that forgiveness she saw in his expression? Certainly he wouldn't be stroking her leg under the table if he were still angry. When he lifted the corner of his mouth, she understood what he was asking in return.

She clutched at his hand for confidence. "Uh, we have an announcement to make. Dalton and I are engaged."

She'd decided to take the plunge, despite the problems they still had to work out. Some risks were worth taking. Dalton and Brianna had become too much a part of her life to deny their importance any longer. Diving into the sea of matrimony came with its own responsibilities, but she wouldn't face them alone. They'd fuse as a team and would come out stronger.

Dalton and Brianna gripped her hands on either side while her relatives showered them with congratulations. She shouldn't have worried about her family's reaction. All seemed genuinely happy for her.

"Have you set a date?" Michael asked.

"Not yet." Although she'd made a commitment, Marla didn't plan to rush into anything, either.

Anita beamed proudly. "Now you can join us at our reunion over Thanksgiving weekend," she addressed Vail. "We're getting together with our extended family. You'll get the full initiation. Besides, it'll be nice to get away. I haven't taken a trip in a while."

A trip . . . Why did those words bother her? Marla brushed aside her misgivings. Now was the time to forge a new future, not to look back at the past. Although she and Dalton faced many challenges, they'd conquer them together. She wanted to experience all the joy their union offered.

Lifting her wineglass, she offered a toast. "May the New Year bring us peace, health, and happiness. *L'chayim.*"

AUTHOR'S NOTE

Having never before had a reading by a psychic, I was fascinated by the opportunities at Cassadaga, Florida. I consulted a woman who said many of the things Hazel told Marla, although I altered my own reading to suit the story. It was an educational experience, and although I subscribe to Marla's healthy dose of skepticism, I'll admit there are phenomena we can't always explain.

Coming next in the *Bad Hair Day* series is *Dead Roots,* where Marla attends the family reunion mentioned in this tale. She encounters many surprises, not all of them pleasant, especially when the psychic's predictions come true. Dalton Vail gets to meet her relatives, and that promises to be fun. Stay in touch for more details as they become available.

I love to hear from readers. Write to me at P.O. Box 17756, Plantation, FL 33318. Please enclose a self-addressed stamped #10 business-size envelope for a personal reply.

Email: nancy.j.cohen@comcast.net

Web site: www.nancyjcohen.com

BONUS RECIPE

SWEDISH MEATBALLS

12-oz bottle chili sauce
18-oz jar grape jelly
15-oz can tomato sauce
½ cup chopped onions
¼ cup marsala wine (optional)
1 large package frozen beef meatballs

(If you want to make your own, get one to two pounds of chopped lean beef, mix with one egg or more to moisten, a sprinkle of garlic powder, and ¼ cup seasoned bread crumbs before forming into small balls).

In a large saucepan over medium-high heat, mix together chili sauce, grape jelly, and tomato sauce until jelly is melted and ingredients blend. Then toss in onions and add wine if desired. When mixture is bubbly, add meatballs to coat. Cover pot and reduce heat to simmer. Lift lid, being careful of steam, and stir periodically. For raw meatballs, simmer for up to an hour until meat is cooked through. For frozen meatballs, heat until defrosted and hot to the taste. Serve over cooked white rice. This recipe also makes a good party appetizer. If you are cooking from scratch, meatballs may be frozen with sauce.